PRAISE FOR *SNAGGED*

"Carrie Harris delivers authentic nerd-dom and impressive cosplay craft details in *Snagged*, a clever homage to the chaotic, campy glory of '80s Saturday morning cartoons. Harris fully embraces *Lady Lovely Locks'* wacky aesthetic, complete with artificer princesses and flirty manga hedge wizards. But beneath the surface nostalgia lies something more intriguing—an ending that reframes everything that came before and sets up what promises to be an even more compelling sequel."

—NIKKI VAN DE CARR, AUTHOR OF *THE INVISIBLE WILD*

"A dazzling retro fantasy romp that will quickly win over fans old and new!"

—SARAH GLENN MARSH, AUTHOR OF THE REIGN OF THE FALLEN DUOLOGY

"*The Princess Bride* meets *Adventure Time* in this magical story that's perfect for fans of cosplay, con culture, and all things nerdy. Fun, fast-paced, and will leave readers eagerly awaiting Leigh's next visit to the colorful Kingdom of Lovely Locks."

—SHANNON TAKAOKA, AUTHOR OF *EVERYTHING I THOUGHT I KNEW* AND *THE TOTALLY TRUE STORY OF GRACIE BYRNE*

SNAGGED

A Lady Lovely Locks™ Novel

BOOK 1

CARRIE HARRIS

RP|TEENS
PHILADELPHIA

This book is a work of fiction. Names, characters, places, and incidents are the product of the author's imagination or are used fictitiously. Any resemblance to actual events, locales, or persons, living or dead, is coincidental.

Running Press Teens
Hachette Book Group
1290 Avenue of the Americas, New York, NY 10104
www.runningpresskids.com
@runningpresskids

First Edition: February 2026

Published by Running Press Teens, an imprint of Hachette Book Group, Inc.
The Running Press Teens name and logo are trademarks of Hachette Book Group, Inc.

The Hachette Speakers Bureau provides a wide range of authors for speaking events. To find out more, go to hachettespeakersbureau.com or email HachetteSpeakers@hbgusa.com.

Running Press books may be purchased in bulk for business, educational, or promotional use. For more information, please contact your local bookseller or the Hachette Book Group Special Markets Department at Special.Markets@hbgusa.com.

The publisher is not responsible for websites (or their content) that are not owned by the publisher.

Cover illustration by Rossi Gifford
Print book cover and interior design by Mary Boyer

Library of Congress Cataloging-in-Publication Data
Names: Harris, Carrie author
Title: Snagged : a Lady Lovely Locks novel / Carrie Harris.
Description: First edition. | Philadelphia : RP Teens, 2026. |
Audience: Ages 13 & up | Audience: Grades 7–9
Identifiers: LCCN 2025032481 (print) | LCCN 2025032482 (ebook) |
ISBN 9798894141640 trade paperback | ISBN 9798894141657 ebook
Subjects: CYAC: Fantasy | Cosplay—Fiction | Magic—Fiction |
Missing persons—Fiction | LCGFT: Fantasy fiction | Novels
Classification: LCC PZ7.H241228 Sn 2026 (print) | LCC PZ7.H241228 (ebook)
LC record available at https://lccn.loc.gov/2025032481
LC ebook record available at https://lccn.loc.gov/2025032482

ISBNs: 979-8-89414-164-0 (trade paperback), 979-8-89414-165-7 (ebook)

Printed in Indiana, USA

LSC-C

Printing 1, 2025

CHAPTER 1

RED AND PURPLE LIGHTS SWIRLED OVER THE small crowd gathered before the main KillyCon stage, and Leigh Carroll peeked through a gap in the backdrop curtain, trying to gauge the audience. Although KillyCon was still too new to draw the crowds of the big regional conventions—let alone a San Diego Comic-Con or Anime Expo—horror nerds filled the tiny auditorium to the brim. Teenagers in store-bought costumes bumped elbows with grandparents in retro nerd shirts, and small children in Halloween gear sprinted up and down the aisles. Over the loudspeakers, the soundtrack from some unidentified slasher film score swelled, the beat galloping to a fever pitch. The audience broke out into raucous applause as No-Face from *Spirited Away* glided stage left. If they liked him, she couldn't wait to see what they'd think of her crazy getup. This was the perfect place to debut a risky new concept.

The stage lights dropped, leaving only a single red spotlight shining from behind. Leigh's heart began to gallop with excitement as the bloody illumination outlined a monstrous figure standing at center stage, where there had been nothing just seconds before. For a moment, it remained motionless. Menacing. Silent. The stage lights slowly began to creep up, giving the audience its first look at the ominous creature that stood before them. Toward the back of the auditorium, a child burst into tears and was hustled out by an embarrassed parent.

A middle-aged woman in a Buffy shirt loudly exclaimed, "What the heck...?"

Leigh's lips twitched, a satisfied grin struggling to break free, but it was showtime. She shut her eyes for the briefest moment, summoning up an expression of fierce strength and icy determination. Her posture straightened, chin lifting as she transformed from average high schooler to monster killer.

She stepped onto the stage next to the twisted creature and savored the collective gasp from the audience as they took her in. Blood streaked her face and long raven hair, which was tied back with a braided thong. She wore a trench coat of black, light-gulping leather, which swirled as she posed next to the hulking abomination. A bandolier of wooden stakes crisscrossed her chest, and a cluster of decapitated teddy-bear heads hung from the belt at her hips.

She pulled a crossbow from the holster on her back. The weapon had clearly seen a lot of use, the grime of years caked into its seams. With a practiced hand, she took a stake from her bandolier, loaded it into the crossbow, and pointed it at the creature.

The music ebbed. The crowd fell silent, transfixed.

"Abraham Van Helsing, I presume?" the beast asked her in a sepulchral voice, its jaws unhinging to show rows of wicked, jagged teeth punctuated by a pair of curved fangs.

A ripple ran through the audience. The jaw moved! It looked so real! Lights flickered across the room as people pulled out their phones to record.

Leigh smiled coldly, her eyes riveted to the abomination before her.

"Van Helsing is my cousin. I am Agatha Van Bearsing. Prepare to meet your maker, Care Bear-cula!" she replied.

The Buffy-shirted woman in the front row let out a bark of laughter, holding her phone high as the audience burst into applause. The duo dropped its act, approaching the edge of the stage to show off the costumes. First Leigh spun slowly to give the audience the opportunity to admire the hours of work she'd spent on the costume before removing her trench to show off the various prop weapons secreted on her person. Then the vampiric Care Bear displayed the fur-covered bodysuit with the bloody fangs on the tummy, moving the jaw of his enormous mask and showing how the bulky foam responded to his movements.

When they were done, a wave of adulation carried them backstage once again. As soon as the heavy curtains shielded them from sight, Leigh pumped her fist as her best friend, Aristotle Jefferson the Third, took off the Care Bear mask and fanned his face. The red flush of his cheeks was clearly visible against the deep brown backdrop of his skin, and sweat glistened at his temples.

"I *told* you," Leigh declared. "I told you it would work if we leaned hard into a *Five Nights at Freddy's* vibe. You should have appreciated my brilliance when you had the chance."

"I bow to your superior intelligence," Ari said, his deep bass voice at odds with his thin, almost delicate features. He'd always said he had a physique made for nerddom, and he kinda had a point. The guy was a beanpole with limbs. "But I wasn't wrong. One misstep and we would have looked like extras in a Nickelodeon Halloween special."

"Hey, I like a challenge, and making a Care Bear scary definitely qualifies. Admit it. I won the bet."

"Fine, fine. I know when I've been beaten. I'll get you something from the Dealers' Hall."

"Deal," she replied, beaming.

After receiving the Fashion Show Judges Award, it took Leigh and Ari a while to work their way through the long line of people who wanted pictures. Everyone was kind and complimentary, and by the time they took their last photo, Leigh's cheeks hurt from smiling.

"Food or Dealers' Hall?" asked Ari, opening his fanged mouth wide to let a little air into the heavy mask.

"Hall. You owe me, remember?"

"How could I forget? You've been bringing it up every four minutes," he replied as they headed down the long hallway toward the dealers' area.

"You were timing me, weren't you? Nerd."

"Blerd. We Black nerds earned our portmanteau. Use it," he said, preening.

"Now if only there was a good word for a nerd of dubious parentage," mused Leigh.

"Hey. I'll throw hands with anyone who suggests that you're of dubious parentage. You know who your folks are," he said.

"Two grainy photos of my mother does not exactly constitute extensive knowledge. I'm not exactly one hundred percent on which demographic boxes to check on my college apps, and I need all the scholarships I can get."

"I didn't search for a dubious parentage category. But anything is possible."

They paused to take in the con map, posted on a sign planted smack in the middle of the floor. The Dealers' Hall was just around the corner in the convention center's B wing. As they pulled up to the doors, he motioned for her to go through first.

"What am I gonna do next year when you go off to college? You are literally my only friend in this godforsaken dump of a city," she said, sighing.

"Not my fault that you're a child."

"Hey! You only have six months on me."

"And yet I'll graduate at the end of this year, and you'll be forced to haunt the halls of North Central High for another year without me."

"Stahp," she moaned. "It's too depressing to contemplate."

"It's fine," he said, patting her shoulder with an enormous paw. "I'll buy you something and make you forget all about it. After all, you did win that bet."

"I am not that shallow," she declared. Her eyes lit up as she took in the booths at the front edge of the Dealers' Hall. "Oooooh. Funko Pops!"

"Aaand here we go," Ari muttered, smirking.

It took them almost two hours to make their way through the vendor tables. Although the con wasn't particularly huge, they took their time at each booth, making a circuit around the edges of the room before working their way methodically through the rows. They sifted through piles of figurines and stacks of comics, admired original art, and examined every prop and costume piece they saw in minute detail. Because of her tight finances, Leigh had a variety of cosplays in various stages of completion, and she was always on the lookout for good deals, especially for items she couldn't make herself, like gloves, footwear, and wigs. Bargain shopping took time. Just as they finally reached the end of the hall, the PA crackled to life.

"The Dealers' Hall will be closing in five minutes," a perky con staffer declared over the speakers. "I repeat: The hall will be closing in five minutes. Please complete your purchases and move toward the exits, and thanks again for coming to Killy in Philly!"

"Okay, strategy time," said Ari, stretching his back as best as he could in the bulky costume. "I'm going to circle back around to the one hundreds to pick up that Pennywise print. Have you decided what you want yet?"

"I don't know. I was thinking I might pick up those striped tights for my cyberpunk Alice in Wonderland..." She trailed off, squinting. "Wait a minute. *What* is *that*?"

He followed her gaze to a vendor tucked beneath a staircase they'd somehow managed to miss. Styrofoam heads cluttered the black-draped table, each sporting a brightly colored wig. At either end of the booth, full-size mannequins displayed longer hairpieces. The one on the far end caught Leigh's eye and held it. The long, wavy locks had been dyed in delicate, cotton-candy pastels. She'd been looking for a wig like this for almost a year now, but she'd either found the right colors without the length or the right length without the colors and never the two combined. But this one was perfect. The vendor had even styled it well, pulling the front section into a pair of tightly wound double buns and leaving the rest loose.

“Finally,” she breathed.

It was just a wig, but she could barely breathe as she approached the table. Her mother had taken off when Leigh was only a few months old, leaving behind two photos and an old storybook about a princess named Lady Lovely Locks and the Pixietails who lived in her magical hair. When she was a kid, Leigh had read that book so many times that it had needed rebinding. Now that she’d grown up a bit, she could admit that the story was incredibly cringe. But that hadn’t stopped her from working on a cosplay that reenvisioned the princess as a warrior maiden. It was further along than most of her other pending projects—about 95 percent done—but she hadn’t managed to find the right wig until now.

The vendor, a rail-thin old lady in a purple beehive wig and cat’s-eye glasses, was already beginning to pack up a display of kanzashi. The traditional Japanese hair ornaments jingled as she removed them from the plastic display case and placed them carefully into a large bin. She paused to bare yellowed teeth in a smile.

“Let me know if you see anything you like, dearies,” she said.

“I’m terrified to ask, but how much is this wig?” asked Leigh, her voice a little breathless.

“The forty-two-inch multi? Now that one is lace-front, handwoven synthetic. I’ll give it to you for $120 since it’s the end of the day,” said the vendor, moving around the table and holding up a length of the hair for inspection. She eyed Leigh with a weirdly satisfied smile as if already anticipating the sale.

Leigh did have an after-school job, but she couldn’t afford to be dropping that kind of bank on a wig. She reserved most of her paychecks for her fashion-design-school fund and daily expenses. After all, rent and utilities weren't cheap, and her dad already worked too much. She had a responsibility to help out. But she ran her hands over the glistening strands, and she wanted that wig. Badly.

"Pretty," said Ari, peering over her shoulder. "Which one's that for again? The Lovely Lady cosplay?"

"Lady Lovely Locks."

The old woman broke out into a coughing fit so hard she staggered into the wig stand, which toppled over in slow motion as she hacked out a lung. Alarmed, Leigh snatched the wig out of the air before it spilled onto the floor, while Ari steadied the vendor. Her beehive had gone crooked, and her glasses hung on the end of her nose. Pale and shaky, she looked like she'd seen a ghost.

"Sit down," Ari urged, his eyes wide. "Should we call someone?"

"I'll be fine. Just got to catch my breath," said the vendor, not unkindly.

Leigh put the wig back onto the stand, smoothing the soft strands. It was perfect, and she felt for the old lady, but it was too much. Responsibility sucked.

"Let's go," she murmured. "I've got to pick up those tights."

"I did owe you..." began Ari, but Leigh cut him off with a wave of a hand.

"If I wanted a comic or something, sure. But this is too much," she replied. "Don't even think about it."

"How about I put forty bucks toward it, and you help me with the wings for King Chrysalis? I've tried them twice, and I'm still not happy with the results."

She hesitated. With Ari's contribution, she could just squeak by on what she had in her wallet without raiding her savings. Could she really justify paying eighty bucks for a wig? She'd have to start rationing shampoo, for heaven's sake! But she'd been working on that Lady Lovely Locks cosplay for so long.

"I'll bump it down eighty dollars total," offered the vendor, nodding in encouragement. "Half from you and half from your friend. It jumped into your hands. Clearly, you're meant to have it."

She must have been desperate to make the sale this late in the day. Leigh hesitated. She knew she ought to do the responsible thing, buy the much-cheaper tights, and congratulate herself on being sensible. But she was tired of having to be a seventeen-year-old adult.

"The sales floor is now closed," said the crackling voice of the announcer over the loudspeaker. "Please exit the Dealers' Hall immediately."

"I'll take it!" she exclaimed, yanking her wallet out of one of her pouches before she lost her chance.

Chapter 2

The new wig looked terrific on the stand near the window. Leigh stood in the middle of her bedroom, admiring it for an embarrassingly long time. In the rush to leave KillyCon before the staffers kicked them out, she hadn't tried it on. But she might as well wait now. Through the thin walls of her bedroom, she could hear her dad getting ready for another overnight EMT shift, and he always stopped in to check on her before he left. After that, she could finish up the cosplay.

She dashed off a little math homework, posted a few pics of the contest to her Instagram, and tidied up her room while she waited. When they'd moved to Philly a little over a year ago, she'd managed to cram all her stuff into the tiny space, but it got cluttered fast. At the end of the bed sat a cube organizer she'd saved off the side of the road, its shelves stuffed with bins and boxes, each labeled in neat writing. The worktable covered the opposite wall, a pegboard rimmed with string lights hanging overhead, full of tools she'd thrifted or bought at the hardware store with her employee discount. On the table sat a cutting mat, a work lamp, a spool tree full of thread, and her pride and joy—a programmable sewing machine she'd gotten from an estate sale. The lady in charge hadn't realized how much it was worth, and Leigh had gotten away with a steal she still honestly felt a little bad about.

Time to get to work. She cleared the scattered foam and fabric scraps off her worktable, putting them into the plastic bins that lined the shelves on the opposite wall. The heat gun and X-Acto knife moved to their respective spaces on the pegboard among the rows of scissors, snippers, and tapes. The plague doctor plushie moved from the chair to the bed. Then she pulled open one of the worktable drawers to reveal neat rows of dollar-store plastic containers, dropping a few buttons and a spool of ribbon into their respective cubbies. As she finished, she heard her dad's heavy steps in the hallway. She sat down at the desk just as he opened the door.

"Hey, punkin," he said.

Leigh had always thought she didn't look one bit like her father. They both had black hair, but that was as far as the resemblance went. He was paunchy and pasty-white in comparison with her tanned lankiness. Sometime in the past twenty-four hours, he'd trimmed his facial hair from a full beard down to a goatee that could have formed the basis of a pretty good Doctor Strange cosplay. She'd offered to make him something a couple times, but he'd never been into it.

"Daddio," she said. "I like the trim."

"Thanks. How'd it go? Your..." He waved a hand around as if the right combination of air drawings might make the word magically pop into his mind. It was giving serious Doctor Strange vibes. Now that she'd come up with the concept, she couldn't unsee it. "Your thing."

"We won the thing, actually."

"Congrats! What did you win?" he asked, beaming.

"I am now the proud owner of a bunch of KillyCon swag. I also get a free ticket to next year's con and bragging rights." She shrugged. "The bigger competitions have better prizes, but it was fun."

His eyes settled on the cotton-candy wig, which trailed all the way down the bookshelf to skim the floor.

"New purchase?" he asked.

"I traded for it, yeah."

"What're you gonna be this time?" He smiled. "One of those My Little Horseys?"

She closed her eyes for a moment, trying to absorb the utter embarrassment that the words "My Little Horseys" stirred up in her. At least Ari wasn't around to hear. He would have never let her live it down.

"Lady Lovely Locks," she said. "From Mom's book."

"Oh."

There was an awkward pause. When she finally opened her eyes, he wore that pained expression he always got whenever she brought up her mom. Maybe the two of them weren't close, but she didn't want to be cruel to the guy. If he would just tell her something—anything—she'd let it go.

She took a deep breath.

"I was wondering if you—"

"I know what you're going to ask, and let's not right now, okay?" he said, looking down at his watch. "I'd better get to work. Did you finish your skeleton yet? I hope the textbook helped."

Leigh's stomach sank to her toes. She'd been excited about her Anatomy and Physiology project, which was to make a model of the human skeleton. Over the course of the week, she'd brought home plenty of EVA foam, and she'd already built a wire frame for the bones to hang from. Then she'd forgotten about it entirely in her excitement for KillyCon. The thing was due on Monday.

“Not yet,” she said, trying not to let her panic show on her face, “but I’ll work on it tonight.”

“You’ll have to show me tomorrow, then. Stay safe, punkin. Call me if you need me.”

“Good night.”

With an apologetic smile, he closed the door behind him. As soon as it clicked shut, Leigh went limp with relief. Of course she loved her dad, but he was just so tough to talk to. She liked cosplay, nerd fandoms, and alternative fashion. His main interests were sleeping and sports like hockey and that weird wrestling show where grown men hit one another with chairs and women in crop tops wandered around holding placards during the intermission. It was like she spoke Klingon while he spoke fluent ESPN sportscaster. The two languages didn’t overlap, although she was pretty sure that the average Klingon would be totally into *Fight Night*.

She twirled in her chair to gaze longingly at her new wig. As desperate as she was to see the finished cosplay, she wanted to take her time. Restyle the wig, maybe. Take a crap ton of selfies. No way was she gonna put all that stuff on and then spend the entire evening carving a bunch of anatomically correct foam bones.

Sighing, she pulled out her school laptop and set it next to the cutting mat. She’d already bookmarked some instructions, and her dad had sent her a couple of pictures from his old anatomy textbooks, so hopefully the project wouldn’t take too long. But she refused to turn in a janky skeleton. Mrs. Koslowski wouldn’t dock her points for a lack of artistic bone carving, but Leigh’s cosplays had taught her the need for visual precision, and those habits were tough to break.

Instead of opening up the project instructions, she typed "Marie Carroll" into the search bar and scrolled idly through the image results, searching for her mother's face. But she'd seen all these pictures before; there was nothing new. Discouraged, she opened up the project page and got to work building Bony Tony.

The next morning, Leigh had an opening shift at Wing It Hardware, which was crammed into a dingy strip mall between a bail bondsman and a travel agent. Overall, she loved her job. Sal, the owner, didn't mind if she used the equipment to work on her cosplays on slow days, and she could even take stuff home overnight if she was opening the next morning. She and Ari usually worked alone on Sundays, because like her father, Sal belonged to the church of sports, or maybe just a real church? She wasn't entirely sure, but he took the day off.

For some reason, Ari was counting out the drawer in the dark when she arrived. She locked the front door behind her and stumbled over a small stack of shopping baskets that had been inexplicably dumped in the middle of the floor. They clattered across the tile.

"That was graceful," Ari observed from behind the register.

"Turn on some lights! Or are you trying to kill me?" she demanded.

"No can do. The alarm's malfunctioning. I had to flip the breaker, or it's nothing but *woop woop woop* until you want to stab something sharp into your eardrums. Sal's on his way to reset it."

"Great." She restacked the baskets before heading to the back room to stash her things. "It's going to be that kind of day, isn't it?"

It was, in fact, that kind of day. It was that kind of day on steroids. After Sal reset the alarm, they were able to turn on the lights, but the one over the registers kept flickering like it was possessed. When Leigh was doing her pre-opening walk-through, she found a single abandoned kids' sock next to the plumbing supplies. It turned out to be stuck to the floor with some unidentifiable goo. She threw it away and washed her hands three times, running the water in the tiny employee bathroom as hot as it could get.

When she came back out, Ari said, "That sock's like something out of a horror movie. I was going to ask what the heck the night shift was doing yesterday, but I don't want to know."

"Maybe it was the rats instead."

He paused, shuddering. "That does not make me feel better. I'll get the mop."

The two of them pitched in to finish the floor just in time to open. Leigh had been hoping for a nice, quiet shift, but the store was busy all day, and not the good kind of busy either. Leigh's first customer was so old that he was practically dust. He insisted that he wanted to buy a plunger and a bucket of fried chicken, which wasn't going to happen since they worked at a hardware store. Then they were slammed with a series of angry DIYers who had either bought the wrong thing, didn't know what thing they wanted, or had broken the thing they bought, probably because they'd been trying to install it incorrectly. One woman with a Karen haircut walked up to Leigh, held her fingers up about an inch and a half apart, and asked for a screw "this size." Leigh showed the Karen the display of screws, tried to explain the difference between, say, drywall and wood screws, or even flat versus Phillips head, but the woman wasn't having it. Finally, Leigh grabbed one at random and rang it up just to make the whole thing end already.

As the door jingled shut again, she pinched the bridge of her nose and wondered if she'd make it to closing without getting fired or arrested for beating someone with the chicken man's abandoned plunger. She just didn't have the patience for it, not after staying up until almost three in the morning trying to carve the perfect femur. It was the cherry on top of an already awful day.

Ari arched a brow at her.

"You okay?" he asked.

"Peachy."

"I'll admit that it's extra weird today, like full-moon weird, but still. You're not your usual sarcastic self." He paused. "You're not a werewolf, are you? That full-moon vibe getting to you?"

"I wish."

He leaned against the counter, folding his arms.

"Seriously, what gives?" he asked.

"It's nothing," she said, hitching a shoulder.

"You are such a god-awful liar."

Leigh hesitated. She'd been deliberately not thinking about the date all day, but it didn't seem to be working. Maybe confessing would help get it off her mind.

"Sixteen years ago today," she said slowly, "my mother left and never came back."

All the breath went out of him in a whoosh, and he sagged against the edge of the counter.

"Daaaamn," he said, dragging the word out into a single shocked syllable. "I didn't realize."

"I try not to think about it. But that's easier said than done today."

"Do you…? Um…" he stuttered. "Man, this is awkward. I've always wanted to ask about it, but it feels like I'd be twisting the knife. But I'm here to talk if you want."

"There isn't much to say. My dad gave me her book and the pictures, and that is literally it. He flat-out refuses to talk about her. Whatever happened, it messed him up good. I used to push it when I was younger, but I caught him crying a few times, so I stopped."

"No photo albums? Cards?"

"Nothing."

Ari straightened, rubbing his hands together with a bright look that suggested he wasn't just going to let this go. A cautious swell of optimism ran through Leigh. Ari was super smart, with a certain level of nerdy tenacity that made him the perfect cosplay partner. For a brief moment, she allowed herself to imagine what it would be like if he helped her find her mom after all this time, but then she had to stop, because she didn't like crying to begin with but especially in the middle of a hardware store next to a display of Goo Gone.

"What about grandparents? They ought to know."

"They died before I was old enough to ask. My dad went through all their stuff. If they had any evidence, it's long gone now."

"Do you think she was…uh…" He trailed off again.

She instantly knew what he meant. After all, it would be naive not to consider it. She picked up a pencil from next to her register and made stabby motions with it like a slasher-film killer.

"*Ree ree ree*?" she asked. He nodded. "Nah. No police report. No missing persons registry. I checked. It's a dead end." Ari wilted, and she could feel tears prickle at her eyes. If she didn't lighten things up, she really was going to cry. "Maybe we can hire a wizard, who will uncover a secret society that captured my mom and forced her to fight in a magical arena hidden underground beneath the SEPTA tracks."

He snickered a little, and the tension slowly ebbed away.

"That's an idea. Or maybe we could go back to the werewolf thing, and you could just bite people until they told you the truth." He paused. "Actually, scratch that. It was funny until I realize you'd have to gnaw on your dad."

"And just like that, I think this conversation is over."

But strangely, she felt better. A little less alone. And who knew? Maybe Ari would come up with some brilliant plan that would answer all her questions about her mother's disappearance after all this time. At the very least, maybe the hope would carry her through the rest of this miserable shift.

Then the bell jingled above the door, and a woman came prancing in with an actual parrot on her shoulder. Maybe a real one. Maybe stuffed. Hard to tell.

"Arr," said Ari, completely unfazed. "Ye be welcome to Wing It Hardware."

After the shift of insanity finally finished, Leigh grabbed takeout and put the finishing touches on Bony Tony, etching the name of each of the larger bones onto the model in tiny, precise letters with her wood burner and writing the smaller bones of the hands and feet onto little flags that she suspended from the appropriate parts.

The work finally done, she leaned back in her chair, swiveling to look out her second-floor window. Rain pattered against the glass, coating the early evening in dingy gray. The scraggly branches of overgrown bushes reached through the bars of the rusty fence separating their yard from the sidewalk. A bus belched out billows of smog as it splashed its way down the block. Across the street, the bright neon lights of a crappy bar cut through the gloom, beer ads flickering on and off in a never-ending cycle. Sometimes late at night, actual grown adults came out of the bar and got into fistfights on the sidewalk. And they said teenagers were immature.

She needed a pick-me-up. Bad. Thoughtfully, she reached a hand out and smoothed it over the shining locks of her new wig. It was time.

The tote that contained the rest of her costume was buried in the bottom of her closet. She lugged it out. Because of the limited space, she had to stay organized, with each costume properly marked and folded in tissue paper, stowed safely away in plastic totes to protect them from bugs, mice, and mildew.

She pulled the pieces of her costume out, removing the paper and arranging them on her bedspread to help keep them straight. The original Lady Lovely Locks had worn a pink fluffy medieval gown that reminded Leigh of an overdressed Princess Peach. Leigh had reenvisioned it with an asymmetrical hem, a vaguely medieval bodice that laced up in the front, and an underdress decorated with a lattice of rainbow-colored pastel ribbons to match the wig. The boot covers were also handmade, with one extending up to her thigh and the other ending at the knee to echo the uneven lines of the dress. To tie the pieces together, the same ribbons crisscrossed their way up the shin of one boot.

She'd also fabricated a staff. When she was a kid, she used to play Lady Lovely Locks with her friends, and she got sick of waiting for the prince to come save her all the time. Young Leigh had taken the battle to the evil Duchess Ravenwaves on her own terms, and teenage Leigh had leaned hard into that idea. The staff was only foam and superglue, with a big resin gem at the top, but holding it still made her feel powerful.

The one thing she hadn't finished was the sheath. Over the past couple of years, she'd learned the hard way that every prop needed to attach to her, or she'd end up losing it. Given the size of the staff, it needed a back sheath, and she liked the idea of the gem poking up over one shoulder. She dug out a similar pattern that she'd used for a *Final Fantasy* cosplay a while back, pulled some scraps of high-density foam out of one of her bins, and snagged the L square off the pegboard to mark off the pieces. Last time she'd made this, she'd bent them over a juice glass, and that had worked well, so she grabbed one from the kitchen after she cut out the pieces, then applied the heat gun to make the foam hold its shape. It would be hidden by her hair, so it didn't need much decoration. She contented herself with adding a thin layer of copper spray and a few rivets, hot gluing them into place.

Done. She grabbed a few pizza snacks while it dried and paused to admire her work. With the wig, she could debut this at one of the larger cons and stand a good chance of placing. It looked damn good.

It took a while to put the costume on, tying endless bows in endless ribbons, but when she looked into the full-length mirror in the corner, she was happy with the result. The sheath fit like a glove. She slid the staff into it, allowing it to poke up over her shoulder.

Now all she needed was the wig, the crowning glory, the source of all Lady Lovely Locks's power. She pulled her hair back, securing it with clips. When she wore the cosplay to a con, she'd apply a full bald cap and secure the wig properly, but this would do for the moment. Her hair wasn't so thick that it would show, especially not with such a gigantic hairpiece.

Her heart beating with eager agitation, she tugged the wig on over her hair. Wavy pastel locks tumbled over her shoulder and tangled in the staff. Perhaps she shouldn't have put the weapon on first, but it was too late now. It took time to delicately extricate herself from the tangle without destroying the precious wig, but finally she pulled it fully onto her head.

It clung to her like it had been custom-built to fit. A thrilled shiver ran over her from the crown of her head to the tips of her toes as she lifted her eyes to glance into the mirror. Strangely, the tingle grew, fogging her vision. It turned her fingers and toes electric, buzzing along her skin.

"What the...?" she said.

Then she disappeared.

CHAPTER 3

WHITE LIGHT SEARED LEIGH'S EYEBALLS. A flash of heat ran from the tips of her toes to the top of her head, like some invisible hand had run an also-invisible hair dryer over her body. The air shifted, the burnt foam and air-freshener scent of her room replaced with a fresh, sweet smell that reminded her an awful lot of her favorite shampoo. Then the electric tingle faded; the brightness dimmed.

Disoriented, she opened her eyes.

She found herself inexplicably plopped in the middle of a forest clearing. Deep shadows cloaked the woods in darkness, but the light of a full pink moon shone down from overhead, bathing her in a pastel glow. The moon seemed much larger than usual, the pattern of the craters unfamiliar. She was no astronomy nerd, but she was fairly sure it didn't normally look like that.

"What the . . ." she said again.

She still wore the cosplay, the staff attached to her back. Ribbons rustled as she looked around wildly, trying to make sense of things. Nothing looked familiar. She patted her pockets only to find them empty. Her phone probably still sat on the workbench in her room, where she'd been just a moment ago.

That made no sense. This had to be a dream, and a lame one too. Did those trees have *hair*?

She stepped a little closer, squinting to make them out in the dim light. Indeed, the trees had luscious locks instead of leaves. One had box braids. Another a bouffant. The wind stirred the curls of a nearby shrub.

This was officially the dumbest dream she'd ever had. She pinched herself hard, hoping to wake up and leave those hairy trees behind, but nothing happened. Then she bit her tongue. Still nothing.

"You're losing it, Leigh," she told herself.

She could plunge into the tangled, braided forest, but where exactly would she go? It didn't really matter, since this was all some nightmare hallucination, probably brought on by the stress of spending so much money on the pastel wig. That would explain the hair theme. Stupid wig. This was all its fault. She reached up, getting a good grip on it, heedless of any tangles she might cause.

She yanked with all her might and let out a shocked screech as pain ripped through her scalp. That made no sense; she hadn't even glued the wig down. It ought to come right off. She jerked at it again to no avail. She couldn't even find the lace at the edge. It had fused to her head.

This dream officially *sucked.*

Suddenly, a trio of creatures dislodged from her scalp. They were about the size of her palm, with rabbity ears and long horsey tails. Oh, and they flew, because her subconscious had decided that the hair trees weren't weird enough, and she needed flying head bunnies too.

A jolt of recognition ran through her as they hovered in front of her face. These were Pixietails, from Mom's book. She must have fallen asleep after putting on the cosplay, and her mind had just filled in the blanks, casting her as Lady Lovely Locks. What a relief!

She'd been seriously starting to worry about her sanity, but this made perfect sense. Even the trees: Everything in the book had been hair-themed.

Well, if she couldn't wake up, at least she could have some fun with this.

The Pixietails made a pretty jingling sound every time they moved despite the fact that she could see no bells anywhere upon their tiny bunny bodies. They were cute, in a flying pastel vermin kind of way. Their tails extended ten times longer than their torsos, and they defied gravity, curling prettily upward. If she could get a wig to do that, she'd easily win Best Hair at one of the bigger cons.

The trio of pastel creatures matched her wig: blue, pink, purple. The blue one hovered a bit closer, clapping its tiny hands with a merry little jingle that made Leigh want to clap her hands over her ears. That was going to get old quick.

"Lady Lovely Locks!" the Pixietail said in a voice like a cartoon character on helium. "We've missed you!"

"You look different!" added the purple one, equally squeaky.

"We missed you, but you look so different!" said the pink one in a surprising bass.

"That was . . . unexpectedly deep and also redundant," said Leigh. "Let me guess. Pixie Shine, Pixie Beauty, and Pixie Sparkle?"

Pixie Shine, the blue one, clapped its hands again, and the other two followed suit, jingle-jangling joyously. Leigh reached beneath the luxurious locks that had been fused to her head and rubbed her temples. This couldn't get much worse, unless they decided to attempt a three-part harmony. Thankfully, this dream didn't seem to include musical numbers. If they let out so much as a warble, she'd hoof it into the hair trees and take her chances.

"Yes!" said Pixie Shine. "You've read our histories!"

"That's good!" added Pixie Beauty.

"It's a good thing you've read our histories," said Pixie Sparkle, whose job seemed to be to repeat what the other two said, only about three octaves lower. Leigh opened her mouth to comment about that when the Pixietail added, "Duck."

Without context, it was difficult to know whether the Pixietail was instructing her to avoid an oncoming attack or observing that an aquatic animal (probably covered in a disturbing amount of hair) had waddled out of the forest. But better safe than sorry. She ducked, and a whoosh of hot air came streaming over her shoulder.

Definitely not a hairy waterfowl, then.

She whirled around to see an enormous creature, hunchbacked and scraggly. It sported a wickedly hooked beak, and its entire face was covered in hard keratin, encasing everything but a pair of beady red eyes. A tangled black mane covered the back of the head and the humped neck, a pair of narrow horns poking out through the mats. It walked on hind legs in a series of loping hops that made her think of the bizarre offspring of a kangaroo and a gorilla. Heck, maybe that's what it was. It was hard to tell since her subconscious had decided that it should also wear a tattered cloak that hid most of its body from view.

It snorted, and curls of flame came out its nostrils.

"What in the fire-breathing kangorilla is *that*?" she asked.

"It's a snagfire!" chorused all three Pixietails. "Run!"

But Leigh had no desire to do that. After all, this was just a dream. Why not play Lady Lovely Locks for a while, just like she'd done when she was a kid? Of course, the princess from Mom's storybook would have waved a hand and let her Pixietails do all the work, but Leigh's version would be a bit more hands-on. She found herself eager to see what she could do; it was a bit like the ultimate cosplay experience. This time, she could be a hero for real...or as real as dreams got, anyway.

She whipped her staff around, twirling it over her head and ending in her best anime warrior pose, crouched and ready for action. Based on the reaction from past competition audiences, she knew it looked great. Too bad she'd never actually trained with a staff, and the weapon in question was made out of a broom handle, EVA foam, and resin. She had no clue what to do next, but that didn't matter. She could whirl the staff around, bop the snagfire on the nose a couple of times, and then wake up safe and sound in her room.

It began to lope-hop toward her, lurching and salivating as steam came out its nostrils. Good thing this wasn't real, or it would have been terrifying. She spun the staff around again, aiming for the head.

Biff! The weapon bounced off the hard beak-head with no apparent effect whatsoever. The beast tackled her, puffing and snarling, knocking the weapon from her hands. Its weight forced the air from her lungs. Curved claws pierced the layers of her costume, pricking her skin. Its breath smelled like a charcoal grill that hadn't been cleaned in years.

She tried to shove it off, but it was much too heavy. It leaned down toward her, its beak click-clicking as if warming up to chew. Hot spittle splattered on her cheek. Ew.

There was nothing to fear, but she was terrified anyway.

"What should we do?" squeaked Pixie Beauty, popping up over the snagfire's shoulder, its tiny face crinkled with concern. "If you need to leave the kingdom, just say all our names aloud."

"Get it off me!" gasped Leigh.

The Pixietail gave her a thumbs-up before whipping out of sight with a cheery little jingle that seemed really inappropriate given the fact that Leigh was about to be eaten. The snagfire's head kept darting closer and closer, its red eyes rolling. She squeezed her eyes shut, trying desperately to wake before it pierced her skin.

"Wake up, wake up, come on, this dream sucks," she babbled aloud.

The pressure on her chest abruptly eased; the snagfire rose into the air. She opened her eyes, expecting to see her darkened room, but she was still in the clearing. The snagfire floated above her, red eyes wide and startled. Around its body wrapped a golden, glowing rope of energy, pinning its arms to its sides. Over the snagfire's shoulder, Pixie Shine gestured and jingled, lifting the creature higher and higher with the magical lasso.

Leigh sucked in a breath of fresh, nonscorched air before struggling to her feet. She felt a bit bruised and battered, and those claws had nicked her in a few places, but otherwise she was okay. No thanks to the Pixietails. All that magical power at their fingertips and no idea what to do with it. They really didn't seem very smart; no wonder Lady Lovely Locks had always micromanaged them in the book.

"What should I do now, Princess?" asked Pixie Shine.

That was a good question.

Her dream, her rules. She was gonna kick some snagfire booty.

She bared her teeth, slamming the butt of the staff onto the ground to psych herself up. The weapon hummed to life in her hand, the wood vibrating. As she stared at it with wide-eyed shock, a lance of energy shot out of the pink, multifaceted gem she'd attached to the top. The resulting weapon reminded her of a spear, but instead of a spearhead, it was topped with a pink beam of energy.

"Now, that's what I'm talking about," she said. "I'm a pastel-spear Jedi, and you're toast, kangorilla."

Magical power crackled and spit out pink sparks as she whirled the weapon experimentally overhead. It twisted in her grip, and somehow she knew that it didn't want to be spun, not like that. It knew what to do; she only had to follow its lead.

"Wow," said Pixie Sparkle, floating closer to take a better look.

"I know, right?" replied Leigh, grinning. "Let it go, Shine. I want to try this thing out."

Pixie Beauty flew up next to Pixie Sparkle and said, "But... violence is never the answer."

"I can name a million anime that would prove you wrong," replied Leigh. "Do it."

With a reluctant wince, Pixie Shine jingled, and the rope suspending the snagfire dissolved in a burst of azure glitter. The confused beast dropped to the ground, making a strange, rusty coughing noise. It crouched, angry eyes locking on Leigh. Clearly unhappy about what had just happened, it intended to take that dissatisfaction out on her.

"Game on," said Leigh.

The snagfire charged, and Leigh's goofy hybrid weapon twitched in her hands. She leaped into action, stabbing, sweeping, whirling.

When the beast swiped at her, the pink blade of energy sheared a line of shaggy fur from its arm. Another cough, this one strangely panicked. It scrabbled backward as she pressed her advantage, slicing the tip off one of its horns with the energy blade.

Now she had the hang of it. The saber-spear felt like an extension of her body, and it cued her less and less as she figured out how to use it properly. Maybe all her training with prop weapons had worked; maybe she was born to wield it. Or maybe she'd finally figured out how to change the rules of this dream in her favor. Didn't really matter, because it was still a blast.

She swung the blade at the snagfire, pushing it off-balance, and then planted her foot right in the middle of its shaggy chest.

"Bam!" she shouted as she kicked it.

Her cheeks flushed in embarrassment—what was she, ten? But at least the kick had its desired effect. The snagfire went tumbling backward. It crouched in the grass for a moment, dazed. Its beak clicked once, half-heartedly, and then the creature turned tail and ran, its tattered cloak streaming behind as it vanished into the shadows of the hair trees.

Leigh dropped her staff, threw her head back, and howled in triumph. Not the most sportsmanlike behavior, but who was going to call her on it?

"Do the sound effects help?" asked a female voice from somewhere in the darkness.

CHAPTER 4

LEIGH WHIRLED AROUND TO SEE A GIRL ABOUT her age with long, wavy black hair hanging past her knees. She had a face like a *Monster High* doll (and not the lame new reboot ones either), with arched brows, tilted brown eyes, and a pouty mouth. She wore the sort of tall black boots favored by super-villains and horse girls with a high-low dress best described as "military medieval." It had a long skirt and the suggestion of a bodice, but also epaulets and piping. All it needed was a few medals and maybe a corset for structure underneath.

She stepped out of the forest, brushing aside the long, hanging braids of a tree, and beamed at Leigh.

"What do you want?" asked Leigh.

"I just wanted to introduce myself to the lady of the hour," replied the stranger. "Which is obviously you. That was impressive. All the banging and powing. Very powerful."

"Yeah, well..." Leigh flushed. "The sound effects help me concentrate."

"I thought they were marvelous. You must be the new Lady. Do you know where you are yet?"

"The Kingdom of Lovely Locks."

"You've been talking to your Pixietails, then. Be warned: They're idiots."

"Oh, I noticed."

Pixie Sparkle flitted up, jangling in anger, and scowled at the interloper.

"Don't listen to her," said the Pixietail. "She's—"

"Only got your best interest in mind," said the stranger smoothly. "Duchess Ravenwaves at your service, Princess. It's not safe to be in the Snarl at night. Would you like to come to my place? It's just through the trees. You'll be safe from the snagfires there."

"Let's see. I could accept the random offer of shelter from a total stranger who mysteriously appears just after I'm nearly brutalized by a fire-breathing mutant thingamabob, or I could wander out in the wilderness and try to eat pin curls off the trees. Let me ponder a moment," said Leigh, pretending to consider. "I think I'll accept."

Ravenwaves hesitated for a moment, clearly trying to decide what to make of Leigh, but eventually she smiled, baring all her teeth. To be honest, the overall effect was more hungry than friendly.

"Great!" she said, pointing. "My tower is this way. We should hurry before the snagfires come back. They usually hunt in packs."

"Let me grab my staff."

Leigh picked the weapon up, noting that the laser-spear at the top had vanished, leaving only the gem again. That was fine. She knew how to activate it if necessary.

She straightened to find Ravenwaves scowling at the staff. As soon as she realized Leigh was looking at her, she plastered another grin onto her face. Did she really expect this bestie act to work? That expression was faker than the gem on the end of Leigh's staff. Besides, Leigh knew whom she was dealing with: Duchess Ravenwaves was the villain in Mom's storybook. She kidnapped the Pixietails, sent giants to destroy the kingdom, and cursed innocent villagers. Anything to get what she wanted. When Leigh was little, she'd been terrified of her.

Brimming with fake cheer, Ravenwaves plunged into the trees via a narrow path crowded with twisted branches. Leigh followed a few steps behind, pretending not to notice the red eyes that followed their every movement from the underbrush. The Pixietails kept darting toward her, whispering urgently only to be repeatedly shushed. Finally, she ordered them back into her hair to make them stop. They didn't want to go, but they couldn't seem to resist a direct order. Strangely, she couldn't feel a thing when they darted toward her scalp. How much did they weigh? This dream didn't have much in the way of underlying logic.

It was also getting a little boring, so Leigh decided to stir things up a little.

"Real pretty place," she observed, looking at all the dead and dying foliage. "Very... uh... scenic."

"It's certainly not as gorgeous as Lovely Locks Castle. But someone had to volunteer to protect the kingdom from the snagfires. Living out here in this desolate landscape is a sacrifice I'm willing to make," replied Ravenwaves with a melodramatic sigh.

Internally, Leigh couldn't stop laughing, but she managed to keep the amusement off her face. Instead, she patted Ravenwaves on the shoulder, trying to look as sympathetic as possible.

"You're such a good person," she said. "You deserve a medal or something."

"Exactly! That's what I said!" Ravenwaves cleared her throat and tried to look modest. "I mean, it would have been nice, but it's not necessary. I'm just trying to do the right thing."

"Sure. What are those snagfires anyway? I don't remember them from—I mean, I don't remember hearing about them before."

Leigh bit her lip, but Ravenwaves didn't seem to have noticed the blunder. Good thing she was so oblivious.

"Years ago, the snagfires were summoned by Lady Knot, an evil sorceress. They nearly killed me," said Ravenwaves, pushing her way through an upward slope full of dead bushes. "But I defeated Lady Knot and barely managed to escape with my life. I was hoping that the snagfires would be banished back to wherever she'd pulled them from, but they remained. Now they infest Tangleland. The Snarl, where you popped up, is completely impassable."

"Except that we're passing through it right now."

"Well..." Ravenwaves paused, preening. "I know a few tricks. But if you brought any of those wimps from Lovely Locks Castle out here, they wouldn't last a day." She coughed then, wiping the satisfied look off her face and replacing it with a sad little smile. "I mean, wouldn't that be a pity?"

"Right," said Leigh.

She didn't remember the Snarl, snagfires, or Lady Knot from Mom's book, and although it had been a long time since she'd cracked it open, she should have at least recognized the names. Perhaps there had been a second volume? Her dad hadn't exactly been champing at the bit to do anything related to her mom, let alone hunt down a sequel.

"Here we are," said Ravenwaves as they crested the hill.

On the other side, a solitary tower jabbed at the red-tinged sky. The tangled shapes of dead vines clustered around its base and climbed up its walls. Beyond them sat a moat, its water black and still. The narrow bridge leading to the tower was studded with broken stone, remnants of a once-majestic road, and overhung with the skeletal remains of the plants that had once grown here. Leigh had to admit that for a lame fairy tale, the place sure did look foreboding.

"I'm surprised more people don't build vacation homes here," she said.

Ravenwaves just blinked at her. Right. These people didn't understand sarcasm.

"It's a joke," Leigh explained.

"Oh. A joke." Ravenwaves forced a laugh. "I guess I'm just a bit oversensitive. This used to be a beautiful place. Just as gorgeous as Lovely Locks Castle, you know. But that was long ago. It's my goal to restore Tangleland to its former glory. Maybe you could help."

"That sounds great," replied Leigh, pretending to ignore the empty look in Ravenwaves's eyes.

"Come on in, and I'll show you around."

Up close, the place looked even worse than it had from far away. The tower walls were crumbling, their surface punctured by lengths of now-dead vines with thick, fibrous stalks. Sickly yellow foam clustered at the edges of the moat, and pallid fish darted hungrily beneath the surface. The scent of mold hung heavy in the air. This was a place where things went to die. It didn't belong in a children's book at all, unless the goal was to set all the kiddos up for a lifetime of therapy.

Ravenwaves didn't give any of it a second glance. She grinned cheerily, keeping up a steady stream of what she seemed to think was encouragement as she urged Leigh across the rickety bridge to the gaping hole that served as a front entrance.

"There you go!" she said. "Watch your step. Those fish are so hungry that they'd gnaw you to the bone, and we can't have that, now, can we? And be careful on the stairs. I keep meaning to fix them, but I never have time because of course I spend hours and hours watching the roads and saving travelers from snagfires. It's a thankless job, but I manage."

"I'm sure you get a lot of traffic," said Leigh, stepping over an unidentifiable pile of sludge just outside the front door. "This is clearly a place to be."

Ravenwaves stopped to stare at her, brow furrowed.

"You're making fun of me," she said, glowering.

Although Leigh had no reason for guilt, her stomach sank anyway. The duchess just looked so *offended*, and Leigh knew what it was like to be embarrassed about where you came from. She hadn't had many friends growing up, because she refused to invite them over after that time in second grade when Ginny Thompson had made fun of her for being "a poor." Although it was a stupid, grammatically incorrect insult, it had stung. Years later, she still hesitated to invite friends over. The only one who had made the cut at her new apartment was Ari, and even though he didn't have a judgmental bone in his body, she'd still felt sick to her stomach the first time they hung at her place.

"Sorry," she said, and meant it. "Just joking again."

Ravenwaves startled, eyes going wide, and for a moment, Leigh wondered if maybe they were going to have a moment. After all, this was a fairy tale, and one kind apology just might have the ability to change everything. The skies would open and the birds would sing, and maybe there would be a snagfire chorus. That last bit might be entertaining, but otherwise it sounded pretty unbearable.

"Okay then," said Ravenwaves. "Whatever."

Thankfully, the moment passed, and she led the way into the creepy tower. The inside was a small step up from the outside. Leigh didn't see a single goo, foam, or unidentifiable sludge anywhere in the foyer. Actually, there was nothing in the foyer at all. Just smooth gray stone as far as the eye could see. No carpeting. No chandelier. Not even an exterior door. If not for the light spilling out the open door on the other end and the faint red gloom that crept in from outside, the space would have been pitch black.

Luckily, the spiral staircase beyond was lit by torches. Ravenwaves gestured for her to follow before locking the heavy door behind them and pocketing the key with another hungry baring of her teeth.

"Got to keep the snagfires out, you know," she said. "I wouldn't want anything to happen to you."

"Oh, definitely not," said Leigh, clutching her staff.

Her heart sped up as they climbed the steps, and not just because she was allergic to cardio. Once they got to the top of this tower, it would be on like *Donkey Kong*. She knew it. If only this dream had come with a soundtrack, it would have been perfect.

"Just up here," said Ravenwaves, gesturing to the stairs. "You'll be safe and sound."

"I trust you," replied Leigh, lying through her teeth.

At the top of the staircase were two heavy wooden doors, both closed. Ravenwaves took the key from her pocket, opened the one on the right, and gestured for Leigh to enter. Cautiously, Leigh peeked in, holding her staff at the ready, but nothing leaped out at her. It was just a study. Bookshelves covered the walls except for a section dominated by an enormous fireplace. A heavy desk sat in the center of the room beneath the flickering candelabra, its surface covered in cluttered junk. A large window had been flung open to let in the cool, moldy night air, curtains fluttering in the wind. A large telescope with clusters of complicated dials sat next to it, its lenses pointed at something far off in the distance.

All in all, not a bad location for a boss fight. Leigh stepped inside, ready for anything. Ravenwaves let out a satisfied cackle before slamming the door shut behind her and locking it with a click.

"Now I've got you!" shouted Ravenwaves through the door, full of manic glee.

"Oh no. Whatever will I do?" gasped Leigh.

As far as performances went, it wasn't her best work. Ravenwaves didn't answer anyway. All Leigh could hear was angry muttering as she tromped back down the stairs again.

"Well, that was anticlimactic," said Leigh.

But really, she didn't have that much to complain about. The tower was pleasantly warm, with plenty to read. The chair looked comfortable too. She still hoped for a quality fight before the night ended, but if it didn't happen, she could entertain herself.

She peeked through the telescope. Although it was dark, she could just make out the outlines of a fairy-tale castle by the light of the moon. In the book, Ravenwaves had spent a lot of time looking at Lovely Locks Castle through her telescope, plotting and scheming. Too bad it wasn't light out so Leigh could see the place better.

Bored, she moved on. Volumes crowded the bookshelves, but their plain leather spines gave no indication of their contents. She'd have to pick one at random. She snagged one with an orange cover and flipped it open only to be greeted with a familiar illustration of Lady Lovely Locks and the giant from her mom's old storybook.

"Oh no," she groaned, grabbing another. "My subconscious can't hate me that much, can it?"

It did in fact hate her that much. The entire bookshelf was crammed with copies of *Lady Lovely Locks,* each with different covers and fonts, but all containing the exact same stories she'd already read a million times before. She got so frustrated that she pitched the last one across the room to land in the fireplace, letting out a shower of sparks.

"Okay, this is lame," she shouted. "I'm ready to fight now."

But the door didn't open, and Leigh couldn't exactly climb out the window. She wasn't sure if this was a flying dream. If it wasn't, she'd splat into that gross water. Even if she couldn't die, she could get a mouthful of foam or be eaten by those freaky fish. No thank you.

"Oh, come on," she muttered. "I'd almost rather have another traumatic school dream where I can't open my locker and my laptop won't charge and we have to run laps in gym."

Complaining about it didn't help. Maybe there was something interesting in the desk? If it contained only copies of *Lady Lovely Locks,* she was going to throw them all out the window.

She pulled out the chair and sat down at the desk, looking at the piles of papers, inkwells, hairbrushes, and other junk piled atop it. Clearly, Ravenwaves needed a cleaner. She picked up a sheet of parchment—blank on both sides—and tossed it over her shoulder. As she reached for another, a painting hanging over the desk caught her eye. She'd missed it before, but now it seized her attention with both hands and held on tight.

The piece depicted a woman in a full-skirted medieval gown in shades of burgundy and dark charcoal. She sat, hands clasped on her lap, looking out at the viewer with a knowing smile that would have put the *Mona Lisa* to shame. All in all, it was an unremarkable piece of art except for one stunning fact.

The woman in the painting looked an awful lot like Leigh's mom.

Leigh launched to her feet, knocking over a small stack of books and papers. They tumbled to the floor, a single sheet of paper sailing all the way to the edge of the fireplace, where it began to smolder. Her staff slid off the edge of the desk, clattering on the tile. She noticed none of this.

She rushed over to the painting, squinting at it. Her heart leaped into her throat, fluttering with an excitement that quickly ebbed. Then her natural skepticism took hold once again; it wasn't real. None of this was. But it sure was convincing—the woman even had a cluster of three moles shaped like a triangle on her collarbone. In one of Leigh's pictures, her mother wore a tank top, exposing a triangle of moles exactly like this. A few times when she was a kid, she'd drawn them on her own shoulder to match. It didn't mean anything. After all, the whole place was populated by her subconscious. If she looked more closely at the other paintings in the room, she'd probably find all sorts of familiar things. But she had no desire to bother.

It was time to get out of this pastel, hairy dump.

"Pixietails!" she barked. "I need you!"

Her hair stirred as the magical rabbit-creatures came sailing out of it, bells a-jingling. They floated in front of her, practically vibrating with agitation.

"You're in trouble!" said Pixie Shine.

"Ravenwaves is a villain," said Pixie Beauty.

"She's—" began Pixie Sparkle before Leigh cut them off.

"I know; I know," she said. "I've got it handled. She's going to try to cut off my hair, because it's magic. She intends to use it to steal you three and take over the Kingdom of Lovely Locks."

"Guess you don't need a warning, then," said Pixie Sparkle. Its matter-of-fact expression quickly faded as it took in the painting, only to be replaced by a growing disgust. "Ugh."

"You recognize her?" asked Leigh. "Why all the groans?"

Pixie Shine and Pixie Beauty both took one look at the painting and dashed behind her head, hiding from it like it might bite. Pixie Sparkle gritted its teeth and held steady through what was obviously some serious effort.

"That," the Pixietail said, its voice dropping even lower, "is Lady Knot."

CHAPTER 5

LEIGH LOOKED FROM PIXIE SPARKLE TO THE PAINTing a few times, trying to figure out what to make of this new revelation. Who the heck was Lady Knot? Her mom was Marie Carroll. Ultimately, it didn't really matter. She was over this stupid dream and everything in it.

The door opened, and a bunch of foul-smelling snagfires came pouring into the room. If a group of crows was a murder and a group of foxes was a skulk, what would a group of snagfires be called?

"A stink," she said aloud. "It's a stink of snagfires."

"What did you say?" asked Ravenwaves, striding in behind the hulking, smoking beasts.

She looked incredibly satisfied with herself, both hands clasped behind her back, bouncing on her toes like a kid who had stolen some candy. Her eyes sparkled. Leigh couldn't scrape up the energy to be amused by it.

"Nothing," she said. "So are you going to try to cut my hair or what?"

Ravenwaves's shoulders drooped as she held up a pair of golden scissors.

"How did you know?" she said, stomping her foot like a toddler having a tantrum. "Darn it; I had a whole speech planned! Well, no matter. It's time for a haircut, Princess. We can do this the easy way or the hard way. And by 'hard way,' I mean that my snagfires will string you up by your toes from the chandelier, and then I'll cut your hair."

Leigh nodded, resigned. She'd fight the stupid fight if that's what it took to get out of this stupid dream. But she'd left her staff on the floor all the way over by the desk. One of the snagfires was standing on it.

Maybe she could avoid the fight altogether. If only this worked...

"Pixie Shine! Pixie Beauty! Pixie Sparkle!" she cried. "Wake me up!"

The Pixietails didn't appear, but the air around her filled with pastel sparkles. Her hair writhed on her shoulders. A familiar magic tingle began to spread through her limbs.

"No, that's not f—" began Ravenwaves, and then everything went white.

Leigh opened her eyes, looking up at the ceiling of her room from the safety of her bed. Scratch that—from halfway on her bed. There was nothing beneath her head and shoulders but air. She fell to the floor with a thump, rattling the Funko Pops on her nightstand. Her funny bone whammed against the bed frame, making white stars dance over her vision. The cotton-candy wig drooped over her face, covering one eye.

"Oooowwwww," she moaned, clapping a hand to the injury.

After she spent a few seconds crouched on the floor, hissing out her breath through pursed lips, the pain finally eased. She climbed off the rug and tossed the wig onto its stand. Normally, she wouldn't treat such an expensive piece with such carelessness, but she was wiped. She'd brush it out in the morning. Speaking of which, it would be handy to know how long she had before her alarm went off. She picked her phone up off the workbench to check the time and groaned. How was it six in the morning already? It felt like she hadn't slept at all.

She eyed her bed, frowning. Good design schools weren't cheap, and she needed all the scholarships she could get. Her grades—and her attendance—could very well mean the difference between going to her dream school and being stuck with one of her safety picks. As tempting as it was to go back to bed, she had to turn in that anatomy project, or Mrs. Koslowski would dock points for lateness.

Sighing, she sat on the edge of the bed, trying to work up the energy she'd need for the day. But visions of that darned portrait hovered there in the depths of her imagination, a reminder of all the answers she'd never have. She wanted to crawl into bed and hide under the covers. Instead, she stood up and began to untie the million ribbons that held her cosplay together. On the way to school, she was going to treat herself to one of those fancy coffees that tasted like milkshakes but had enough caffeine to fuel a small island nation, and she wasn't going to feel guilty about it either. Not after the night she'd had.

After that dream, she was over the stupid cosplay. She tossed the bodice into the bin and kicked it under her bed.

If there were justice in the world, the day would have been great to balance out Leigh's karma. But that didn't happen. Ari was out for a college visit. When she left Bony Tony on her desk and went to the bathroom, someone tore off his arm. She had to talk herself out of a detention for dozing in health class, and during lunch, she fell asleep in the library and drooled on her math worksheet.

By the time she got home, the only thing she wanted in the world was sleep, although perhaps it was more accurate to say that it was the only item on her wish list she was likely to get. She fought with the sticky front door lock for a good couple of minutes before she finally dislodged it, dumped her satchel two steps inside the tiny living room, and shut the door quietly behind her to avoid waking her dad. After shoving a protein bar down her throat, she trudged to her bedroom for a well-earned nap.

Her dad was sitting on her bed.

She stopped in the doorway, looking up and down the hall in momentary confusion. Her tired brain struggled to make sense of this new development—Dad had been working nights for months now; he slept during the day. On the rare occasions when he had to do something during daylight hours, he woke up long enough to take care of it and then conked back out on the sofa. Usually snored loud enough to wake the dead too. This was a serious break in tradition, and the shock was almost enough to jolt her to consciousness.

"Hey, punkin," he said, patting the wrinkled bedspread next to him. "Have a seat."

She sat down at the desk instead, giving him a thorough once-over.

"What's wrong?" she demanded. "What happened? Are you okay?"

"I'm fine. There's no need to panic."

Even though he'd scared the crap out of her, she couldn't deny her relief. If something happened to him, what would she do? She had literally no one else. No family. A few old friends, but they'd moved around so much that her initial plans to keep in touch with her former besties had slowly faded away to the occasional like on social media. And Ari was moving away to college in a few months.

"Okay," she said cautiously. "What's up?"

He leaned forward, elbows on his knees. This was his earnest, you-can-talk-to-me look. He saved it for special occasions, like the time he gave her the mortifying birds-and-bees speech. The mere sight of the knee elbows gave her flashbacks, and she stiffened, trying to brace herself for whatever was about to come out of his mouth.

"Where were you last night?" he asked.

She blinked.

"What do you mean?" she asked. "You talked to me. I was right here."

"I know that," he chided. "But when I got home from work, you weren't here. Where did you go?"

"I..." She trailed off, confused. "I was sleeping. I fell out of bed and everything. Maybe I was cocooned up in my blankets, and you couldn't see me?"

He shook his head at her, mouth pushed into a firm line.

"Don't try that with me, young lady," he said. "I'm trying to be understanding, but that's not going to last if you lie to me. I turned on your light. I called your name. You weren't here."

She stared at him for a long moment before realizing that her mouth was hanging open like an idiot. But she couldn't process this. Had she been sleepwalking? Could she have left the apartment, locking and unlocking the sticky front door, without ever waking up? Didn't seem likely.

But the only other alternative was ridiculous. She refused to believe that she'd been magically transported into her mother's storybook. That was the stupidest thing she'd ever heard in her life, and she wasn't even going to dignify it by considering it.

Which left...what exactly? She had no other explanation. Not one that made sense.

Her dad clenched his jaw and raised his eyebrows. He was growing impatient. She had to tell him something, but she didn't know what.

"It's been...hard lately," she finally managed. "I just needed some air. I didn't want to worry you."

"Where did you go? This neighborhood isn't safe for you to go traipsing around by yourself," he said, relaxing a little.

"I didn't. I wouldn't." Now that she'd gotten started, the lies came with disconcerting ease. Her acting abilities would put Ravenwaves's to shame. "I walked over to Ari's. That's all. I wasn't doing anything stupid."

He nodded, finally unclenching his jaw.

"Ari's a good kid. He wouldn't get into any messes," he said.

What about me? she thought. *I'm good too.* But she didn't say anything, didn't dare risk a slip that would clue him in to the fact that she was lying through her teeth. Instead, she just nodded.

"Look, punkin," he continued, "I know things have been tough. I'm working long hours, and this place is a dump. But I'm doing my best. I want you to know that."

"We're doing okay, though, right?" she asked. "I can take on more hours at the store if I need to. Sal said he'd give me another shift or two if things get really rough."

"School comes first; you know that."

"Yeah."

"I know..." He struggled for words, visibly uncomfortable. "I know yesterday was a tough day."

The reference to her mom's disappearance, no matter how oblique, took her by surprise. Such things were simply not spoken about in this household. If she didn't know better, she'd think he was some sort of clone, and not the cute *Neon Genesis Evangelion* kind.

"Yeah...?" she said tentatively.

"If you need to talk to someone, I understand," said Dad.

He slapped his hands on his knees and stood, as if to signal that the conversation was over now that he'd delivered that stunner. She couldn't restrain herself. She was confused, exhausted, and just plain done.

"That's it!?" she exclaimed, the words bursting out of her. "That's all you've got to say? After all these years, can't you tell me something? I don't know why she left or who she was or... anything. Are you really going to let me go through the rest of my life thinking it was my fault?"

His eyes widened, but she wasn't finished. Now that she'd started, everything she'd ever wanted to say kept pouring out. Maybe because she was so unsettled by her dream that maybe hadn't been a dream after all. Or—more likely—because she wasn't willing to accept the excuses any longer.

"I'm sorry if it hurts you, but keeping me in the dark is hurting me, Dad. I deserve to know the truth," she said, her eyes beginning to well up. "You're going to have to tell me what happened sometime. I'm old enough now. I can take it."

She fell quiet then, blinking hard to keep the tears at bay. He stared at her as if seeing her for the first time.

"You're growing up..." he said, standing over her. "I don't have to like it."

"Please," she whispered. "Tell me."

He gritted his teeth, hesitated, and then shook his head.

"I... can't, punkin. I just can't. I've got to get some sleep, or I'll be a zombie at work tonight," he said, hurrying toward the door like he thought she might bite him. Frankly, it was tempting. But she said nothing as he rushed out like a coward, shutting the door behind him. As soon as the latch clicked, she threw her plague doctor Squishmallow at it, but that didn't make her feel any better.

She threw herself onto the bed, but sleep eluded her. She stared at the ceiling, obsessing over it all—the maybe-dream, the argument, the teeth-gritting annoyance of all those mysteries piled atop one another—until her dad left for work. For once, he didn't come in to bid her good night.

CHAPTER 6

LEIGH SPENT THE NEXT DAY IN A DAZE, WORRYING in endless circles. What had happened the other night? If she didn't come up with a logical explanation, she would be forced to believe that her cosplay was magic, her missing mother was an evil sorceress, and magical bunnies lived in her hair. But nothing else held up under scrutiny. Around and around she went, with no forward progress whatsoever.

She bombed a pop quiz in Anatomy and Physiology, and Mrs. Koslowski pulled her aside, face pinched with concern, to check on her. For one wild moment, she considered confessing that she was starting to question her sanity, but she couldn't do that. Mrs. K actually cared; she'd worry even more. Or call home, which would be even worse.

"I'm sorry," she said. "I'm just stressed. I'm dealing with some stuff." She paused, but Mrs. K kept staring at her, expecting more. "Stuff at home, I mean."

Mrs. K squeezed her shoulder, her eyes sad.

"I'm not going to pry," she said, "but my door is always open. If you ever need anything, you know where to find me. You can retake the quiz tomorrow during your lunch."

Leigh thanked her, hightailing it out of the classroom and running smack into Ari, who was waiting outside the door. He grabbed her by the shoulders, steadying her, his brown eyes crinkled in concern.

"You look like crap," he said.

"Haven't been sleeping," mumbled Leigh.

"If you need to call off work tonight and catch up on some z's, I won't hold it against you."

"I can't afford to cut my hours; you know that. I'll just drink some of Sal's coffee. That stuff would raise the dead," said Leigh, heading down the hall. "We'd better go or we'll miss the bus."

They walked in silence until they reached the doors, pushing out into another dingy gray day. Clouds hung low in the sky, the watery sun barely poking through. Shallow puddles dotted the pavement, and a cold wind whipped right through the thick fabric of her hoodie. She shivered, hugging her arms close to her body.

"So your dad called me," said Ari.

Leigh muttered a swear word under her breath.

"Don't worry. I told him that you were hanging out with me the other night," he continued. "You should be good."

"Thank you. He was really freaking out."

"Yeah." They reached the bus stop, hovering just outside the cluster of kids waiting there. Leigh exchanged nods with a girl from her art class, trying to pretend that everything was fine and normal. Then Ari asked, "So where were you?"

She didn't know what to say, so she faked a cough. Then she *still* didn't know what to say, so she took a deliberate step backward into a puddle, soaking her shoe. It didn't feel good at all, but it was the best she could come up with on short notice.

"Damn it!" she exclaimed as water filtered into her socks.

"That was a brilliant move," observed Ari, his eyes narrowed. "Why'd you do that?"

"Because I'm an idiot?"

"Right," he replied, clearly unconvinced. "About that question . . ."

"There's the bus," she said, looking over his shoulder. "Let's hustle. Yesterday, this creepy old dude kept breathing down my neck. I'd like to grab a seat if we can."

"Right," he repeated.

Throughout the subsequent four-hour shift, he kept asking, and she kept evading. After all, what was she supposed to say? He was already worried, but that would be nothing compared with how he'd feel if she explained that she'd either sleepwalked or vanished, but she wasn't sure which. Maybe she could forget all about it. After all, if it didn't happen again, none of it mattered. All she had to do was concentrate on not disappearing. Simple.

Luckily, the shift was a busy one, leaving little opportunity for discussion. Late in the evening, when things finally began to slow down, the employee toilet overflowed. She'd never been so happy to have plumbing issues than she was at that moment. She fetched the chicken man's plunger and took care of the problem.

When she got home, she found a white takeout carton on the kitchen counter with her name written on it in sloppy Sharpie. Dad must have been feeling really guilty; he'd gotten lo mein. She took the box and a fork to her room and slurped it down while chugging through her math homework.

As she was finishing the last problem, he tapped on the door.

"Yeah?" she responded.

"I'm heading out," he said, sticking his head in. "You okay?"

She was not in fact okay, not anywhere near it, but she nodded anyway. He looked her up and down, hesitating, and then shut the door behind him. A few minutes later, the apartment door slammed shut.

"Nice talk," she said aloud to the empty room. "I really feel like we made a breakthrough in our relationship."

She fished the last few noodles out of the bottom of the container and threw away the empty carton. Her empty bed beckoned her, and she quickly changed into an old tee and a pair of sweats. Sure, it was early, but she needed to catch up on sleep big-time.

As soon as her head hit the pillow, she began to worry. Should she set up her laptop camera to make sure she actually stayed in her bed this time? She had to know. Otherwise, she was left feeling like the world had somehow tipped off its axis. Left was right, up was down, and shoulder pads and neon were in again.

The camera wasn't a half-bad idea, though. She set up her laptop. Unfortunately, by the time she toppled back onto the pillow, she was wide awake. She made a cup of tea, hoping that it would soothe her into dreamland, but afterward she found herself staring at the computer screen, watching herself not sleep at all. That wasn't particularly helpful. What else helped people doze off? She googled it but discovered nothing useful. She didn't have any melatonin in the house, had no desire to work out, and didn't practice sleep hygiene, whatever that was.

Perhaps she could try one other thing: putting on the cosplay in front of the camera to prove once and for all that it didn't whisk her off to a magical kingdom full of hairy trees. Maybe then she'd be able to rest.

She might as well, because she wasn't going to fall asleep anytime soon. So she got up and retrieved the Lady Lovely Locks bin from beneath the bed. All the ribbons had wound into a tangled mess that took a good five minutes to unravel, and the costume pieces had gotten extremely wrinkled after being shoved in there all willy-nilly. She heated up her little handheld steamer and smoothed them out before turning her attention to the mangled wig. Ever since the dream, she'd studiously ignored it. Now she got out the wig spray and a wide-toothed comb and worked out all the snarls, restoring it to its former glory.

Much better. She put on all the pieces, her laptop recording the whole time. Once she'd verified her sanity, maybe she could use parts of the video for her social media channels. Time-lapse cosplay tended to do pretty well with her viewers, and she could use the ad revenue.

She finished tying the last ribbon. This time, she wasn't going to make the same mistake she had before; she'd put the staff into its sheath after she put the wig on. She pulled her hair back, securing it to her head with some flat barrettes. Then she retrieved the wig from the stand and hesitated.

There was just one problem with this plan—her mirror was attached to the wall, and her laptop didn't have enough battery to unplug. If she used the mirror, the edge of her bookshelf would block her almost entirely from view, but if she wanted to use the video later, the wig had to be straight. She leaned down in front of the laptop to see herself on the screen, but every time she bent over, the hair got caught and pulled the wig back off. After the third try, she gave up on that plan.

Huffing in annoyance, she grabbed a hand mirror off the pegboard. It had been a part of her evil Valkyrie queen cosplay two years ago, and although she'd sold off the dress, she'd kept the mirror. Filigree and spikes covered the back and sides, and she loved the idea of a makeup mirror turned blunt weapon. Good thing, because she needed it now.

She held up the hand mirror, tugging the wig more firmly onto her head. The part was off-center, and details like that made all the difference when it came to a final look. She shifted it slightly and then pulled the wig snug.

The room vanished. There was a flash of light and an electric shiver, and then she found herself standing in the middle of another clearing. As before, the pink moon hung low in the darkened sky. Grass tickled her ankles, and the sweet scent of flowers filled her nose. Disoriented, she looked around, trying to remain calm despite the nerves that choked her throat. Was she really here? She'd have to wait until she saw the video to be certain, but she had to at least admit that there was a possibility that she really owned a magic wig that carried her off to the Kingdom of Lovely Locks every time she put it on.

"Aw, come on!" she exclaimed, kicking at the ground. "You've got to be kidding me."

"On the contrary," replied a pompous voice from somewhere near her waist, "I am quite serious."

That didn't sound like one of her Pixietails. The voice was neither helium squeaky nor bass deep. She whirled around, trying to spot the whatever-it-was. As she did, a flash of movement in the mirror still clutched in her hand caught her attention.

When she looked into its depths, a face peered out at her. Not her reflection. A whole different face entirely.

It had the blank white features of a mask, with black holes for the eyes and mouth. But despite its lack of detail, it managed to give the impression of snobbish superiority. Those pointy cheekbones could cut glass, and the mask tilted back as if its invisible wearer looked down its nose at her. The rudimentary mouth twisted in a smirk.

"Like the dress," it said. "You look like an explosion in a ribbon factory."

"Hey!" she snapped, affronted. "You're a floating mask in a magic mirror. You don't have any room for sartorial insults."

"So touchy. What has all your ribbony knickers in a bunch?"

"You really want to know?" she demanded, her voice climbing higher and higher as her agitation grew. "I'll tell you! I'm pretty sure I have a magical cosplay that transports me into another world, but is it a world full of cute anime boys I'd like to date? No. Instead, I got the one where the trees have bangs. If all this nonsense is real, I nearly died the last time I was here, because I thought I was dreaming and almost jumped out a window. The magical vermin that live in my hair didn't bother to explain anything useful; the only other person I met was only interested in shaving me bald, and now that I'm back, I've got a judgy magic mirror giving me grief. Honestly, if you don't lay off, I'll beat the crap out of you with…wait a minute. Where's my staff?!"

She reached over her shoulder to where the staff ought to be, opening and closing her hand on a big bunch of nothing. She flailed around for a moment, trying to bend her elbows backward and grope her own back. Finally, she held up the mirror, snapping at the mirror man.

“That’s empty, right?” she said. “No staff?”

The mirror man bobbed, somehow communicating the fact that it had just rolled its eyes despite the fact that there were no orbs to roll.

“Not unless it’s invisible,” it said. “Did the poor magical princess forget her eensy-weensy wittle staff?”

“Keep it up, bub. I’ll step on you.”

The mirror stuttered for a moment before glaring at her.

“You wouldn’t dare,” it said.

“Oh, I’m about a millimeter away from full-on violence. Try me.” It didn’t respond, and somehow, that made her feel a little better. “That’s what I thought. Why am I arguing with you anyway? I have stuff to do.”

“Oh, yes. Important things like whining and floofing your hair. I know how you girls are.”

She opened her mouth to start the whole argument all over again, thought better of it, and stuffed the mirror into a pocket. She could hear its muffled protests through the thick layers of tulle but couldn’t make out the words. Much better.

Now what? She considered going back home to check the camera, but ultimately decided against it. She couldn’t resist the urge to get one more look at that painting. If this place wasn’t some sleep-deprived hallucination, it would be the first clue she’d ever gotten about her mom. Electric excitement numbed her fingers and cheeks as she thought about what it would be like to finally have some answers, to live without that mystery hanging over her like a sword about to fall. Before now, the possibility had been . . . well, impossible.

Fists clenched in determination, she began to march toward the red glow of Tangleland, barely visible through the branches of the forest. Although she didn't have her staff, she'd punch her way through Ravenwaves if necessary. She wasn't a violent person, but the idea appealed more than she wanted to admit. She daydreamed about it at length as she tromped over the uneven ground, forging a path through the thick trees. Tangleland really deserved its name. She had to backtrack a few times.

After cresting a jagged hill, she paused at the top, folding in half with her hands on her knees to gasp for air. In all her eagerness, she'd pushed a bit too hard, and now the plains of Tangleland appeared to undulate in her swimming vision. The sight was enough to make a girl seasick on dry land, so she tore her gaze away.

As she descended down the far slope, a few rocks near the bottom got up and began to lope toward her, emitting a familiar barking cough. Not rocks, snagfires. With a pang of alarm, she realized that the field hadn't been moving just because her vision had gone wobbly; it was covered in snagfires. Even if she'd brought her staff, there were too many for her to fight. There must have been hundreds of them. No, *thousands*.

The snagfires scrambled up the loose slope, rocks skittering down behind them. The terrain would buy her only a few seconds at the most, and then she would have to face them unarmed. Although maybe not. Maybe the mirror had a secret power too. After all, she hadn't realized how to use the staff until she was faced with an enemy. It was a magic mirror; it had to do something other than annoy her, right? She whipped it out of her pocket and held it up so the mirror man could see the small herd of snagfires as they quickly closed the gap.

"Yeeeeees!" exclaimed the mirror man in malicious delight. "A fight! That's what I'm talking about! Violence! Gore! Blood on the rocks! Entrails hanging from the—"

"Ew! Shut up!" snapped Leigh. "You're supposed to be helping here!"

"I'm helping you have a little fun."

"Fun? You call entrails *fun*?"

"I'm the magic mirror of an evil Valkyrie queen. Violence is literally what you made me for, and entrails are my favorite," declared the mirror man. "I know! Beat them with my spikes! Ooooh, I can practically taste the gristle!"

The snagfires loped closer. She could see the wild red orbs of their eyes and smell their sharp stink. Her magic mirror was obviously determined to be no help whatsoever. Acting on instinct, she dropped down into a full-on Chris Pratt *Jurassic World* stance, holding her hands out to stop the charging beasts.

The snagfires skittered to a stop, heads cocked in confusion. Leigh's heart thumped a wild beat in her chest as they stared at her, steam curling from their beaks. It was working! The Chris Pratt stance soothed velociraptors *and* snagfires! Who would have thunk it?

"Death!" howled the mirror man, still clutched in her hand. "Dismemberment! Defenestration! Some other violent word that begins with the letter *D*!"

The snagfires jerked out of their stunned reverie, hissing and barking. Leigh stumbled, nearly dashing the mirror against the rocks as she fell. A not-insignificant amount of hair tangled in her face, blocking her vision. The mirror man shrieked, babbling in wordless fear at its almost-demise, and for a moment, she considered smashing it on purpose just to shut it up. But there was no time. Even if she couldn't see them, she could hear the snagfires coming.

"Pixietails, get me out of here!" she yelped.

The responding jingle was immediate, and for the first time, she welcomed the obnoxious racket. She lifted into the air, but it wasn't until she heard the frustrated barking of the snagfires far below that she began to relax.

"Can one of you fix my hair?" she asked. "I'm flying blind here."

"A hairstyle!?" exclaimed Pixie Beauty, excitement raising its voice to an eardrum-piercing pitch. "I thought you'd never ask!"

"I never got my entrails," moaned the magic mirror.

Leigh wanted to tell off the whole lot of them, but she held back for the moment. She needed to know more about that painting, so for now, she'd have to grin and bear it. Or just bear it, anyway. As the Pixietails and the magic mirror kept up their endless chatter, she couldn't find the strength to grin without murdering someone.

CHAPTER 7

BY THE TIME THE PIXIETAILS FLEW HER AND THE mirror man back to the castle, Leigh had been through four different hairstyles, including a giant bouffant, and she had gritted her teeth nearly to nubs trying not to scream in frustration. Or maybe it just felt like it. Hard to tell. But when she landed outside the walls, her jaw sure throbbed.

"I still don't understand why we had to leave," said the mirror man. "It's so booooring here. I might diiiiiie."

Without a single word, she stuffed the mirror back into her pocket, muffling its continued complaints. She didn't quite trust herself to speak. The Pixietails would probably be scandalized if she swore. Maybe that would shock them into silence? She sank down onto a smooth stone near the gates, put her throbbing head into her hands, and tried to wait it out. There couldn't be that much to say about braids, could there?

Apparently, this was an untapped subject. They went on for a good five minutes without taking a breath, and she couldn't take it anymore.

"Enough!" she said, cutting off a long debate between Pixie Shine and Pixie Beauty about waterfall braids. "We have important things to do."

"Oh," said Pixie Shine, mouth curved into an O of shock. "Really?"

"What do you need, Princess?" asked Pixie Sparkle, floating up to hover near her shoulder.

If only she knew. She pinched the bridge of her nose, trying to think despite the pounding of her head. It had been so long since she read *Lady Lovely Locks*, but there had to be something within its pages that would help her get past all those snagfires. But what?

Maybe she could bypass the fight altogether. That would really get the mirror man's knickers in a twist. She grinned to herself. It would be very disappointed by the lack of entrails in the plan, and the more she thought about it, the more that tickled her. That decided it: She'd try the Looking Room. With its magic, the princess could see all the way into Tangleland. She could bypass Ravenwaves's defenses and examine the painting from the comfort of her own castle. Why hadn't she thought of this before?

"I need to use the Looking Room," she said. "I can do that, right?"

"Yes, Princess," replied Pixie Sparkle. "You're the only one who can enter it, so it's been closed up for a long time."

"I hope it comes with a manual," muttered Leigh.

"Shall we take you there?" piped Pixie Shine, jingling with excitement. "First, you go through the Princess Door, and then the Room of Challenge, and on to the Floating Stones, and... oh, it's so exciting, I can barely stand it!"

The blue Pixietail jingled itself right into a bush in its excitement. Leigh rolled her eyes. She didn't have time for this nonsense. The stories had described some security measures to protect the Looking Room from Ravenwaves and her minions, with an illustration of the princess hopping across a series of enormous floating stones, but she hadn't realized how much of a production it would take to get through them. From the sounds of it, the maze of obstacles would take forever. It sure would have been easier to lock the room behind a door and plop some guards in front of it, but no one had asked her.

"Can't you just fly me past all that?" she asked.

"Fly... past?" asked Pixie Beauty, frowning.

"Which word didn't you understand?" Leigh waited, but the tiny purple bunny just gaped at her. They really were idiots. She'd need to be more specific. "Does the Looking Room have a window?"

"Yessss...?"

"Fly me into it."

"But you can't... that's not..."

Overcome with emotions, Pixie Beauty also flew into the bush. Leigh waited for a moment, but neither of them came back out again. She would have been worried if not for the fact that she could hear them jangling and shushing each other. Cowards. She turned to Pixie Sparkle, who floated off to her left.

"Well?" she asked. "I don't know what the big deal is. You guys flew me here, so why not fly me up there?"

The Pixietail pursed its tiny lips thoughtfully.

"It's against the rules," it finally said. "The obstacles are designed to ensure that you're really the princess and not an impostor in disguise. Only the true Lady Lovely Locks can get through them all; it's a way to protect the power of the Looking Room from Ravenwaves. It would be bad for the kingdom if she got her hands on it."

"Oh, no kidding. There would be no privacy at all. Every time she learned a new secret, there would be a villainous monologue to go with it. Ugh." Leigh shuddered. "No thank you."

"Exactly," said Pixie Sparkle.

"But I have you," she said. "If I have Pixietails, then I'm the princess, right?"

"Other maidens have Pixietails," replied Pixie Sparkle.

"Right. Those two morons—I mean, girls—from the storybook. I know they have Pixietails, but that's not the point. The point is that I'm asking you to take me to the Looking Room. You know who you are. You're a real Pixietail, and you belong to the real princess. So if you're real, then you know I'm real, and it's not a problem to take me past the defenses. They're still working as intended by only letting in the true Lady Lovely Locks."

As she spoke, the Pixietail's eyes began to cross with the effort of following her convoluted logic. Although the tiny pink beast was the smartest of the three of them, she'd apparently reached its limits. She was surprised that steam didn't start coming out its ears. It blinked at her and then nodded hesitantly.

"I'll get them," it said.

It dived toward the bush in a flurry of pink sparkles. The leaves rustled for a moment, and the high-pitched voices of Shine and Beauty let out yelps of pain, but then Sparkle dragged them out by the tips of their long, pointed ears.

"We're taking her up to the Looking Room," declared Pixie Sparkle.

"But..." Beauty's eyes dashed toward the bush, but another yank from Sparkle kept it in place. "Ouch!"

"That's our princess. We're taking her," said Sparkle, cracking its tiny knuckles one fist at a time. "Now."

The other two Pixietails exchanged a worried look, gulping audibly. Then they nodded in desperate eagerness.

"Right!" said Pixie Shine. "The Looking Room. Why didn't we think of that?"

"Happy to help, Princess!" piped Pixie Beauty, not to be outdone. "Up, up, and away!"

An aura of purple glitter surrounded her, and she found herself lifting up off the ground and soaring through the air. Her hair streamed in the wind; the ribbons trailed off her dress. Maybe this was real, or maybe it wasn't, but that didn't matter right now. It was a blast. She whooped as she flew toward the dark bulk of the castle, wishing with all her heart that it was light out so she could enjoy the view. Flying was much less nerve-racking than she'd expected. She used to have nightmares about falling from the sky, but she felt completely secure. Maybe she was a natural.

She soared through the window at the top of a tall tower, gently coming to rest on the white marble floor of a large chamber. Hundreds of translucent bubbles with flickers of movement deep in their depths floated in the air above her. She looked around, but there was no obvious control panel. In fact, she saw no furnishings whatsoever. Luckily, she remembered this bit from the storybook, and she knew exactly what to do.

"I'd like to see Ravenwaves Tower," she said.

In the book, the Looking Room had responded to verbal commands, and it thrilled Leigh to see the magic she'd dreamed about in action. The mass of bubbles jostled as one worked its way out and floated down toward her. It bobbed before her, color rising to the surface and coalescing into a vivid image whose clarity would rival the latest iPhone. She could see the red-tinged sky of Tangleland and the jutting finger of the tower in perfect detail.

"Closer, please," she said.

The image blurred as the perspective changed. Now the tower filled the bubble, a writhing mass of black at its base. Had Ravenwaves flooded the moat? She directed the image again, zooming down to get a closer look. As it cleared, she swore aloud. Hundreds of snagfires clustered around the tower, fighting, sleeping, lighting things on fire. There would be no sneaking around the snagfires to get to the painting. Not when they reached all the way to the tower door. Good thing she had the Looking Room and its magic bubbles, or she'd have been toast.

"Looking Room, show me the study at the top of the tower," she ordered.

The image wavered again before resolving into the outlines of a familiar chamber. She found herself staring at the window, where the telescope still pointed toward the very castle where she now stood. For a brief moment, she wondered if she could look through it and see herself, but this was no time for games. She steered the bubble around to face the desk and pushed it into the corner where the painting had hung, her breath ragged with excitement.

But when the image cleared, there was nothing in the corner but a small placard. Leigh's brow furrowed with confusion as she examined it. Perhaps she had the wrong one? She tried the other three in quick succession, but two contained bookshelves and one was too narrow. This had to be the spot. She returned to it, squinting into the bubble. There! Ravenwaves wasn't exactly great on the housekeeping front; she could see the outline on the wall where the painting had hung. So why had this particular painting been moved?

Perhaps the placard would offer some clue. She zoomed in, jittery with nerves.

In spidery handwriting, the placard read: *If you want the painting, come get it. I'll trade it for your hair.*

It wasn't signed, but she knew full well who had written it. She whirled her bubble around, half expecting Ravenwaves to pop out of the walls and start monologuing at her. But that didn't happen. She returned to her contemplation of the empty wall, unsure what to think. Did Ravenwaves know about her connection to the painting, or had she just seen Leigh look at it and grabbed onto any bit of leverage she could find? It was impossible to know for certain. Even if she could wrench any answers out of the duchess, she wouldn't be able to trust a word of them.

She sighed, stretching out her stiff neck, and dismissed the bubble. This was useless. She needed to go home and check the camera. It wasn't worth putting a bunch of effort into making a plan when she didn't even know for sure if any of this was real. Stupid kingdom with its stupid villains. She should let her mirror man feast on their entrails. It would serve them right.

"Augh! I am so over this! Pixie Shine! Pixie Beauty! Pixie Sparkle! Send me home before I do something I'll regret!"

A shimmer of magic surrounded her, depositing her unsteadily back into her room, where she stumbled into the desk and knocked the laptop off the workbench. Once she'd righted the mess, she sat down in her desk chair and took out the mirror. Its surface reflected nothing but her own face, without a single sociopathic mirror man in sight. Chuckling to herself, she hung it back on her pegboard. Wherever the mirror man was, it was probably so pissed at her.

Working with careful precision, she took the cosplay off and stored it neatly away. The process took longer than it had any right to. Although she didn't want to admit it, she was stalling. She wanted it to be real. Lovely Locks was one of the lamest places she'd ever been; the trees were stupid, and the Pixietails and the duchess were all morons. After all, the genre wasn't exactly known for its realism and character development. But Leigh still wanted to believe. Partly because she was desperate to know what had happened to her mom, but that wasn't the only thing that drew her to Lovely Locks Kingdom. There, she could fly. No matter what happened, she'd always remember how it felt to soar through the sky and not fear falling for a single moment. If it was real, she wanted to know more. How in the heck had this happened? She still struggled to believe in it herself, and she'd seen the place in all its pastel glory with her own eyes.

She tried to prepare herself for disappointment. She probably had narcolepsy, or maybe a brain tumor. Maybe she'd hallucinated the whole thing—the fairy-tale world, the snagfires—heck, even the chicken plunger man at work. She reached out to the laptop and shifted the mouse, her finger hovering over the button.

She squeezed her eyes shut and clicked. Hesitantly, hopefully, she peeked.

The frozen video showed nothing but an empty room. She stared at it for a long moment, her mouth hanging open. It didn't mean anything, not yet. Maybe she'd stepped out of frame for a moment. Maybe she really did sleepwalk. The only way to know for sure was to start at the beginning. She restarted the video and watched in fast-forward as she put on the cosplay, tying ribbon after ribbon. Video Leigh tried to tug on the wig, crouching in front of the camera. Then she picked up the mirror.

As soon as she pulled the wig on, she disappeared in a shower of sparkles.

Leigh couldn't help it; she whooped aloud. Despite all the evidence, she could barely believe it. She watched her disappearance over and over again, and it was undeniable. Lovely Locks Kingdom was real. She sat back in her swivel chair, stunned.

Maybe, just maybe, she'd finally figure out what had happened to her mom.

CHAPTER 8

LEIGH FLOATED THROUGH THE NEXT DAY ON A wave of caffeine and adrenaline, but by the time she got to work, both had worn off. She kept yawning with such frequency that her jaw started hurting. Every minute felt like an eternity, but she focused on the prize. Only three hours and fourteen minutes until she could go home... three hours and thirteen and a half minutes...

The clock above the registers ticked off the seconds, and each one felt like an eternity. The shop was dead; the bell above the door silent. Normally, she'd chat with Ari to make the time go faster, but she couldn't concentrate enough to hold a coherent conversation. At one point, she found herself standing in the tapes and fasteners aisle with no idea what she'd intended to do. She whirled around to check the clock again, but only a minute had passed since the last time she'd checked. Three hours and nine minutes left.

She turned back to the tape display, hoping the sight would jog her memory, but no luck. Shrugging, she decided to pour herself another cup of coffee, but Ari blocked the end of the aisle, his arms folded. He'd never been particularly intimidating—he was too thin and gangly—but he sure came close now. What he lacked in mass, he made up for in sheer stubborn determination.

"Spill it," he said.

Her addled brain registered only the word "spill," and she looked around blankly at the floor. Had she come here to clean up? If so, she'd forgotten to get the mop. But she saw nothing. Not even a random mysterious sock like they'd found the other day. She turned a questioning look in his direction.

"Seriously, you're freaking me out," he continued.

"Sorry." Another enormous yawn cracked her jaw. "I'm just so tired. Where's the spill again?"

But he just looked more worried.

"There's no spill, you moron," he said, his brow furrowed. "Sit down. I'll get coffee."

"You think we could improvise an IV so I could pour it directly into my veins?" she asked, but he was already gone, muttering to himself as he disappeared into the back room.

He'd told her to sit, and that sounded delightful. She plopped down right there, perching on the edge of the shelving unit and propping her tired head up on her knees. She couldn't see the clock, which was probably for the best. The slow progression of time was ticking her off.

Sometime later—could have been two minutes or maybe an hour, who knew?—Ari returned with two cheap Styrofoam cups of coffee. It was steaming, the cup warm in her hands. She guzzled it anyway, burning the roof of her mouth. The whole time, he stared at her, brow arched. When she was done, she spiked the cup on the ground, paused, and then picked it back up again just in case a customer came in.

"Better?" he asked, sitting down on the bottom shelf opposite her.

"Yeah. I'm awake for at least the next two minutes."

“Good. Mind telling me what’s going on?”

“Huh?” It took a moment for her to process what he was talking about. “Oh. I’m just exhausted. It feels like my brain has been replaced with Jell-O. And not even a good flavor. I’m thinking orange.”

“Not sleeping?”

“I got, like, three hours last night, and zilch the night before. Sorry I’m such a zombie.”

He nodded, staring into his cup for a minute. Finally, he said, “I don’t buy it.”

She snorted. “Okay.”

“No, I mean it. You’re tired and spacey, sure. Fine. Been there. But you’ve been putting me off for days. You disappear in the middle of the night, use me as your alibi, and refuse to tell me where you went. Now you’re exhausted because you’re not sleeping. I don’t have to be Sherlock to put this one together. You’re still sneaking out.”

She stared at him, mouth hanging open. Telling him the truth was out of the question. It was one thing to believe she owned a magical cosplay after seeing the video evidence, but if she told him that, he’d think she’d snapped. Her secret would develop legs—once she spilled, she wouldn’t be able to unspill it.

But she didn’t know what to say. She stared at him helplessly, unable to think straight enough to concoct a believable story. After a moment, his lips firmed, pressing into an angry line.

“So that’s how it is, huh?” he asked. “I sure hope you know what you’re doing. If you get yourself in too deep, I’ll be there for you, but you better be prepared to answer some questions.”

She snorted. “Jeez. It sounds like you think I’ve developed a nice new fent habit or something.”

“Are you telling me you haven’t?” he asked evenly.

“I’m not doing drugs. Or dealing drugs. Or anything related to drugs. I’m just tired. Going through some stuff. I didn’t realize that was a crime.”

“And that’s the problem!” Ari threw up his hands, the coffee sloshing over the rim of his cup. “Ow.” He stuck his hand into his mouth, wincing. Wordlessly, she got up and went to the registers, returning with a roll of paper towel. He took it, wiping up the spill. “Thanks,” he continued. “But like I said, that’s the problem. I thought we were friends. Friends support each other. Either we’re not as close as I thought we were, or you’re doing something really stupid that you know I’ll call you out on. So which is it?”

She had to tell him something. Maybe a partial truth would satisfy his curiosity without making her feel like a complete and utter jerk.

“Okay, look. So you remember my mom?” she said.

“. . . Yeah?” he responded, drawing the word out into one long, uncertain syllable.

“I might have found something. A clue about what happened to her. I don’t know what to think of it. Heck, maybe it’s a dead end. I’m almost afraid to hope, you know?” That was more truthful than she wanted to admit. She couldn’t look at him. Instead, she began to tear pieces of Styrofoam off her cup, dropping them inside it. “As soon as I’ve figured things out, as soon as I’m ready to talk about it, you’re the first person I’m coming to. But I’m just not ready yet. It’s a lot to digest.”

He let out a long, slow breath. Took a sip of coffee. Sat with that for a moment.

"Wow," he said. "I didn't…I guess I can't blame you for that. That's huge."

"Yeah. I'm sorry again about my dad pestering you. I know I put you in a tough position, but I didn't think he'd ask you. I can't tell him about this, because…well, you know."

"He gets all twitchy whenever you bring her up. I get it." Ari nodded. "But I wouldn't rat you out. You know that, right?"

"Of course I do. I just…I've got some choices to make. Like, I've been rushing into this headlong, but last night, when I finally tried to go to bed, I couldn't stop worrying. If I dig into this and it turns out not to be her, then I'm pretty much back where I started. But if it is her, I can't unlearn whatever I find out. What if it sucks? What if she's an awful person?" she said, tearing another piece from the ragged edge of the cup. "Like, really awful? Maybe I should just let sleeping dogs lie."

"I mean, but what if you get your mom back?" he asked. "I understand the fear, but think about it. Your dad is biased. She probably broke his heart, right? That doesn't mean she's a bad person."

"I guess…"

"I'm not trying to push you in any direction, because Lord knows what I'd do in your shoes. Whatever you do, you've got my axe. I protec. I attac. You know the drill."

"You're such a nerd." She snickered.

"Yeah, yeah. Tell me something I don't know." He pushed up to standing. "I'd get you more coffee, but you murdered that poor cup."

"Pour it right into my mouth," she suggested, clamoring to her feet. "I could use it."

“Why? Are you sneaking out again tonight?” he asked. “I’ll come with. I won’t ask questions. We can glue my mouth shut if necessary. But don’t go wandering around the Badlands searching for your mom alone. If you get shot, I’ll be really pissed.”

As much as she appreciated the offer, she still wasn’t ready to confess everything else. She hadn’t been lying. The more she’d thought about it, the more complicated this situation became. Besides, as badly as she wanted answers, she needed sleep more. The smart thing to do would be to rest up tonight and return to Lovely Locks once she didn’t need a coffee IV to stay awake.

“I’m hitting pause for tonight,” she said. “Promise. I’ve got a mountain of homework, and if I don’t get to bed at a decent hour, I’m going to start hallucinating.”

“Fair enough. My ringer’s on all night if you change your mind. I meant what I said, Leigh. Let me be the Robin to your Batman. The Patrick to your SpongeBob. The Donkey to your Shrek.”

“Get out of mah swamp!” yelled Leigh, throwing the mangled coffee cup at him.

Bits of torn Styrofoam went flying everywhere. One landed in his hair. He looked somber as he surveyed the damage.

“I have your back, but you’re cleaning that up,” he said.

By the time Leigh got home that night, she felt nauseated and exhausted, and although she wanted nothing more than to crawl into bed and sleep for a year, she had math to do. She threw together a quick box of mac and cheese and took a bowl into her room so she could eat and work at the same time.

As she was finishing up the last polynomial, her dad tapped on the door and peeked inside. His expression brightened when he saw the bowl on her desk.

“Is there any more macky cheese?” he asked.

When she was little, she couldn’t pronounce “mac and cheese” and had insisted that the correct term was “macky cheese.” The name had stuck. Although she was still frustrated with him, it reminded her of the good times they’d had when she was younger. He’d spent hours at the neighborhood park, pushing her on the swings and the ancient metal merry-go-round. That thing had been a death trap; she’d lost her first tooth after taking a header off it, and he hadn’t even blinked at all the blood. It had been her and Dad against the world.

“Yeah,” she said, her voice thick with more emotion than the moment deserved. She cleared her throat and continued in a more normal tone. “There’s about half a pot left on the stove.”

“Yes!” He pumped his fist. “I’m gonna snag some on my way out if that’s okay. Promise not to eat it all.”

“Go for it.”

He surprised her then by crossing the room to plant a kiss on the top of her head. Afterward, he squinted down at her screen, wrinkling his nose in disgust.

“Ugh. I sure am glad you’re smart, because I can’t remember how to do half that crap,” he said.

She didn’t say anything and instead leaned her head against his chest. After a moment, he put an arm around her.

“Yeah, I hate math too,” she said.

“It runs in the family.” He paused. “We okay?”

Maybe she should tell him about the painting. Not where she found it, but just that one existed. Maybe it would shake some answers out of him. But she couldn't make herself speak. She was too afraid of what he might say, or even worse, that he might not say anything at all.

She nodded.

"Good." He shifted his wrist to check his watch. "I'd better skedaddle. You working this weekend? There's an Eagles game on Sunday. I was thinking about getting a pizza."

"I'm closing, but save me a slice."

He nodded, his eyes roaming the equipment on her pegboard, the sketches pinned to the walls, the wig stands and bins and swatches. She braced herself for one of his forced but supportive comments. He didn't get her fandoms and never would, but at least he sometimes tried.

"When did you start growing up so fast?" he murmured.

Her cheeks went red.

"Daaad," she said, drawing it out. "Stop. I'll die from embarrassment."

"Well, then you'd be one of those zombie things, right?"

He made vague zombie motions.

"I think you're going to be late for work," she said.

"Damn. You're right, punkin. Have a good night; stay safe; lock up."

He rushed out of the room, leaving her conflicted but smiling anyway. After a moment, she heard the clatter of silverware against the cookware. He was eating out of the pot again. Another clatter, this one of the fork in the sink. Then, finally, the apartment door slammed shut.

Finally. Peace and quiet.

Now that she had the place to herself, she put some music on her Bluetooth speaker and dashed off her last math problem before submitting it through the student portal. Then she finished off the dinner and scrubbed up the dishes, setting them in the rack next to the sink. She took a shower, hoping that the warm water would settle her down so she could catch up on a little rest. But with every passing minute, she grew more and more awake. Again.

After the shower, she sat down at her desk and combed out her hair, frowning thoughtfully. She'd spent the day circling over the same questions, making the same arguments, worrying about the same things. Ultimately, she'd gotten nowhere. But at some point, she was going to have to decide what to do.

She was going back in; that was for sure. If she didn't, she'd always wonder. But she had to be careful. Her dad and Ari were both on high alert, and her flimsy excuses wouldn't hold up for long. No more Lovely Locks all-nighters. Besides, if she kept this pace up, she really would get so tired she'd start hallucinating. She needed to be well rested if she was going to get to the bottom of the mystery about her mother. It was a catch-22. She needed rest to get the answers, but she couldn't rest without them.

Okay then, middle-of-the-road approach. She'd go to the kingdom every night, but she'd spend only an hour or two there. That way, she could continue to investigate and still get a decent night's sleep. Could she bring her phone with her to keep an eye on the time?

Only one way to find out.

Chapter 9

Leigh appeared back in the Kingdom of Lovely Locks with her staff strapped to her back. She'd tucked her phone into her bodice, but a quick pat was enough to confirm that it hadn't made the jump. Damn. Maybe tech couldn't pass into the fantasy world? She hadn't spent much time inside the castle, but she felt like it was safe to assume it wasn't full of microwaves and PlayStations.

She found herself on a cobblestone road just outside the walls of what looked like Lovely Locks Castle, and she took the time to admire it in the waning light. The structure was made of majestic white stone that sparkled in the light of the setting sun. Pastel flags fluttered from every turret. Instead of a foamy moat, flowers and ribbons wreathed the castle walls, and the gates stood wide open and unguarded, which seemed rather careless to Leigh given the presence of fire-breathing kangorillas in the nearby forest.

The road was deserted. It would have been nice to see someone, if only to confirm that she was in the right place. She didn't have time to waste by waltzing into the wrong castle, and she appeared to be popping up in different parts of the kingdom without much rhyme or reason. With her luck, she might teleport into the foamy moat, a snagfire lair, or some random person's bathroom. She wouldn't be able to show her face in public if she popped up foot down in a privy.

"Pixietails!" she called. "I've got a question!"

The three perky pastel Pixietails came zooming out of her hair, jingling with all their might.

"Lady Lovely Leigh!" said Pixie Beauty. "It's so good to see you!"

"Just Leigh, please. Why do I end up in a different place each time I come here?"

"Oh. It's…" Pixie Beauty waved its little hands around as if that were at all helpful.

"Exactly," said Pixie Shine.

Exasperated, Leigh turned to Pixie Sparkle. It seemed to be as annoyed as she was. It rolled its eyes before answering.

"When you shift over, you appear wherever your Pixietails are," it explained. "If we know you want to go somewhere, we can stay in the area. Without direction, we go where we please when you're not here."

"That's handy. Although what were you three doing in the Snarl the day I met you?" asked Leigh.

"Duchess Ravenwaves caught us," said Pixie Shine.

"And tried to make a stew out of us," added Pixie Beauty.

"We were on our way home when you first popped up," said Pixie Sparkle.

"You don't seem to be all that surprised by all my questions." Leigh frowned thoughtfully. "You've done this before."

"We train all the new Ladies," said Pixie Sparkle. "We're experienced."

"Most of the villagers don't even notice when there's a new Lady," Pixie Shine scoffed.

"The sillies!" added Pixie Beauty.

"Weird," said Leigh. "Let's table that for the moment. I've been thinking. I need advice, so I thought I'd go see the wizard. Am I at the right place? He's there, right? I don't have any time to waste; I've got to get back home at a decent hour."

"Done," said Pixie Sparkle. "This way."

Pixie Sparkle jingle-jangled down the road, pausing to look over its shoulder. Leigh followed it through the gates. Based on the sound of bells behind her, the other two were bringing up the rear, but she honestly wasn't sure she needed them. Sparkle was winning the Favorite Pixietail Award by a landslide so far.

Inside the castle walls stood a large courtyard which ended at a tall series of steps leading up to the castle door. No defenses whatsoever. No moat. No guards. Not even one of those big heavy bars for the front door. Good thing Ravenwaves was completely incompetent, because she could wander right in if she wanted.

At one end of the courtyard, a small group of villagers was holding some sort of celebration. One of them juggled to the delight of a herd of small children. A pair of bearded young men played fiddles at the center of a circle of villagers who whirled around hand in hand, laughing as they spun in a complicated dance. Off to one side, a couple canoodled in the shadows, the girl blushing as the boy murmured something in her ear. Leigh had never been much of a party person, but even she couldn't deny that it looked rather fun.

Then one of the kids—a little girl with chubby cheeks and sticky hands—yelled, "Lady Lovely Locks!"

Everything stopped like someone had thrown a switch. The juggler dropped his balls. The musicians fell silent. The dancers ceased their whirling. They all stared at her.

"It's so good to see you, Princess!" said one.

"It's been too long," added another.

She didn't know how to react, so she just smiled and nodded in what she hoped was a royal sort of way. The little girl began to close in on her, beaming. The rest of the villagers followed suit.

"What are they doing?" she asked Pixie Sparkle out of the corner of her mouth.

"It's good luck to touch your hair," the Pixietail explained.

"They're so sticky..." Leigh moaned, thinking about all the work she'd have to do to clean out the wig later.

But the kids looked so excited. All she could think about was how thrilled she would have been to meet the real Lady Lovely Locks back in the day. So she held fast as the kids clustered around, bracing herself for tugs and yanks. But they each patted her respectfully, even the littlest one with the sticky hands.

When she looked back up, everyone was smiling at her like she'd done something marvelous. She'd expected bowing and scraping, but none of them went down on one knee or hesitated to meet her eye. Instead, they seemed genuinely happy to see her. Although she still thought this world was pretty lame in general, this bit was... nice.

They kept staring at her. She had to say something.

"If you need anything, I'll do my best to help you," she said awkwardly. "Just ask."

As far as inspiring speeches went, it sucked, but they didn't seem to notice. They just murmured their thanks until one of the dancers said, "Would you like to join us, Princess? We'll teach you if you don't know the steps."

"Thanks," she said, "but I'm good."

The villagers exchanged glances, obviously confused.

"Of course you're good," said the dancer. "You're Lady Lovely Locks."

"Oh boy..." said Leigh. "What I meant to say was that I appreciate the offer, but I'm on my way to consult with Shining Glory...?" She trailed off, uncertain but hoping that she hadn't stuck her foot in her mouth.

"Of course, Princess!" exclaimed the dancer. "If you need anything, you come ask. I say, do you need directions? I could take you to Glory Manor."

"My Pixietails will guide me. Thanks." Leigh smiled, but the villagers kept staring at her. Did she have to dismiss them or something? "Please, carry on with your celebration."

The fiddlers lifted their instruments once again, filling the air with music, as the Pixietails led Leigh past the castle entrance to the right. The courtyard opened up here, exposing a small collection of buildings. These were the sorts of outbuildings one would expect to see in a fairy-tale castle: stables, a chapel, a hair salon. Okay, so that one stood out, but it made sense. Someone needed to take care of all the magical manes around here.

Beyond the scattered outbuildings stood a structure that looked a bit like a shrunken pastel Taj Mahal. A long gray carpet stretched out the open front door, and matching banners flapped from the tiny, bulbous towers. Nothing moved in this corner of the castle grounds, and somehow, the place had a forlorn, abandoned air that stood in stark contrast to the pleasant bustle near the entrance.

"Glory Manor?" asked Leigh.

"Yes!" said Pixies Shine and Beauty together.

"Thanks. I've got it from here. You can return to my hair now; I'll call if I need you."

Grumbling in high-pitched disappointment, the two Pixietails zoomed toward her head. Pixie Sparkle paused to catch her eye and sigh before following suit. Leigh couldn't help but grin. Could Pixietails get promotions? If so, Sparkle deserved one simply for being so darned entertaining.

She wandered through the open door, examining the expansive entryway. The tall, open space was cluttered with artwork—paintings and statues had been crammed into every possible space and sometimes layered atop one another. They stretched up all the way to the ceiling, so high that no one could possibly make out the contents of the shelves and frames. Leigh paused, scanning the wall next to her. Perhaps Shining Glory also had a Lady Knot painting. Anything was possible. After all, this medieval castle had a hair salon.

She scanned the walls. The paintings were completely unfamiliar, and although she wasn't much of an art person, she thought she'd recognize famous paintings from the real world. But there was no *Mona Lisa* or Monet water lilies. She did, however, spot a bunch of dragons, a few snagfires, and the castle. More than a few paintings featured Lady Lovely Locks, and she gave those a nice close look, but they were all true to the original story and provided no hints to what the heck was going on here.

Well, that was a dead end, but no matter. Hopefully Shining Glory would be able to fill in some of those gaps. In the original stories, he served as a mentor to the princess, advising her on where she needed to go or what she needed to do in order to defeat Ravenwaves. If anyone knew anything about Lady Knot, he would.

"Hello?" she called out. "Anyone home?"

There was no answer, so she moved toward the door at the other end of the room. It led into an antechamber dominated by a pair of curving staircases. Enormous floating globes of light illuminated the space, hanging with no apparent mode of suspension like the magic balls in her Looking Room. They just floated around by themselves like giant glowing balloons, pinging gently whenever they bounced off one another. She stared at them longer than she might have liked to admit before shaking herself out of the awed reverie. There was still no sign of Shining Glory, so there was no choice but to climb what looked like a never-ending staircase.

As she approached, she noticed a plain wooden door tucked into the shadowy recesses between the two stairways. It had been left cracked open, and a cold, flickering blue light played around its edges. That seemed awful wizardy to Leigh, and if investigating it meant she might avoid having to climb a million stairs, she was all in. She crept toward the door, putting a gentle hand to it and pushing it open.

Inside was a bright chamber made entirely of glossy white stone. On a plinth at its center sat an enormous crystal ball, which roiled with blue smoke and bolts of electricity. The entire ball flashed and dimmed over and over again, lighting up so bright that it illuminated the entire room before fading again. She crept toward the plinth, the back of her neck crawling. Could it be!? Was this the crystal from the book?

"Shining Glory?" she shouted, but again there was no answer.

She was wasting time she didn't have. In the book, Shining Glory and Prince Strongheart had been imprisoned in an enormous crystal. Leigh couldn't remember all the details—there was some sort of curse involved—but the gist of it was that the two characters were perfectly healthy inside the crystal. Outside it, Shining Glory was blind and the prince turned into a lovesick dog with a crush on the princess.

When she was a kid, she'd pictured a giant, jagged crystal formation big enough to fit an adult inside, but this ball would also fit the bill. There was just one problem: If Shining Glory and his royal canine were stuck in there, she didn't know how to free them. There had to be some sort of safety mechanism on this thing, or else someone like Ravenwaves could just walk in and steal it.

She hesitated, electric blue light flickering over her skin. The smart thing to do would be to ask for help, but her Pixietails were idiots, and she was tired of second-guessing herself. She needed answers, and she needed them now. So she gritted her teeth and put her hands on the ball, hoping that she wasn't about to fry her own head off.

Electricity zapped her fingers, making her long, lovely locks crackle with static. Then a wave of bright magic flooded the room with a loud *whoom* like a plane taking off. It slowly faded, leaving bright spots dancing across her vision.

Standing next to the crystal ball was a tall man with long silver hair and eerie white eyes. Leigh pegged him as somewhere around her dad's age, although he looked like a cool hipster dad, in contrast to her father's paunchy midlife-crisis vibe. He had a man bun and a goatee, and instead of wizard's robes, he wore a slouchy sort of suit in shades of gray and black, with a weird cloak–trench coat hybrid over top. Overall, it was a look she could get behind.

The click of nails on tile announced the arrival of an animal, but instead of the expected mutt, it turned out to be another odd creature she'd never seen before. It looked a bit like a fox, and in fact it had the same red-and-white coloring, but its ears had been stretched to almost comical lengths. Like most of the creatures in this hair-obsessed place, it was remarkably well coiffed, with a fancy multicolored ruff and a long, luxurious tail that dragged on the floor.

"That's not a dog!" she exclaimed.

The cool hipster dad who was probably a wizard arched a brow.

"That's . . . astute," he said, clearly meaning the exact opposite.

"But I thought he was supposed to . . ." She trailed off. Maybe this wasn't the prince. Really, it didn't matter, because she didn't intend to go all gooey over some stupid boy just because he was royalty. She didn't believe in insta-love. Declaring eternal devotion to someone immediately after meeting them was a nice way to end up with a stalker.

So she waved it off. "Never mind," she said. "Are you Shining Glory?"

"As a matter of fact, I am. I take it that you're our new princess? Welcome to Lovely Locks Kingdom. How can I assist you?" he said, sketching a little bow.

"Y-yep, that's me," Leigh stuttered. It really would have been a good idea to write down her questions, because now that she was here, her mind had gone blank. "I—I could use some information. I spent my first few visits blundering around like an idiot. If not for my magic staff, I probably would have gotten myself killed."

"Magic staff?" he asked, perking up. "Mind if I examine it?"

With a swift gesture, she pulled the staff from its sheath and held it out to him. They stood there for a moment before she realized he couldn't see her. Her cheeks flamed with embarrassment.

"Here," she said. "I'll give it to you."

He held his hands out, completely unaware of her mortification, and took the staff gently from her hands. As he examined it, murmuring to himself, the fox thing sidled up next to her, rubbing the side of its head against her boot like a cat demanding pets. She leaned down and ran her fingers through its silky pelt as the creature nuzzled her hand. Honestly, if this really was Prince Strongheart, she hoped he stayed in this form. She'd take animal snuggles over some pompous, swaggering princeling any day.

A bright glow jolted her out of her reverie, and she looked up to see her staff bathed in more of that blue light. It faded quickly, revealing Shining Glory's satisfied smile. He held the weapon back out to her, nodding to himself.

"It's as I expected," he said as she took the staff and resheathed it. "Did you make this yourself?"

"I did. What did you do to it?"

"Just a little incantation that reveals magic items. The staff should work normally. What exactly are its powers?"

"It turns into a lightsaber-spear," she explained, but of course he wouldn't get the reference. "A blade of magic comes out the top when I bang it on the ground. I haven't gotten to play around with it much. I've been too busy trying to figure out what the heck I'm doing."

"Sorry about that. I keep trying to teach the Pixietails some of the relevant information to help our new princesses, but I'm afraid they're not much smarter than the average animal. Pixie Sparkle might have absorbed a bit more than its companions, but that's a low bar. If ever I need to create a set of magical guides, I think I'll pick smarter animals to serve as the template."

"No doubt." Leigh relaxed a little. Out of everyone she'd met here, Shining Glory was already the easiest to talk to. He also appeared to have a head on his shoulders. Finally, she'd get her answers. "But I'm here now. Can I ask you a few questions? Is now a bad time? I'm not sure how long you've been stuck in that crystal."

"Honestly, me either. I've been in there since the last princess came to us, but I have no real way to know how long that's been. The villagers won't notice any difference, by the way. They see what they expect to see. Only those of us with magic can tell that there's a new Lady."

"I'm sorry. That must be tough to deal with; you've got no one to talk to inside the crystal, and no one to talk to outside it too. I think I'd go nuts."

"Not at all. I have Prince to keep me company."

She looked down at the fox thing, which had curled up at her feet.

"What is he?" she asked.

"He's a locksfox. Beautiful creatures, aren't they? But they require quite a bit of brushing. Otherwise, they turn into tangled messes."

"Speaking of tangles, I've already been to Tangleland. Ravenwaves took me to her tower and tried to cut my hair. Big shocker, I know. While I was there, I saw a painting in her library. It's Lady Kn—"

"Don't say that!" he barked, interrupting her. "Best not to tempt fate."

“Because if you do, she’ll appear?” Leigh frowned as Shining Glory nodded gravely. “Okay, well, she looks like someone I know. The... lady we don’t mention. Tell me about her?”

“I—” Shining Glory broke off abruptly, freezing in place. After a moment, he continued, “I cannot.”

“But she looks like...” Leigh trailed off. It didn’t seem good to admit that the evil sorceress that terrified the pants off everyone might just be her mom. She didn’t know what to think. Was this whole thing a frame job by Ravenwaves? She could believe that in a heartbeat. The only other alternative she could come up with was that her mom was pretty much Voldemort, which would be mostly awful but just a tiny bit cool as heck. “Are you sure you can’t tell me anything?”

“I’m sorry; I can’t. But that person whom we do not discuss hasn’t been seen for a long time. I’m hoping she’s gone for good.”

Leigh hoped not, but she wasn’t about to say so.

“Well, what if I’m on a quest to find out more about her?” asked Leigh. “That’s a thing that princesses do, right? Quests?”

Shining Glory pressed his lips together, his brow furrowing in frustration. Next to her, the locksfox stood up, snarling. Maybe he had indigestion or was about to bust out some dope magic. But he simply slumped after a moment, seemingly exhausted.

“I’m sorry,” the wizard said panting. “I can’t.”

“Can’t what? Can’t talk about quests? That doesn’t make any...” She trailed off thoughtfully. “Wait a sec. You’re cursed, aren’t you?”

“You’ve read our histories, I see. Or rather, I don’t.” He offered her a thin smile. “That was a joke. A rather dark one, I admit.”

She wasn’t sure if it would be rude to laugh, so she just let out a brief “hah.”

"But you are right. The curse has multiple effects. Stealing my sight was the least of its damage. It ties my power to the crystal, effectively blunting my powers. To make matters worse, it strangles my speech. There are certain topics I cannot discuss. Trust me; I've tried. I cannot push past the bounds of the curse."

"Why not?"

"I'd tell you if I could. All I can say is that the creators of the curse had a specific goal in mind."

Leigh frowned thoughtfully. That was a puzzle worth unraveling. Clearly, whoever had cast the curse on Shining Glory had wanted to keep him from saying something. Probably from identifying them, for starters. Could Ravenwaves do that? Or—and she hesitated to think it—Lady Knot? She would have to think that through later. She needed to find out about that painting. If Shining Glory couldn't tell her, he would have to point her toward someone who could. Once she'd found out what the heck was going on with her mom, she could circle back and help him undo that pesky curse.

"Man, that sucks. I'll help with that if I can."

"That is kind of you, milady." He inclined his head. "But don't you worry; there are still plenty of things I can talk to you about. For example, I suspect that you're an artificer, which is quite thrilling. Artificers create magical artifacts."

"I do like making things. In addition to the staff, I created a mouthy magic mirror with violent tendencies, but I'm not sure that's a good thing. That darned mirror man nearly got me killed."

"That...sounds like a story. You'll have to tell it sometime. But it's still delightful. I don't think we've had an artificer princess before."

"So I should just make things and bring them here to see what they do?"

He considered, frowning.

"I'm not so sure about that," he said. "I don't have the skill myself, but I've known a few artificers in my time. A few wizards I know have had the knack for it. They're very careful about creating random objects. I'm told they can often have unintended effects."

"The mirror sure did," she offered. "It was a bloodthirsty little beast."

"Well then, there you go. I think it's better to create objects for specific needs. That should help keep you from repeating the problem with the... how can a mirror be bloodthirsty? Do I want to know?"

"Probably not," she admitted. "Okay, so I'll look into this artificing thing. That'll be a good tool to have in my back pocket for later. But that still takes me to my main question. I need to find out more about the nameless one. Whom can I ask?" She sighed. "You probably can't even answer that, can you?"

He considered for a moment before forcing out a single sentence. "Think about what I've said..." he choked out.

Leigh frowned. Maybe he'd slipped some sort of clue into their conversation. If she was right, the reference would be tough to spot. She'd have to put on her Sherlock hat. Unfortunately, she was so tired that her brain felt like congealed glue. What had he said when he first appeared? She walked back over to the crystal and put her hand over it, trying to use movement to stimulate her exhausted neurons. They'd introduced themselves and talked about the fact that the Pixietails were morons, and they'd talked about the curse—or she'd talked about it, since he couldn't, and then...

Then he'd brought up the artificer thing. Was that it? Was she supposed to make some sort of magical artifact that would help? That idea was an interesting one, but she had no idea what to make. But she had to be on the right track, because it was the only conversational topic he'd volunteered out of nowhere. What exactly had he said? She paced back and forth.

"I'm an artificer. I made the staff, and what does it do?" she muttered to herself. A quick glance in Shining Glory's direction earned her an encouraging nod. She was on the right track! "The items have unintended effects. Does that mean that the staff might do something else?"

"Probably not," said Shining Glory. "Advanced artificers can create more complex artifacts, but you're still rather young to the craft."

"Okay." She paced some more. "Maybe I could ask... maybe I could apprentice under one of these other artificers? If they're not cursed, they could help me?"

"We haven't had an artificer in Lovely Locks, or in our neighboring kingdoms, for a long, long time," replied Shining Glory.

"You said a few wizards you've known have had the skill..." she murmured. "Other wizards? Ones who aren't artificers? Do you know of any other wizards in Lovely Locks or the neighboring kingdoms?"

He opened his mouth, scowled, and then shut it again. The locksfox rubbed up against his leg, yipping sadly, and he caressed the creature's head absentmindedly.

"I know; you can't answer that. No worries. I know what to do now. Thank you." She tossed her head. "Pixietails! I need you!"

Out zoomed the three magical rabbits, whirling around the locksfox with delighted giggles before they returned to hover before her.

"How can we help?" asked Pixie Shine.

"I have to go home and get some sleep before my math test," said Leigh. "While I'm gone, I need you to find another wizard. When I come back tomorrow evening, I want you to take me to him."

"Another wizard? Not Shining Glory?" asked Pixie Beauty skeptically.

"What's a math test?" asked Pixie Shine.

Pixie Sparkle flew up in front of them, shaking its little pink head.

"We'll search for you," the Pixietail said.

At least one of them had some brains. She gave Pixie Sparkle a grateful smile as Shining Glory beamed with pride.

"I think you'll do just fine, Princess," he said.

"I'll come back if I get stuck so you can *not* help me again," she replied, grinning.

"Well then, I look forward to not assisting you in the future," he said.

CHAPTER 10

LEIGH FLOATED THROUGH THE NEXT DAY AT SCHOOL, and by the end of it, she was hard-pressed to remember a single thing that had happened. She'd managed to scrape together a few hours of deep, dreamless sleep, so her head no longer felt like it had been stuffed with cotton balls, but she couldn't stop thinking about everything that had happened ever since she put on that cosplay. It sounded like the plot of a shoddy anime, the sort that she and Ari liked to make fun of. But she had to take it seriously, at least until she got to the bottom of the mystery about her mom. Time to do some research.

It had all started with the wig. The vendor who'd sold it to her might have some answers. After a power nap and a quick PB&J, she searched through her gear from KillyCon in the hopes of finding the receipt, but she came up empty, and to be honest, she couldn't even remember if she'd gotten one. A con staffer had pushed her out the door as soon as the money changed hands, repeatedly reminding her that the show floor was closed. Maybe she'd recognize the vendor's name. She pulled up the KillyCon maps online and searched the vendor hall layout for a random table tucked beneath the stairs, but she didn't see one.

Odd.

Bringing up the vendor list and searching for "wig" or "hair" popped up a couple of results, but none of them looked familiar. It was a frustrating dead end. Maybe Ari would remember something helpful.

As she closed her laptop, her dad tapped on the door and stuck his head in. He looked a little ragged today, with dark circles beneath his eyes.

"Just checking in before I head off to work," he said.

Sometimes she wondered why he bothered. After all, they had the same conversation nearly every night and barely spoke to each other otherwise. For a moment, she wondered what would happen if she told him that her magic wig transported her into a fantasy world themed around hair, where she'd seen a painting of an evil sorceress who looked an awful lot like her mother. Would he react at all, or would he just say, "That's nice, kiddo. Be safe, and don't forget to lock up"?

As tempting as it was to find out, she kept her mouth shut. She didn't want to risk another attempted intervention that could mess up her nightly travel plans.

"You okay?" he asked, brow furrowed.

"Yeah. Just..." She waved at her workspace. "Got homework to do."

"I'll let you get to it, then," he said. But he didn't. He just stared at her in a way that made her nervous. She was fairly sure he hadn't caught her again; she'd returned home to take off the cosplay well before his shift ended last night. But there was always the possibility that he'd swung by partway through his shift to check on her.

"Everything okay?" she asked as casually as she could.

"Yeah. Sure. It's fine. I'd better go," he said, even though they both knew the tension between them wasn't fine at all. He just didn't have the guts to talk about it. Never had. "Be safe. Lock up—"

"Behind you. I know."

He left. She stared at the wall, deliberately not feeling a dang thing. She had no time to sort through her jumbled emotions about her dad, and no real desire to either. She had better things to do. As soon as the front door of the apartment closed behind him, she sprang into action. She'd put on the cosplay so many times now that it had become quite easy, and her fingers flew over the ribbons. Once she had the dress on, she paused before her cosplay bins, considering the collection of props and devices she'd created over the years. As tempted as she was to bring her Van Bearsing crossbow, she decided to hold off until she figured out more about the whole artificer thing. Plus, that weapon really didn't work with the whole pastel vibe. She gave it one last appreciative glance and left it on the shelf.

She pulled the wig on.

When her vision cleared, she found herself standing in a marketplace beneath a darkening sky. Just beyond the trees, she could see the tall spires of Lovely Locks Castle, which made this the nearby village. A row of stalls had been arranged around a central well in what appeared to be the town square. Bright pennants flapped over most of the stands, and a variety of shoppers still browsed despite the late hour. Draped around the well, a hand-painted banner read: "The Night Market."

Her eyes roamed the tables, which were covered with standard fantasy-world goods. Leather-bound books and housewares sat next to a stall full of fresh produce. Beyond that was a table full of metal cups and plates overseen by a hulking blacksmith in a singed leather apron. All the way on the end sat a table covered in hairbrushes, ribbons, and rudimentary curlers, which didn't fit the standard fantasy vibe but was still completely unsurprising. Of all the displays she'd seen so far, it was the busiest.

But the far end of the market was even busier, with a large group of new shoppers just emerging out of the shadowy depths of the hairy forest. She took a few steps in that direction, snickering to herself as she scanned the tables to figure out what was so popular down there. Was there a Lovely Locks version of the Hair Club for Men, maybe?

Then, with a sense of dawning horror, she realized who those newcomers were. A single scream pierced the air as one of the vendors got a good look at them too.

"Snagfires!" shouted Leigh. "Everyone scatter!"

They kept pouring out of the trees, dozens and dozens of them. Too many. The last time she'd fought one, she'd thought this whole thing was a dream, and she'd welcomed the battle. But now her stomach curdled at the thought. If she died here, what would happen to her in the real world? She'd forgotten to ask Shining Glory.

Screaming, the villagers fled, tossing their packages and housewares and sprinting for cover as the snagfires charged. The blacksmith upended his table to block the onslaught, metal cutlery clattering to the ground. The two girls manning the table of hairbrushes threw armfuls of them to cover their customers' retreat. But the numbers didn't look good. Leigh wasn't sure if the village buildings would be strong enough to withstand a full stink of enraged snagfires, and the castle was too far away to take shelter inside.

The timing of the attack was all too suspicious. Was it a coincidence that the snagfires had shown up moments after she'd arrived, or had they been waiting for her? The latter seemed more likely, and she didn't have the time or the patience to deal with whatever stupid trap Ravenwaves had up her sleeve this time. The smart thing to do would be to avoid this nonsense altogether. After all, the villagers would survive, right? They always had.

She took a single, regretful step backward. Then she saw the little girl with the sticky hands—the one who had been so desperate to touch her hair—cowering before a hulking snagfire, tears streaming down her face as it loomed over her. Smoke curled from its hungry mouth, long ropes of spittle dripping from its jaws.

No way was some mutant fire-breathing kangorilla going to eat a kid on Leigh's watch. Cold fury stilled the nervous tremble of her hands, steadying them as she pulled her staff from her back. She sprinted across the marketplace, slamming the butt of the staff onto the ground as she ran. The blade hummed as it shot out of the crystal at the top, and the weapon came alive in her hands as if sensing the presence of evil.

The snagfire reached toward the cowering child. Leigh wasn't going to make it in time; she was too far away. She would have to watch that little kid get devoured.

"Not on my watch," she muttered. "Eat spear, snagfire."

She pulled back, sighted, and threw.

Over the years, Leigh had always been one of the last people picked for teams in gym. Not the absolute last, but definitely somewhere in the final five. She could make choreography look good, and she'd put that skill to good use in her cosplay, but she had the mass of a toothpick and no strength to put to use in a sportsball environment. In basketball, her form was decent, but her shots fell decidedly short of the rim. On the tennis court, she had the grace of a wannabe Williams sister so long as the ball wasn't involved.

She'd tried to throw a javelin only once and nearly impaled her own foot. With that in mind, hurtling the spear was a bad idea, a desperate Hail Mary doomed to fail. Or it would have been, if not for the fact that her spear was freaking magic.

It twisted in the air, arcing toward the giant, shaggy beast. The shot would have gone embarrassingly wide—anyone could have seen so—but the glowing spearhead blurred, redirecting itself. It plunged into the snagfire's back. The creature stiffened, falling toward the little girl. She stared up at it, frozen with fear.

But Leigh was still running. She snatched the kid up just in time to avoid being crushed. The snagfire toppled to the ground, its beak snapping shut one last time before it went still, her spear sticking out of its back.

She whirled, the kid clutched in one arm. The little girl grabbed onto her neck, squeezing her with panicky strength. Snagfires trampled over the stalls and chased the helpless villagers. The hair stall had caught fire, setting up plumes of inky smoke into the darkening sky. The dimming light only made things worse. As she watched, a fleeing townswoman tripped over something on the ground, the snagfire behind her growing closer.

"I'll take her," said the blacksmith, running up to Leigh with one hand out. In the other, he carried an enormous sledgehammer like it was a baseball bat.

"Go!" Leigh peeled the kid off her neck and thrust her toward the burly man. He heaved the girl over one shoulder as she looked around wildly, eyes wide in her tear-streaked face. "Get her to safety. I'll . . . take care of this."

He obeyed without question, rushing away and shouting for others to follow him. As Leigh yanked her spear free and set off to help the woman on the ground, she heard the loud thwack of the sledgehammer as it struck a target followed by a yelp of snagfire pain that made her grin in grim satisfaction.

She reached the prone woman a millisecond before the snagfire did, sweeping at its legs with a long stroke of the humming blade. It toppled backward as the young woman scrambled to her feet, gasping out a thanks. Leigh reversed the stroke, stabbing through the creature's thick mane and into the chest below.

"You're welcome," she said. "Get out of here!"

The young woman hesitated for just a moment before a new fear flashed over her face. Eyes widening at something over Leigh's shoulder, she turned tail and ran. Leigh whirled around to see three snagfires closing in on her with that weird loping stride of theirs.

She had to buy the young woman time. So even though the numbers weren't in her favor, she had to stand her ground. She extended the spear to its full length, swaying it to and fro to keep the beasts from flanking her. But it was only a matter of time before one of them broke through her defenses. Sweat slicked her palms as she looked desperately for some way out of this mess.

A lock of lavender hair fell in front of her eyes, and she blew it up out of her field of vision with a grimace. Being blinded by her stupid hair was the last thing she needed—she was already in hot water as it was. But it gave her an idea—the sort of thing she should have thought of long ago.

"Pixietails!" she shouted.

Zip zip zip jingle! The trio of pastel bunnies floated up between her and the snagfires. Pixie Shine and Pixie Beauty both put up their tiny fists, despite the fact that the enormous beasts could have eaten them with one gulp. She had to admire their guts if not their logic. Pixie Sparkle trailed behind, its little jaw tight with tension.

"Leave our princess alone!" shouted Pixie Shine.

"Leave Lady Lovely Locks—Leigh—Lady Lovely Leigh! Leave her alone!" echoed Pixie Beauty.

"How can we help?" said Pixie Sparkle.

"Can you restrain the snagfires? There are too many to fight off on my own!"

"Don't ask us. Tell us," said Pixie Sparkle. "That's how the magic works."

Finally, some clear instructions! Leigh nodded, relieved.

"Pixietails, restrain the snagfires! Protect the villagers!"

All three of them began to glow with power, turning into tiny balls of pastel light. Pixie Shine gestured, and a long golden lasso wrapped around the three snagfires facing her, lifting them off the ground in a shower of blue sparkles. The Pixietail began to tow them away back into the trees. Not to be outdone, Pixie Beauty flew toward a pair of snagfires, levitating them up in a cloud of lavender glitter. As it closed around the snagfires, they both screwed their faces up, sneezing. Gouts of fire streamed from their noses.

Pixie Sparkle zipped off into the trees. But of all the Pixietails, Leigh didn't worry about Sparkle. The little pink bunny with the deep voice was intelligent enough to work unsupervised. The other two Pixietails followed their magical friend, dragging their snagfire captives along with them.

Whew. She paused to take a breath, wiping sweat and soot from her stinging eyes.

The market was deserted; all its occupants had fled. Down at the end, the burning stall collapsed with a crash, the banner next to it lighting aflame. She'd better put that out before it spread any farther. Luckily, the well was still intact, and she drew up some water and duckwalked it over to the fire, hoping that no one would show up to see her struggle beneath the weight. The water splashed over the flames, dampening but not putting them out entirely.

She pulled up another bucket from the well, her shoulders burning from the exertion. But when she turned around, she found herself face-to-face with ten snagfires, who had either dropped down from the sky or were secretly ninja. She hadn't heard a thing over the creaking of the well and the sloshing of the water in the bucket, but here they were. Their red eyes fixed on her hungrily; steam curled from their open mouths, wicked beaks snapping on empty air.

As if on cue, they began to advance on her as one.

CHAPTER 11

For a moment, Leigh stood frozen as the snagfires advanced on her and the marketplace burned to cinders. There was no way out; there were simply too many of them. Why weren't there any guards in this kingdom? She hadn't seen a single uniformed sentry on any of her visits. Didn't they know their neighbor was a psycho with a kangorilla army? She needed backup, like, *now*.

"Pixietails!" she called, but there was no response.

The snagfires continued to advance. They'd tear her to pieces or maybe cook her like a burger on a grill. Neither option sounded particularly pleasant. Her heart hammered in her chest; her hands shook. It was taking every ounce of nerve she had not to pee on herself in complete and utter terror; she didn't have a whole lot of brainpower left for higher reasoning.

She needed a distraction, but all she had was a bucket of water.

Then again, they were fire creatures.

She heaved the bucket at them, swinging it in a wide arc to splash as many of them as possible. The creatures let out their coughing barks, backing away from the spray, but she didn't stick around to see what the impromptu shower did to them. She spun, sprinting toward the trees with all her might, arms pumping, ribbons streaming.

Although she wasn't much of a religious person, she found herself praying wordlessly that she'd get out of this mess alive.

"Up here!" said a voice, as if summoned by her prayers.

A hand thrust down through the dangling spiral curls of a nearby tree, gesturing her closer, and although she wasn't in the habit of shaking hands with random tree creatures, this seemed like a good time to make an exception. She rushed toward it and grabbed on, looking up through the snarled branches and dangling hair to see whose hand she was holding. A boy about her age stared down at her, with tousled sandy hair and a face pinched in worry. He gritted his teeth and heaved, pulling her up. She lifted off the ground but stopped halfway up, the boy's arm shaking with effort. Her feet windmilled through open air. If he dropped her into a snagfire's mouth, she would be very, very ticked off before she was very, very dead.

"Pull!" she snapped.

"Oh, thanks," he replied, shooting an exasperated look in her direction. "Didn't think of that myself."

He yanked again, grunting loudly. She could just reach the branch; her fingers scrabbled at the wood and finally latched on. Her feet still swung at snagfire level. It was only a matter of time before one of them pulled her down. She had to climb up. They both strained, but he didn't seem to be much stronger than she was.

"Help me!" she gasped.

"I know what to do!" he exclaimed.

Then he let her go. It took her by such surprise that she slid back down again, losing what little precious ground they'd managed to gain. Her fingers shook, her grip strength ebbing. This was a losing battle. She was going to fall.

The boy didn't even seem to notice her continued struggle. He had his eyes shut, his hands held up in front of him like he was about to belt out a song that would soothe the savage snagfires. She was about to die to the sound of bad Taylor Swift karaoke, and she couldn't have been more pissed about it.

The tromp of heavy feet nearby announced the arrival of the snagfires. She still dangled from the tree, well within their reach. She desperately tried to raise herself onto the branch, but she could barely hold on anymore.

"Be quiet!" he whispered.

"I don't want them to eat my feet!" she babbled, frantic with fear.

"Shut up," he continued. "They won't see you, but they'll hear you. See?"

He pointed, and she followed his finger as quick footsteps crunched through the underbrush. But they were too light to be a snagfire. Instead, she saw... herself.

Fake Leigh paused to look over her shoulder at the snagfires in hot pursuit. Then she looked up at Real Leigh and winked before dashing off into the woods, brush crackling beneath her feet. The snagfires howled and coughed before thundering off after her. None of them looked up to see Real Leigh hanging from the tree branch high overhead, and soon, the tumult of their passing faded away.

"See?" said the boy, grinning at her. "Problem solved. Now let's get you up here, shall we?"

Now that she wasn't so panicked about potential foot removal, Leigh managed to worm her way up beside him, although she was panting and sweaty by the time she was done. He crouched next to her on the branch, the details of his face muddled by the thick shadows of the tree.

"Sorry about that," he said, and sounded like he meant it. "If you want to be hauled up into a tree, you're much better off choosing one inhabited by one of those beefy lunkheads who lift meat and chew iron."

She snorted, almost lightheaded with relief.

"Don't you mean lift iron and chew meat?" she asked.

"I have no idea. Do I look like a beefy lunkhead to you?"

"Honestly, I have no idea either. It's dark."

"Oh yeah. Come on in."

There was the creak of wood, and then an honest-to-goodness door opened up, spilling out a pleasant yellow glow. A tree house? Her savior stood silhouetted in the doorway, holding a hand out to her.

"Come on," he repeated. "We can wait out the attack in here."

She hesitated. It felt a little selfish to be hiding out while the villagers ran from the snagfires. But she'd done all she could for the moment, hadn't she? She'd instructed the Pixietails to help. Once they were done, they'd come find her for further instructions. She deserved to take a break, at least until she stopped shaking.

She stepped inside, and the boy latched the door behind her. The space was cramped—smaller even than her tiny apartment. To the left sat a pallet atop which rested a pillow and a rumpled blanket. At its end was a desk, its surface covered in stacks of books. A small stove and some cabinetry dominated most of the far wall, and in the corner was an overstuffed chair with some clothes thrown over top.

The boy swiped the clothes off the chair and gestured toward it.

"Have a seat," he said. "I'll get you some water."

She curled into the chair, which was surprisingly soft and comfy. If not for the fact that her limbs still jangled with adrenaline, she might have fallen right asleep. Instead, she took the opportunity to examine her rescuer properly. The shock of sandy hair she'd noticed in the tree topped off a handsome face that belonged on an anime bad boy, with large eyes, sharp cheekbones, and a thin, delicate mouth. He was tall and lanky, although not as pole-thin as Ari, with long limbs and deft fingers. He wore a simple outfit of all black that set off the paleness of his skin, with an interesting asymmetrical cut and a variety of straps and belts that held a variety of dangling pouches and pockets. A pair of tall leather boots completed the ensemble.

"Here you go," he said, offering her a terra-cotta cup of water.

"Thank you," she said, taking it from him and trying not to stare. "I'm Leigh. What's your name?"

"Oh, right," he said. "Brandish the Distractor at your service."

He bowed with a theatrical flourish before looking up at her through the fringe of his hair and grinning. Uh-oh. That lopsided grin grabbed onto her with both hands and held on tight, although she tried her best to resist its lure. Everyone knew that the charming boy with the lopsided grin was trouble with a capital *T*. That was one trope she needed to avoid at all costs, but what other choice did she have? She could go out there and get turned into a shish kebab by the snagfires, or she could stay here with the boy with the dangerous grin.

"What kind of name is that?" she asked, sipping her water and trying to ignore the rapid beat of her heart.

"Honestly, not one I would have chosen for myself." He leaned against the wall next to her chair, all casual-cool. "I would have gone with Brandish the Mostly Competent, or maybe Brandish the Guy Who's Great with Spells But Not So Good at Hauling Pretty Girls into Trees. But they didn't ask me. You can just call me Brandish."

"I expected another hair-themed name. You've got to admit that you stand out."

"Hopefully it's not the only reason I stand out," he said, the corner of his mouth twitching.

"Well, the part where you almost dropped me on my head is also notable, but I didn't think you'd want me to draw attention to that," she replied archly.

"Touché. I'm glad I saved you. I like a girl who can stand up for herself."

"You *barely* saved me!" she protested. "I did at least half the work."

"But I wove the illusion. At the very least, you have to give me credit for that," he said.

"Wait a minute. Illusion? What illusion?" She paused before answering her own question. "You cast an illusion spell and drew the snagfires away."

"They do call me the Distractor. I've got to live up to the hype."

"I've been looking for you!" she exclaimed, setting the cup down on a little table and twisting in the chair to face him more fully. "Wizard, right? I need your help. Do you know Shining Glory?"

"I know *of* him; everyone does. But he spends most of his time polishing the inside of that crystal ball. He hasn't been out ever since I got here." Brandish paused thoughtfully. "I suppose he's out now, then?"

"Yeah, I talked to him yesterday. He's under some sort of curse that limits what he can tell me, so I've been trying to find other wizards to consult. My Pixietails have been searching for you. I assume they would have introduced us if not for those stupid snagfires."

"Not a fan?"

"They stink." She sipped her water, overcome by a pang of guilt. "You know, we should go out there and help. Between your magic and my enchanted staff, we could kick some snagfire booty."

"I'm sorry, but you were just running from the snagfires, weren't you?"

"Yeah, but I was alone then. The odds are much better now."

"Oh, delightful. Instead of a thousand to one, now it's a thousand to two," he scoffed. "You're nuts."

"But you're a wizard, and I'm Lady Lovely Locks. We each count for multiple people."

"Mathematics aren't my strong suit, but I'm still not sure that either of us counts for enough people to make those numbers even remotely close. But what do I know, Lady Leigh? Your wish is my command."

Brandish offered her a hand up, but she ignored it, leaping to her feet like she had something to prove. Now that she had backup—any backup—she felt much more confident. Teeth clenched with determination, she marched outside with her staff in hand, only to have to resheath it in order to climb back down to the ground via a handy rope ladder.

During the short time they'd been inside, full night had fallen, and clouds cloaked the pink moon, hiding it from view. She squinted into the darkness but saw no signs of the snagfires. The market had burned itself out, with only a few embers letting out a fitful glow. The silence should have been comforting, but instead, it felt ominous. She drew her staff once more and stood guard while Brandish descended, dropping to the ground with catlike deftness.

"Would have been nice to use that on the way up," she said as he tied the ladder up out of sight.

"Next time, veer left around the trunk instead of right, and the ladder's all yours," he replied, teeth flashing. "Where to?"

"You know where the smithy is? I sent some of the villagers there to hide."

He nodded, his eyes roaming the trees. Although he didn't appear to carry a single weapon, his presence still reassured her.

"So you don't carry a gnarled wizard's staff? No magic crystal ball tucked into those pockets? Or a wand? I hear they're all the rage these days," said Leigh as she followed him into the brush.

"My wand is in the shop," he said, so deadpan that she wasn't sure if he was kidding or not. "There are a variety of different types of wizardry. You're thinking the prim and proper sort, like Shining Glory. Wizards who counsel royalty and that sort of thing. I'm more of a hedge wizard. No wands or pointy hats for me. I can't even grow a passable beard."

"And a hedge wizard is what exactly?" she asked. He held a large branch up for her to walk under, and she sidled past, all too aware of his closeness on the path. He was too damn handsome for his own good, and definitely too good-looking for hers. But she kept her expression neutral, trying to let no sign of her continued agitation show on her face. "Thanks."

"Don't mention it. Hedge wizards are about as common as they come. I used to make a living as a traveling performer. I can do some mean tricks with a little wooden ball and a few cups, and I wouldn't advise betting on a card game against me. One day, I started making the balls and cards actually disappear. It ruined my show."

"You poor wittle baby."

“Young lady, I will turn this car around and take you home,” he joked.

She stopped in the middle of the path, confusion rooting her in place. He continued on without her for a couple of steps before realizing she was no longer behind him. Then he dropped to an instant crouch, his head swiveling as he scanned the area.

“Snagfires?” he hissed.

“No, not that,” she said, stepping closer in a vain attempt to make out his face. “How do you know about cars?”

“Did I get it wrong?” he said. Although she could make out only the barest outline of his face, his voice sounded rueful. “I’ll admit it freely; I stole that line from a book.”

“You have books from my world here?”

“Now, that’s an interesting story. One of the previous princesses had a book thing. She kept bringing them over, and they’re somewhat of a collector’s item among wizards. I’ve gotten my hands on a few over the years. I’ve been trying to collect more of them. Your world is a fascinating place.”

“Yeah.”

Interesting. Now she understood why he sounded so different compared with everyone else here. If she closed her eyes, she could almost believe that he was just another boy from her high school. For a moment, she wondered what he’d read and what ridiculous ideas he’d developed based on the contents of his library. A horror reader would have a much different sense of the world than a fan of magical girl manga. If he read manga, he’d be expecting her to fly into the air and pose while little creatures flew around her trailing sparkles. Come to think of it, that wasn’t too far from the truth.

“The smithy is right around this bend,” he said, gesturing toward a large rock outcropping. “Quiet.”

They both stopped in place, huddled together on the path. For a moment, Leigh heard nothing. But then a loud, familiar thwack split the silence.

“They need help!” she exclaimed, sprinting past him, her staff in hand.

“Leigh!” said Brandish, surprised. “Wait up!”

CHAPTER 12

LEIGH DASHED AROUND THE STONY HILL LIKE A charging barbarian, staff held high, up until the moment when she stepped on a loose rock and nearly went down. After that, she crept around the outcropping like a tentative wimp. At least Brandish didn't say anything. He barely seemed to have noticed in his constant need to scan their surroundings. No one would sneak up on them, if only because he spent at least half his time looking over his shoulder.

The smithy was a squat building with an open forge next to it. Red embers still glowed from the central pit. Although the hot coals didn't emit a ton of light, they still illuminated the shadowy outlines of snagfires moving in the darkness.

She froze in place at the sight of them, and Brandish stumbled into her back. The stones clattered beneath their feet as she clapped a hand over his mouth to muffle his startled curse. The snagfires had to have heard that. Her heart hammered in her ears, so loud that it would drown out any signs of pursuit. But the seconds ticked away, and no fire-breathing beasties came to investigate the ruckus. She released him, leaning close to whisper in his ear.

"Snagfires near the building," she breathed.

She could feel him nod, wisps of his hair tickling her face.

"I'll distract them," he whispered back. "You knock their heads off."

She nodded in return, trusting that he would sense her response as she had his. She heard a faint rustle as he rummaged around in one of his pouches, probably fetching some spell components, a potion, or something along those lines. A surprising excitement thrummed through her veins. Whatever happened here, at least she'd get to see some real magic. Hopefully she wouldn't die before she had a chance to properly appreciate it.

"Ready?" she murmured.

"Always," he responded, his breath tickling her skin.

As they drew closer, she could smell the carbon stink of the snagfires and hear the scrape of their wicked claws against some hard object. Were they trying to tear down the door? She had no idea, but she intended to stop them.

Leigh and Brandish reached the side of the building, flattening themselves against the wall. She had no idea how well the creatures saw in the dark, but they probably had better night vision than she did. Better to use what cover she could in the hopes of taking them by surprise.

There was a click from the wall immediately in front of her, and a dark blur of movement as something—a window?—swung open. The faint, watery light of the moon was just bright enough for her to make out the outline of the heavy sledgehammer as someone inside swung it out at her. She scrambled backward, letting out a startled scream.

So much for surprise.

"Princess?" called the shocked voice of the smith, the word half drowned out by the barking coughs of the snagfires. "Is that you?"

"We're here to rescue you. Close the window," she snapped, banging her staff on the ground to activate its magic.

The magical spear hummed to life, spreading a welcome pink glow. It didn't illuminate much, but at least she'd be able to see what she was stabbing.

"Whoa," said Brandish. "Nice."

The snagfires rounded the corner, three or maybe four of them, but this time she wasn't alone. She thrust the spear out to buy Brandish time to throw around his magic, and he didn't disappoint. He gestured, muttering to himself so low that she couldn't make out the words. An electric shiver of magic ran over her; she could feel it pass her. The snagfires barked again, the tone higher this time.

They sounded afraid.

Two of them slammed into each other, before one let out a gout of flame that hit the other in the face. It howled. For a moment, Leigh stood there, watching with stunned interest, but then Brandish shook her, breaking the shocked reverie.

"They're blind!" he explained. "Hit them now, before it wears off."

She needed no further encouragement. She stabbed at the panicked snagfire in front, the magical blade sinking into its flesh like melted butter. The burning snagfire bolted off into the darkness in a panic, leaving only one, which was too close to stab. She spun smoothly, hitting it with the haft once, twice, a third time, beating it mercilessly until it began to back away. Then she smoothly reversed the weapon, impaling and killing the beast.

She waited for a moment then, her weapon held at the ready, but nothing else moved in the dark recesses of the smithy. All the frantic energy drained out of her as the reality of what had just happened sank in. She could have died. Brandish could have died. The more she thought about it, the more she shook.

Brandish didn't say anything. As the staff fell from her hands, the blade sinking back into the gem at the top, he pulled her in close, resting his face in her hair. Normally, she wouldn't snuggle up against some guy she'd just barely met, but he was shaking too. It was only natural that they should comfort each other. It meant nothing. She would keep reminding herself of that until she believed it.

Then the window swung open again with a creak that suggested the hinges needed oiling.

"Is it over?" asked the smith. "Or do you need my sledgehammer?"

The smith had been busy. He'd collected at least ten kids en route to the smithy and hid them all inside, attacking the snagfires through the windows. When he finally unbarred the sturdy doors, the kids all came spilling out. Most just wanted to touch Leigh's hair for luck, but the little girl she'd saved seemed to think they were besties now. She climbed right into Leigh's lap, eager to show off her favorite stuffed cat and the scrape on her elbow. Once she started, she just kept talking without any apparent need to breathe.

Leigh had never been much of a kid person. She babysat when she was too young to get an actual job, but she didn't love it. Little kids made her feel like she was cosplaying as a person who knew what to do in an emergency. But this little girl somehow put her at ease, so she listened and nodded in what seemed like all the right places until her Pixietails finally returned with a small herd of villagers in tow.

One exhausted-looking lady rushed over to sweep the kid up and cover her with relieved kisses.

Leigh stood then, stretching out her stiff legs. As she did, Pixie Shine and Pixie Beauty came over, all atwitter and talking a mile a minute. Once she realized they were just spouting relieved nonsense, she tuned them out and didn't feel an ounce of guilt over it either. But when Pixie Sparkle joined them, she snapped back to reality.

"Are all the snagfires accounted for?" she asked. "Anywhere else we need to be?"

"They retreated back to Tangleland," said the Pixietail. "The villagers begged us to help find the children. I told them to follow us to you, because you would be with them."

She blinked. "How did you know?"

"Because you're a hero!" interrupted Pixie Shine.

"A real natural," said Pixie Beauty. "So brave and lovely."

Weirdly, Leigh had to admit that the label kind of fit. She *was* a hero. As she watched the grateful villagers reunite with their children, she realized that none of this would have been possible if not for her and Brandish. Instead of hiding away in his safe tree house, they'd gone to help simply because they could. Because it was right.

A strange warmth spread through her. Leigh had always been a bit of a wall hugger except where cosplay was concerned. She didn't like being the center of attention. She wasn't smart or gorgeous or athletic or any of the things that made people popular. She abhorred bullies, and she'd stood up to a few, but she'd never really been in danger from them. Not until today. She could have gotten badly hurt.

But if she had to do it again, she would have made the same choices. Otherwise, she wouldn't be able to look at herself in the mirror.

A steady stream of villagers came up, pressing their foreheads to her hands and thanking her. Some of them cried. She found herself tearing up a few times but managed to pass it off as dust in her eyes. They described burnt homes and terrifying moments, but they'd survived. They would rebuild.

By the time the last villager disappeared, she was wavering on her feet. She looked up to see Brandish standing opposite her. Quickly, she brushed at her leaky eyes with the back of her hand and tried to look casual, but based on his expression, he wasn't buying the act at all.

"Stupid onion bandits," she said.

"Sorry?" he asked, wrinkling his nose in confusion.

"Oh. That must not be in your books. Onion bandits—onions make you cry. It's . . . never mind. It's not important."

"You're okay, though?" he asked.

"Yeah, thanks to your help. I feel like a bit of a jerk. I soaked up all the credit when I should have shared it with you. I'm sorry. I'm just exhausted. But I'll tell them—"

"No worries." He brushed it off with a wave of a hand. "You know, and that's what's most important. They tell me that pretty girls are impressed by heroics. Did it work?"

She huffed in amusement, but he didn't stop staring at her expectantly.

"You don't expect me to really answer that, do you?" she asked.

"I earned a little flattery, don't you think?"

"Oh, fine. We make a pretty good team."

"We make a *spectacular* team. Our exploits will be legendary, our reputations impeccable," he declared.

"I don't know about that. When that hammer swung at me out of nowhere, I screamed like Markiplier in a FNAF video." She paused. "Which means nothing to you. Never mind."

"Don't sell yourself short. I know what screaming is, and you weren't that loud," he said. "I'm only half deaf."

She elbowed him as he snickered, blushing for the umpteenth time that day. Speaking of days and times, she looked up at the sky, trying to judge how much time had passed based on the position of the moon, but she'd been running around in circles for so long that she honestly couldn't tell.

"Can I come back to see you?" she asked. "Maybe tomorrow night?"

The corner of his mouth quirked up.

"And why would you want to do that?" he asked. "More snagfire hunting? Do you want to brainstorm more names for me that are better than the one I currently have? Or am I just that irresistibly attractive?"

She swung the butt of her staff around, bonking the side of his leg, and he yelped, laughing aloud. His face lit up with amusement, and she couldn't help it. She burst out laughing along with him. It felt good after so much fear and tension, and once she started, she couldn't stop. Maybe she was a bit hysterical.

"Sorry," he finally said. "I'm a bit hysterical."

"Same," she replied, blushing. Again. She wished she knew how to make it stop, but the more she thought about it, the more she did it. The only thing left to do was to act casual and hope he was color-blind. "But I mostly wanted to ask you questions."

"What kinds of questions?" he asked, stepping closer, his voice low and intimate.

She could feel her palms sweating. She had to get ahold of herself. Normally, she was helpless when it came to out-of-character flirting, but she'd been doing so well.

"Wizard questions," she replied, trying and mostly succeeding to keep her voice from wavering.

"Right. Of course." But he seemed nonplussed, and when he stepped back, she swore she saw a flicker of disappointment flash over his face. "Anything in particular you want to know about? I might have to read up a bit. Hedge wizard, remember? Unless you've got questions about the old ball-and-cup routine, in which case I'm your man."

"There's this painting of a lady in Ravenwaves Tower. I'm pretty sure I know her from when I was young. Before I ever came here."

He tilted his head thoughtfully.

"Oh?" he asked. "That's odd."

"Exactly. I'm trying to figure out how that's possible, but Ravenwaves hid the painting from me, and she's not exactly president of my fan club. The person in the painting is missing, and it could be a clue to her whereabouts."

"So many possibilities..." Brandish trailed off, running a long finger thoughtfully down his jaw. "Right. I say we steal it."

"That's a good—wait. What?! I was looking for expert wizard advice."

"I'm not sure why that matters, but fine. My advice as an expert wizard is to steal the painting. If you really want to, you can return it after you're done with it. I won't judge." He took in her shocked expression and held out his hands. "I told you: hedge wizard. We're not the prim and proper fellows with the pointy hats and long beards, but we're great to have at your side if you're planning a heist."

"But..." Leigh hesitated.

"I understand the reluctance, but look at the facts. Ravenwaves isn't going to just hand over the painting to you; she's nuts, and according to the rumor mill, she hates you. If you want it, you're going to have to take it."

Leigh hesitated. She wasn't a total fed; she'd broken a few rules here and there. After all, didn't everyone? But it was one thing to cross the street in the middle of a block or pirate a movie online. Theft was another thing entirely.

But Brandish did have a point. The only way she was going to get her hands on that painting was by force.

"Maybe...?" she said. "But I don't even know where it is."

"Like I said, we make a good team. I'll help you find it, and then we'll liberate it from its current owner."

"Why?" she asked, narrowing her eyes.

"I suppose I find you irresistib—"

"Cut the crap, Brandish. There's no reason for you to go to all this trouble to help me. Either you're too good to be true, or there's something here I don't know. Which is it?"

"Pretty and smart? Be still my beating heart," he murmured, putting the back of his hand to his forehead. Before she could kick him in the shins, he straightened. "But seriously. I suppose there are a few ways to answer that question. I'm tired of the constant snagfire incursions. The villagers just grin and bear it, but that's not in my nature. Besides, I'm not ashamed to admit it; I'm here to make a name for myself. This seems like it could be a step in that direction."

The explanation held up well enough no matter how hard she tried to poke holes in it. Sighing, she nodded.

"Okay, okay. Sorry," she said.

"I still think my first response is probably the most accurate." His mouth twitched. "I'm a sucker for a pretty girl with a big stick. But if those other explanations make you feel more secure, let's go with those."

"I will hit you over the head," she growled.

"See?" His eyes danced. "Who could resist that? All the village girls swoon when I walk by, but there's nothing like a challenge. So what will it be, Lady Leigh? Is this painting worth getting your hands a little dirty?"

He leaned toward her as he spoke, his voice pitched low. She had the feeling that no matter what she said, he'd take it in stride. If they were going to do this, she'd have to trust him, and she barely knew him. Perhaps she should wait. Go home. Think things over. That would be the most logical choice to make in this situation, but for some reason, she found herself taking a total leap of faith instead.

"If you're honestly offering to help, I'd better lay all my cards on the table. The painting looks like my mom," she blurted.

"Whoa."

"It's a painting of Lady Knot."

"Whoa."

"You sure you want to help?"

"How could I not?" he responded without hesitation. "This is the sort of thing that legends are made of. If I bow out, I'll regret it for the rest of my life. But are you sure it's her?"

"I only got one look at the painting, but the resemblance is uncanny. My mom had a pretty distinctive birthmark, and it's in there. It really could be. I've got to get my hands on it, but I can't walk around telling everyone that I think I might be Lady Knot's daughter. To be honest, I'm surprised you didn't run away screaming."

"Ah, but I'm not from here. I've heard tales about her, but there's no way to know which are real and which fantasy." He smirked. "Also, I'm known for two things: my charming good looks and complete inability to back away from a challenge."

"Are you sure you're not known for your ego?" she teased.

"See? You're a challenge, and I like it."

The look he gave her was frank and admiring, and she could practically feel it on her skin. He was so charming but self-deprecating at the same time. The combination was lethal in a completely unexpected way. Good thing she didn't believe in insta-love, or she would have been swooning. Instead, she fumbled for a change of subject, trying to ignore the flaming of her cheeks.

"Yeah, so, uh..." she fumbled. "My mom disappeared when I was young, and I don't know what happened to her. My dad says she left us, but... there's got to be more to the story. I need to know."

His lips quirked, but he didn't comment on her incredibly rosy complexion. Instead, he leaned back against the wall of the smithy, stuffing his hands into his pockets.

"Take the painting," he urged. "If robbery really strains your morals, leave it outside Ravenwaves Tower when you're done with it. But if you don't, you'll always regret it. I know I would."

He was right. She felt it down to her bones.

"Yeah." She took a deep breath, trying to tamp down the nervous excitement that welled up in her the moment she made the decision. "Yeah, let's do it."

"At your service, Princess," he said with another of his flourishing bows.

"Leigh. If we're forming a criminal enterprise, you should call me Leigh."

"And you can call me Brandish the Irresistible," he suggested, eyes twinkling.

"I thought it was Brandish the Distractor?"

"Sadly, yes, but you can't blame me for hoping."

Their eyes met. A single lock of hair flopped into his face, and she had the incredibly intense urge to reach up and brush it away. She resisted it, but that was more of a struggle than she liked. *He's just a flirt,* she told herself. *He probably pours on the charm for all the girls.*

She knew it was true, but that didn't stop her from wishing otherwise.

CHAPTER 13

AFTER LEIGH MADE ARRANGEMENTS TO RECONVENE with Brandish the following night, she called out to her Pixietails to send her home. She had no idea what time it was, but she knew she'd stayed much later than intended. For the first time, she wondered what she'd say if she popped up in the middle of her bedroom to find her dad waiting for her. What would he do? Take her to the doctor? Confiscate her cosplay? Would he believe her about the painting, and even if he did, would he stop her from returning to investigate?

Once the possibility occurred to her, she became convinced that it was going to happen. Why hadn't she been more careful? She should have locked herself in the bathroom to avoid any chance of being spotted. She squinched her eyes shut as the magic whooshed her from the bright excitement of the fantasy kingdom back into the dull gray of the real world. If her dad was in the room, he'd shout at any moment.

The silence stretched out, unbroken.

She cracked open an eyelid. She'd appeared right in front of the open window, looking out through the open blinds, backlit by her desk lamp. Beyond the overgrown bushes that grew outside the window stood Ari. He was staring straight up at her, his face clearly illuminated by the streetlight and the neon glow from the bar across the street. The wideness of his eyes and the round O of his mouth made it clear—he'd seen everything. She couldn't hear him through the glass, but it was all too easy to read his lips when he spoke.

"What the..." he said.

This was bad. Not as bad as her dad, but still bad. She gestured for him to come inside before pulling the cheap metal blinds closed, thinking furiously. She had to tell him something, but what? The truth?

The sticky front door took a few good yanks to get open. When she finally managed to do so, he stood there gasping on the mat like he had sprinted inside. Above him, a single bare bulb emitted an electric hum. The door to apartment 1C remained closed, but she was fairly sure she saw a flicker of movement from behind the peephole.

"Ari," she said, a bit too loudly. "Thanks for coming over to help me study for that anatomy quiz. I really want to ace it."

"I..." Confusion flickered over his face as he fumbled for words. "I don't know—"

"Come on in," she interrupted before he could ruin everything.

She closed the door behind him, jerking on the knob a few times before she could engage the dead bolt. When she finally turned to face him, he already had his arms folded.

"Explain," he demanded.

Since he didn't specify, she decided to go with the easier of the two explanations.

"The old lady in 1C likes to tattle," she said. "And I don't think she sleeps, like, ever. When I was cramming for exams at the end of last year, I went out for a Monster late at night, and she told my dad precisely what time I left and when I got back. At least this way, we'll have an alibi."

"You think she'll snitch?"

"Oh yeah. But my dad likes you, and he really wants me to ace Anatomy and Physiology. If I tell him we were drilling tarsals and metatarsals and rattle off all the names, he'll be chill."

"Okay..." said Ari. Then he turned around and flipped off the door. "Screw that lady, though."

Leigh nodded, trying to avoid his gaze. She still didn't know what to tell him, so she went to the kitchen to stall for time. There wasn't a ton of food—neither she nor her dad knew how to cook things that didn't come in boxes with simple directions—but she did scrounge up a bag of unopened tortilla chips and some shredded cheese that didn't look moldy. She held them up with an expression of triumph and shook them for effect.

"What are you doing?" he asked, exasperated.

"Nachos. You want some?"

"It's two in the morning."

"And you're about to interrogate me. That'll suck, but it'll be slightly more bearable with nachos."

She shook the chips out onto a paper plate, covered them liberally with cheese, and popped them into the microwave. Resigned, he sat down on one of the wobbly kitchen stools, elbows on the counter, and waited. The microwave dinged. The nachos came out steaming, but she was too hungry to wait. All that fighting and running had worked up an appetite.

She still didn't know what to say, or even why she was so reluctant to tell him. She'd confided in Brandish, whom she'd just met, but not in her best friend. It didn't make sense. Ari had always had her back. If anyone was going to believe all this insanity, he would.

She had to say something. Anything.

"Why were you in the bushes outside my apartment?" she blurted. "Are you cosplaying as a stalker now?"

His expression darkened, his brows drawing down into an angry V. Maybe she *shouldn't* have said something. In fact, maybe she should have kept her stupid mouth shut, but it was too late now.

"Don't even try that," he said, shaking a nacho at her to punctuate every word. "Don't try to turn this around on me. You've been squirrelly all week. Where were you tonight?"

"Uh..." She blinked. "Here?"

He threw the chip down, disgusted.

"You no-showed at work, Leigh. Did you even notice? I covered for you, *again,* because I figured you were trying to track down your mom and you'd spill eventually. I ignored the fact that you've been a total zombie at school and haven't heard three-quarters of the things I say to you. You don't respond to my Snaps. I was starting to think that maybe I'd pissed you off—"

"No, it's not like that—"

"—but that was before I saw you *appear out of thin air*. What the hell, Leigh!? Will you please tell me what's going on?"

"Look, I..." She had never lied to him, not about anything important, but she found herself staring straight into his eyes and lying through her teeth. "I didn't appear out of thin air. I've been working on some new illusions for my cosplay. You know, like stage magic. I thought it would be a neat effect."

She plastered on a smile that felt faker than a Real Housewife. Desperation and shame rolled in her belly along with all those nachos. What was she doing? Why lie? She didn't know, but now it was too late to take back.

"How'd you do it?" he asked.

"Oh...well...uh...isn't that a rule of magic? You're not supposed to say."

"But I'm your partner." His eyes narrowed. "Unless we're not doing contests together anymore either. Is that it?"

"No, it's—"

"Then tell me. How'd you do it? Mirrors? You don't have a trapdoor in your bedroom floor. I don't buy it."

"What, you think I really disappeared?" she asked, her grin shaky. "That's nuts."

He stared at her for a long moment, his mouth pressed into a thin, furious line. Then he stood, brushing crumbs off his pant legs. She'd never seen him angry before, not like this. If he walked out that door, there was a good chance that their friendship would never recover. But she didn't know what else to do. Tell him the truth?

She didn't want to share Lovely Locks. Parts of it were ridiculous, but it was hers. Next year, Ari would go to college, where he'd make a bunch of new friends. A new life. He'd stay in touch, but it wouldn't be the same. She needed Lovely Locks. What if Ari wanted to go with her, and she broke whatever magic allowed her to keep returning? What if he thought it was too dangerous and tried to talk her out of continuing the search for her mom? She couldn't risk it. Not just because of the link to her mom. Because there, she was a hero. Special. Somebody.

Ari stared at her for a long moment as if expecting her to say something. When she didn't, he huffed and headed for the door.

"You know what?" he said. "Never mind. If you're not willing to trust me, our friendship isn't what I thought it was. I'll see you around, Leigh."

At that moment, she realized that of all the things she could lose, his friendship would hurt the most. Ari had always accepted her just as she was. He helped her with her math homework, covered for her at work, made stupid jokes to cheer her up on bad days. He gave her space when she needed it. Most people assumed that they must be dating because guys and girls can't just be friends, but it wasn't like that. Over the summer, he'd been deep into a talking stage with a cute Kawaii girl he'd met online, and he'd broken it off with her when she started demanding that he spend less time with Leigh. Leigh hadn't even known about it until it was all over.

With a pang of regret, she realized she'd been selling him short. Yes, it was scary to think about facing down next year without him, but if anyone would stay in touch, it was Ari. He was loyal to the bone.

"Wait," she said, launching to her feet so quickly that she knocked the bag of tortilla chips off the counter. Chips skittered across the cracked tile, but she ignored them. She couldn't let him leave. "I just—I'm scared to tell you."

He stopped but didn't turn around.

"I'm listening," he responded.

"You're going to think I'm nuts."

"Let me decide for myself."

She took a deep breath, trying to figure out where to start. But there was no way to soften this. Best to rip the Band-Aid off as fast as she could.

"My cosplay is magic," she said. Ari turned to stare at her, one eyebrow raised. "When I put it on, it teleports me into Lovely Locks Kingdom, which is insane, I know, and I didn't believe it myself at first. I thought I was dreaming. But it kept happening. I even recorded myself, so I had to believe it even though it's nuts, right? So I've been trying to figure out how it works—why it works—because I saw a painting in there that looks like my mom, but I couldn't tell you any details about it because I was worried you'd think I was Joker levels of mentally unstable."

Panic made her babble. She clamped her mouth shut and stared at him, trying to determine how he was taking all of this. For a long moment, he didn't speak. Then he opened his mouth. Closed it. Opened and closed it again. Clearly, he wanted to say something, but he couldn't scrape up the words. She knew the feeling, so she waited.

"Well, that wasn't what I expected," he finally said.

"What did you expect? Did you come up with some rational explanation for teleporting that I missed?"

"I was going to go with one of the basics. Bit by a radioactive bug. Cursed by an ancient demon. Or maybe possessed by a sea hag. That's one of my personal favorites."

"You sound like a bad anime."

"No, that would be if you got transported to the magic kingdom and promptly met a boy and instantly decided that someday, you'll marry him and have his babies."

Her cheeks flamed again. Ari took one look at her and sighed.

"There's a boy, isn't there?" he asked.

"I'm not going to marry him and have his babies. I'm seventeen, for god's sake. I'm not having anyone's babies. And I don't believe in insta-love any more than you do, so get off my back," she declared.

"Okay, so there's a boy, and he's really cute. Does Mr. Cute have a name?"

"Brandish," she said.

"That's definitely a lame fantasy name. But let's table that for a minute and go back to the rest of it. One: I would never compare you to the Joker, because I actually like you. Two: Tell me more about how this works, and what your mom has to do with it, and what it's like over there."

"You do realize that number two on your list should really be numbers two, three, and four, right? Like, that's three things."

"Quit being a semantic jerkwad and tell me everything," he ordered, walking back toward her. Chips crunched beneath his feet, and he stopped in place, staring down at them like he'd forgotten that chips had ever existed. "Scratch that. Get the broom first, and then tell me everything."

"You're so demanding," she teased, but inside, she was brimming with relief. He'd listened. He'd believed.

Everything was going to be okay.

Once she got over the initial fear, confiding in him became easy again. She told him everything—well, pretty close to everything. She glossed over some of the flirty bits, because they made her look a little desperate, and she didn't want him to start teasing her again. He gave her a few significant looks every time she mentioned Brandish, but he didn't say a thing on that subject. Instead, he asked intelligent questions about how the cosplay worked and what made this one different from all the others, the same sorts of questions she'd asked herself.

After a good half hour of Q&A, they turned their attention to the wig. In her bedroom, Ari pulled it off the stand, examining it minutely as she explained.

"I've stared at that thing so long I see it in my dreams, but it sure looks normal to me," she said. "Nothing hidden inside it, no magical sigils stitched into the base. No clues that would make sense of all this weirdness. But it's obviously the key."

"Yeah, I don't see anything either," he admitted, his disappointment clear. "It just looks like a normal wig to me."

"I was thinking the vendor who sold it to me might know something, but I didn't see her on the floor map, and I haven't had the time to follow up."

"Yeah!" He perked up. "I could take the lead on that. My friend Spider is in a talking stage with a girl on con staff. Let me see what I can find."

"I would love you forever," she declared melodramatically.

"We both know you'll do that anyway," he said, but his attention didn't waver from the wig. "Besties for life."

"Yeah." They stood there in silence for a moment, staring at the hairpiece. She'd picked it up off the floor and arranged it on its stand. It needed a good brushing, but she didn't have the oomph for that. A quick glance at the clock told her why—it was almost four thirty in the morning. Her dad would be home soon. “Crazy, isn’t it? I still can’t believe I own a magic cosplay.”

“I want to see it in action,” said Ari, still staring at the wig.

“Sure, but not now. My dad’s gonna be home in a little more than a half hour, and we’ve got to get up for school in less than three.”

“Crap.” Ari jolted, looking at the clock in shock. “I totally lost track of time. I can see why you always look like an extra from *The Walking Dead.*”

“I’ve been waiting until my dad leaves to suit up, and my cell doesn’t make the jump with me, so it’s hard to keep track of how long I’ve been there. I’ve been mainlining caffeine, but it’s a losing battle.”

“Okay,” he said decisively. “Here’s what we’re gonna do. Last half of our shifts is always dead, right? So when we’re at work, I’ll cover for you. Just stay through the rush, and once we hit the lull, you can suit up, and I’ll hold down the fort until you get back. Then you can catch up on sleep a little.”

Leigh nodded eagerly. “Sleep, yes. In fact, sleep *now.*”

A yawn cracked his jaws.

“Same. If you stop for a Monster on the way to school, get me one? I’ll pay you back,” he said.

“Nah. I owe you one for not laughing at me outright. I still can’t believe how well you’re taking all of this.”

He shrugged. “I mean, I saw you disappear. This convo would have gone very differently if not for that. Besides, I’m not sure it’s the weirdest thing that’s happened to me recently. If I can believe in lunatic customers like the chicken plunger guy, then I can believe anything. Some things are inexplicable, and we just have to be okay with that."

"If you're gonna rant like that, you should start streaming. Viewers eat that crap up. Now get out before I hit you with my staff."

Snickering, he hurried toward the door, and she locked up behind him before toppling into the bed with half of her cosplay still on. By the time her dad arrived home about a half hour later, she was already snoring.

CHAPTER 14

AFTER SCHOOL THE NEXT DAY, LEIGH STOPPED AT home to grab her stuff before heading off to work. As a long-time cosplayer, she was used to lugging around enormous props and bins full of costumes, and she'd taken steps to save her arms. A few months ago when Sal threw out an old hand truck with a shaky wheel and broken handle, she'd snagged it. After a few repairs, it now maneuvered the cracked curbs with ease.

When she arrived at Wing It, Ari hurried to hold the door while she wrestled the bin inside. The bell above the door jingled as she tried to dislodge the box, and the incessant noise kept making her look over her shoulder like her Pixietails might be stalking her. But of course that wasn't the case.

Ari didn't notice. He was examining the hand truck, which she'd repainted and covered in vinyl Transformers stickers.

"Is this the one you took from the dumpster out back?" he asked.

"Yeah. I'm thinking of naming him Megatron."

"I wonder why. Sal's still in the break room. Don't let him see it or he'll try to take it back."

"Over my dead body," she declared, but she still took the advice, hiding the hand truck in the corner with all the mops. Sal hated doing the floors; he'd never look there.

After clocking in, she began to work her way through the stack of special orders by the phone. Sal came stomping out of the back room before she'd made much progress. If Mario were an old man, Leigh thought he'd look exactly like Sal—balding and rotund, with a big bristling mustache. Normally, he was a happy grump; he complained all the time but seemed to take immense pleasure from it. But at the moment, he glowered at her from beneath his shaggy old-man brows. Had he seen the hand truck after all and was pissed that she'd taken it? Or had he realized that she'd completely flaked on coming into work last night? She froze, racking her brain for excuses. She couldn't afford to lose this job.

"Those IRS yahoos can shove their paperwork up their tuchuses!" he declared. "I'm going home."

"IRS...?" she responded weakly.

"Yeah! You got a problem with that?!"

"N-no...?" she sputtered.

"Should we do anything?" Ari asked from the safety of his register.

"Naw, I'll be back. Unless you know a hit man..."

Sal trailed off, muttering to himself as he stomped out the door. As it swung closed behind him, Leigh and Ari exchanged a glance.

"What's going on?" she asked.

"He got a letter from the IRS, and it nearly sent him into cardiac arrest. Something tells me that his system of throwing all receipts into a shoebox has finally come back to haunt him."

She gritted her teeth. "You think I should hold off on the..." She jerked her head in the direction of the bin, all too aware of a single customer with a soul patch over near the spackle. He probably couldn't hear her all the way over there, but better safe than sorry. "The thing? In case Sal comes back?"

Ari pursed his lips thoughtfully as the spackle guy finally made a selection and brought it up to the counter. After the purchase was completed and the door jingled closed, he said, "I think you should go. Now. Make it quick. I'll cover for you if he comes back before you do. Just lock yourself in the bathroom. I'll tell him you got another burrito from Taco Planet."

"Please don't bring that up again. I have trauma," she said, shuddering.

"But it's useful trauma. Just..." He trailed off. "Let me watch this time? I'll lock the bathroom door for you after you're gone. I just want to see the teleportation up close. I gotta admit; I'm a little jealous."

"Yeah, of course. You know I'd share if I knew it would work, right? But I'm not sure what the rules are. Maybe once I pass the wig on, I can't use it anymore. I'm too afraid to risk it."

"I get it. You've got to find out about your mom. No big. I'm not sure I'd look good in that wig anyway. Pastels just aren't good for my complexion. I'm much better in jewel tones."

He fluttered his lashes at her, and she snickered.

"I'll go change," she said.

This time, the transition from the real world to the magical kingdom of Lovely Locks went smoothly, although she did have a bit of a rough time getting the wig on in the tiny employee bathroom without dropping the end of it into the toilet. The last thing she saw was Ari's delighted expression as the real world faded away. Her vision cleared, revealing the castle courtyard.

Sighing, she looked around. Bright afternoon light filtered through thin clouds, and a warm breeze stirred her long hair. There were no signs of the snagfire attack, at least not that she could see here. A few villagers hurried about, pausing to smile and greet her before continuing on with whatever they'd been doing. She paused to gaze up at the glittering expanse of the castle and considered going inside to take a peek, but she had things to do and little time to waste.

Everything looked different during the day, but her Pixietails claimed to know exactly where Brandish's tree house was. They led her through the bustling market, and although many of the villagers offered her samples, she turned them down as politely as possible. But honestly? This place was better than Costco. One year, her dad won a membership from a raffle at work. They used to go there every Sunday to fill up on samples.

To her immense relief, the market had been fully repaired. None of the villagers brought up the snagfire attack or even seemed to remember it. She wasn't sure if snagfire attacks were a daily occurrence, or there was some weird fairy-tale rule that everything defaulted back to normal while the main characters weren't looking. It didn't really matter so long as everyone was okay.

She spotted the tree house easily, although it took her a moment to find the ladder tucked among the branches. Her cheeks were already flaming as she climbed up.

Brandish wasn't home. She tapped on the door and eventually stuck her head inside just in case.

Once the door was open, she couldn't resist looking around a little. She stopped next to the desk and eyed the piled books and papers for a moment. The temptation to rifle through them pulled at her, but she turned away firmly. She refused to stoop so low. Besides, what did she think she was going to find? A diary in which all the recent entries were about the mysterious girl who had popped into his life and his undeniable feelings toward her? Barf.

What now? She should try to start working on this heist of theirs. They needed a crew.

Her mind made up, she hurried back into the tree house to scribble a note on one of the blank pages atop Brandish's desk. It read:

> HAD TO COME EARLIER THAN EXPECTED. SORRY I MISSED YOU. I'M GOING TO SEE ABOUT GETTING US SOME HELP FOR THAT THING WE WERE PLANNING. WILL ASK MY PIXIETAILS TO HANG AROUND WITH YOU TOMORROW SO THAT I DON'T MISS YOU AGAIN. —LEIGH
>
> PS—I SWEAR I DIDN'T GO THROUGH YOUR STUFF, EXCEPT TO FIND SOMETHING TO WRITE WITH. I'M NOT A STALKER.
>
> PPS—A STALKER IS A CREEPY PERSON WHO—YOU KNOW, NEVER MIND. FORGET I SAID ANYTHING.

She forced herself to put down the pencil and leave before another postscript occurred to her. Her scattershot thinking translated well to DMs, but in print, it made her look a bit like an idiot.

This time, she returned to the castle without the help of the Pixietails. She was beginning to learn her way around, and a few of the villagers she passed were somewhat familiar. They all wore the same homespun, simple clothing in muted shades, but she remembered that guy's bulbous nose and that woman's crystal clear complexion. She didn't really know anyone here, and approaching random strangers to ask them to help with a little theft seemed like a poor choice. Besides, she had a better idea.

When she rapped on the door of Glory Manor, it swung open on its own. She crossed through the entry hall with its jumble of paintings and into the crystal room. The place had changed since her last visit. A set of overstuffed pastel couches had been arranged around the glowing crystal plinth, and Shining Glory sat at the end of one with a book in his hands. On the other end sat the locksfox, posing prettily on a silver pillow, its fur fluffed to perfection.

Shining Glory set the book down, smiling in her direction.

"Princess," he said warmly. "How good of you to drop by. Are you in need of my services?"

"Advice, mostly. If I'm not interrupting?"

"Come in and be welcome."

She sat down opposite him, the soft sofa nearly swallowing her. The wizard set his book down, patting its cover appreciatively. His empty white eyes seemed to fix on her, and she wondered how much he could really see. He must not be completely blind if he'd been reading, right? But it would be tactless to ask.

"The books read themselves," he said.

"Beg pardon?"

"I said the books read themselves. You were wondering how I'm able to consume them. They'll read to you, if you only know how to ask. I'm quite lucky. The objects in Glory Manor often pitch in to make my existence a little easier; isn't that right, Prince?"

The locksfox rested its head on its front paws with a sigh.

"You don't happen to have a beast and a talking candelabra with matchmaking tendencies, do you? If so, I've heard this story before."

"No beasts here unless you count the locksfox, but I wouldn't use so coarse a term for him, personally."

Maybe because the locksfox was actually a guy, like in the story? Leigh almost asked, but she had no desire to open that can of worms. In the book, Prince Strongheart had clearly been set up as a romantic interest, and she wasn't about to encourage that. She had her hands full with Brandish anyway.

"Right." She took a deep breath. "So I wanted to ask you a question. Hypothetically. If I were planning a heist, would you be able to help me?"

"Hypothetically, you say?" He grinned in approval. "Oh, I love a good hypothetical. No link at all to reality, is there?"

"No, never."

"Well, *hypothetically*, I'd wish you the best, but I probably wouldn't be of much assistance. Remember, I cannot leave the crystal. The further I get from it, the weaker I grow."

"That's not good. Couldn't you take it with you?"

"The crystal used to be mobile, but Ravenwaves kept trying to steal it. Succeeded a few times, which isn't a surprise given the abysmal security around here. Once, a new princess came to the kingdom, and I wasn't available to help her, because Ravenwaves had absconded with my crystal, and I'm still quite miffed about it. That poor girl had no idea what had happened to her, and it didn't end well, I'm afraid. As soon as the crystal was returned to its proper place, I secured it to this plinth so I'll always be available to each new princess. It does limit my travel somewhat, but that's a sacrifice I'm willing to make. I'm afraid that if you were going to go on this hypothetical heist, you'd have to go without me."

"And that's it? You wouldn't counsel me against it? It's not against the princess rules?"

"Ah, but you're a hero. If you're taking something, it's for the right reasons. If you were an evil princess... well, that would be a different story."

There was that fairy-tale morality again. Leigh briefly considered arguing against it, because if anyone here could grasp the complications of real-world ethics, it would be the wizard. But it wasn't worth the time or effort.

Besides, said a small voice inside her, *Brandish understands.*

"Okay. I did find a new wizard friend who can help give me advice," she said. "So, hypothetically, I'd be okay if I was going to do anything silly."

He jerked upright, excitement suffusing his features.

"Stellar!" he asked. "What are they called?"

"Brandish the Distractor."

His excitement vanished beneath a wave of obvious confusion.

"Never heard of them," he said. "I'm concerned. I wouldn't want you to get bad advice."

"Huh. That's odd. Although... he's young like me. You've been stuck in your crystal ever since the last princess showed up, right? I think he arrived here after that."

"Oh. Well, I suppose that makes sense." But he kept on frowning. "I just would have liked you to—"

He froze in place, an exasperated expression moving across his face. His throat worked as if trying to force out the words, but no sound escaped his lips. Up until this moment, Leigh hadn't realized that the curse might be physically painful, but every muscle in his body appeared to have seized up as he struggled to speak. Watching it alone was agonizing; she couldn't imagine what it must be like to have to live with it.

"It's okay," she said, gently patting his hand. "I'll figure it out."

Prince padded over, settling his fluffy body next to the wizard as he relaxed in slow stages. Leigh couldn't have felt worse. He'd endured that pain because he wanted to help her. Until now, she hadn't realized how bad it truly was.

Shining Glory sagged against the couch cushions, patting Prince on the back. His breath was ragged.

"I'm sorry... Princess," he gasped. "Just a... moment."

"Take all the time you need."

She retreated to the antechamber, tucking into a corner, and called to her Pixietails. They zipped out, their expressions grave. Even though they'd been in her hair, they knew what was happening. Good. That would save time.

"Can you remove Shining Glory's curse?" she asked.

Pixie Shine sighed, and Leigh's heart sank.

"We don't work with curses," said Pixie Sparkle. "They go against everything we stand for. If we're magic, they're... not magic, if that makes sense."

Leigh pressed her lips together in disappointment, but it wasn't surprising. Things were never that easy. Besides, curses seemed like a job for wizards. Brandish didn't seem to know much about them, but he was a hedge wizard, and that distinction seemed to matter. She'd have to find one that specialized in curses.

Prince padded out into the antechamber and stared at her as if in summons. She ordered her Pixietails back into her hair and returned to the crystal room. To her immense relief, Shining Glory appeared to have fully recovered. His color was good and his voice lively as he apologized for the dramatic display more times than necessary.

"I should be apologizing to you," she insisted, settling back down opposite him and leaning back into the comfy cushions. "Please, don't worry about it."

"Well, I hope I can be of service in some other way. It's dreadfully frustrating to be locked up like that."

"I do have some other questions, if you feel up to them."

"Gladly!" he exclaimed. "What knowledge I possess is yours."

She paused to think through her question before she asked it, hoping to avoid triggering the curse again. Unfortunately, she didn't know exactly how it worked, and he certainly wouldn't be able to tell her. The last time they'd spoken, he'd gotten around the curse by using subtext, so maybe she ought to try that.

"Do you miss your friends?" she asked, picking each word with deliberate care. "Being stuck in here, I imagine there are a lot of people you used to see in your travels. Friends. *Coworkers.* You know...?"

"Coworkers? What are—oh, of course!" She could practically see the light bulb go on over his head. "Let's see, now... the last time I set off on the road, I visited my friend Plummerly from the Color Kingdom."

"The Color Kingdom? You mean to tell me that everything in this world isn't hair-themed?"

"Obviously. Our kingdom is called Lovely Locks because of the trees. And the Pixietails, of course. But other places don't have those things."

"Huh. I hadn't even considered the possibility," she admitted.

"I'll have to see if I can hunt up a geography book for you, if you have the time or interest. Plummerly is a bit neurotic, but he's a wiz with—er… he's a smart fellow." He cleared his throat, choosing his words with a bit more care. He must have ventured close to one of those forbidden topics. "The Color Kingdom borders Lovely Locks to the south. Then I swung up to see Sadamel from Emotion Valley."

"Sad-a-mel? Let me guess; he's depressing."

"You'd be depressed, too, if the Judgmental Knights had taken over your homeland. I'm not sure how that sorry situation has developed; Sadamel hasn't responded to my most recent letter. But last I heard, things in Emotion Valley weren't good. I'd avoid it myself." He sighed. "But the Color Kingdom would be a great place to visit. See some sights. Get some advice."

"How long does it take to get there?" asked Leigh.

"Oh, about three days or so. Of course, I'm old and creaky. You'd probably make better time."

Even if she shaved it down by a third, there was no way. She didn't spend a lot of quality time with her dad, but he'd notice if she was gone for multiple days in a row.

"Thanks for the suggestion, but the trip's a bit too long. I suppose I could send my Pixietails there while I remain in my world and then travel straight to them, but—"

"I'm afraid not. Outside the borders of Lovely Locks, their magic is limited. You won't be able to travel back and forth between your world and ours outside our borders. And the neighboring kingdoms are no place for unattended Pixietails. They're rather vulnerable without you. Not to mention the threat of the duchess and her snagfires on our lands. The Pixietails have good reason to remain near the castle, I'm afraid."

"Darn it. Well, I hope you hear from your friend soon. If you do, let him know he is welcome in Lovely Locks anytime. I'm sure we could make space in the castle if you don't have enough room for him here."

She was sure of no such thing; in all her wandering, she still hadn't managed to explore the castle. Fancy bedrooms and expensive furnishings didn't particularly interest her. But she was the princess, after all, and if anybody had a problem with her offering shelter to someone in need, they could tell her to her face.

"Thanks, Lady Leigh. That is a kind offer; I'll pass it along when the opportunity presents itself."

Although she felt good about offering to help Shining Glory's friend, this new information left her a bit in the lurch when it came to planning that heist. They needed bodies, and she didn't relish the idea of drafting the villagers. The smith seemed to have his head on straight, but if she took him along, that would leave the village without his much-needed leadership. Ravenwaves had plenty of snagfires; she could be poised to attack the minute Leigh left the area. She couldn't risk it. Perhaps she could recruit Prince, but how much help could he be? He didn't even have opposable thumbs.

She sighed, her shoulders slumping. Hopefully Brandish had some fancy magic up his sleeve, because the odds were definitely not in their favor. She was trying to resign herself to this fact when a bolt of inspiration struck her, jerking her upright.

"Wait a minute," she said. "Where are the maidens?"

In the storybook, the princess had two best friends with two ridiculous names. Leigh fumbled around in the depths of her memory before coming up with them—Fairhair and Curlycrown. They were the stereotypical damsels in distress, but they had Pixietails. If Leigh could get the maidens to use their magic for more than party decorations and fancy hairstyles, they might just get into Tangleland unscathed.

"Maiden Fairhair and Maiden Curlycrown? In the castle, I hope. We have plans later. They're supposed to give me a hair mask," said Shining Glory. "But plans with the maidens must always be flexible by default. The poor things have such awful luck when it comes to kidnapping."

Leigh snorted.

"Enjoy the hair mask," she said, standing.

"You know," he mused, "I do feel sorry for those girls. They've been captured so many times by Ravenwaves that I believe they must know that tower as well as she does."

Leigh's heart leaped. She was getting good at this whole subtext thing, and it didn't take much effort to understand what Shining Glory was trying to tell her. The maidens could get her into Tangleland. Heck, they might even know where the painting was. All she had to do was talk them into helping.

She saw herself out, trying to be hopeful. But as she walked toward the castle entrance, one thing nagged at her. Shining Glory's words echoed in her ears. The idea that there were places in this world where she could be stuck with no way to return home disquieted her. Although she was beginning to enjoy her time here, she couldn't imagine never returning to her real life. To Ari, to cosplay, even to her dad and their crappy little apartment. Sure, her favorite hobby required her to pretend to live in various fantasy worlds, but that didn't mean she wanted to leave the real one behind.

Did it?

CHAPTER 15

WHEN SHE ARRIVED AT THE CASTLE STEPS, SHE found Brandish standing at the bottom, staring up at the doors as if trying to psych himself up to enter. She stopped in her tracks, trying to figure out why she'd gone so annoyingly gaga over him. Yes, he had delicate-anime-hero good looks, but she'd seen cute boys before, and they usually left her cold. Sure, his tousled hair glinted in the fading sunlight. He had a certain thin-hipped swagger that she particularly enjoyed. But she was usually able to shrug those things off. Why couldn't she do that this time? If she could figure it out, she could put an end to it before she made a total fool of herself.

He spotted her and grinned, his mouth twisting in that annoyingly charming way. For all she knew, he was doing it on purpose, the jerk.

"If I didn't know better, I'd think you were stalking me," she teased, trying to pretend that her cheeks weren't flaming. Again.

"Not sure yet. Would you like me to?" he replied, his grin widening.

"Don't tease." She flapped her hands at him and swiftly changed the subject. "I've got an idea. Not a plan, but maybe a kernel of a plan."

"I love a good kernel. What's the play?"

"Shining Glory is a wash; he can't leave the castle grounds. That curse is the absolute worst. You don't know anything about curses, do you?"

"Not my thing, I'm afraid. But I'm here if you need a pretty young maiden swept off her feet. Like, say... you?"

She had to admit that the idea had a certain appeal, but she wasn't about to admit that out loud. Based on his arch expression, she was pretty sure he was teasing. So instead, she said, "Funny you should mention that. I think we should recruit the maidens. Perhaps you already know them since you're such a ladies' man."

"I don't think I've had the pleasure," he said.

"You'll love them," she said. "They're experts at picking flowers, braiding hair, and getting kidnapped."

"I'm not sure those are the skills we're looking for," he said, wincing. "And they definitely don't sound like my type. I like my women capable."

"They've been kidnapped a lot. In this case, it's an advantage. As in, they've seen the inside of Ravenwaves Tower. The only person who knows the place better is the duchess herself, according to Shining Glory."

"Oh..." He brightened as he considered this. "So they might know of some secret entrances or hiding places. Smart, Princess. Very smart."

The compliment warmed her. Most guys tended to get stuck on physical details; they complimented how she looked in her cosplays instead of the work she'd put in to create them. She couldn't think of the last time a guy had complimented her brain.

"Uh... thanks," she said, fumbling awkwardly for words. "So I'm headed inside to look for them. You want to come?"

"Let's see. Would I like to be the lone male in a group of eligible young women? Let me think..." He put his hand to his chin and pretended to ponder. "It's such a difficult conundrum."

"Come on, Romeo," she said, tromping up the stairs.

He hurried to catch up, and they climbed the lengthy approach to the castle doors together. About halfway up, he frowned thoughtfully, his steps slowing.

"I've been meaning to ask: Why aren't there guards here? Is there a hiring shortage? With all the snagfire attacks, guards would be a wise choice," he observed.

She snorted. "I've been thinking the same thing. Maybe I should start a training program."

"I'd volunteer to head it up, but I'm not sure that would help. Hedge wizards don't exactly inspire the same instant confidence as the pointy-hat types."

"Why not?"

"Well, because we get involved in things like heists, I imagine. But just because I *can* use my illusion magic to steal from random innocent people doesn't mean that I will, any more than you'd walk up to some random villager and wallop them with your staff. Some things you just don't do."

"I get it. People can be judgy. Especially here. This is a very black-and-white sort of place."

"What do you mean by that?" he asked.

"If you ask anyone, they'll tell you that Ravenwaves is a villain. She'll always be a villain, and villains live in Tangleland," said Leigh, picking her words carefully. "It's like you said; the people here don't understand shades of gray. In their mind, being a princess makes anything I do automatically good. Being a villain makes Ravenwaves always wrong. And being a hedge wizard makes you . . . suspect, I suppose. I don't know if people are like that where you're from? I know you're from a different village."

Brandish stopped entirely, just short of the door. She couldn't read him. Was he upset? Thoughtful? Had she offended him?

"Yeah, the people where I'm from are like that too," he said softly.

She took one glance at him and was shocked to see the pain clearly written on his face. Whatever had made him uproot his entire life and settle here hadn't been good. She had no intention of prying, but her heart went out to him nonetheless. Without thinking, she reached out and squeezed his hand. It wasn't a flirtatious gesture; she didn't blush at all this time. But he was hurting, and she empathized with that.

Surprised, he looked at her, folding his fingers over hers.

"Thanks," he said.

They stood there in silence for a moment as the colors shifted across the sky with the setting sun. Leigh was surprised at how comfortable she felt—she was completely content in this moment with him.

Slowly, reluctantly, he released her hand and took a deep breath, rubbing at his eyes. Had he gotten teary? She didn't want to embarrass him by asking. Instead, she looked out at the sky while he composed himself.

"I think we should head in," he declared with a fraction of his usual jaunty confidence. "If you're ready?"

"I'm game," she said. "Maybe you can charm them into helping us. I can't do all the hard work around here."

She softened the barb with a grin, and in response, he broke out into a relieved one himself. Now they were back on familiar ground, the awkward emotional moment ebbing away.

"I'm wounded!" he exclaimed, putting a hand to his chest. "You don't appreciate all the value I bring to this operation. I'm good with illusions, and I'm pretty to look at. Just ask me." He preened.

"Maybe you should be the pretty, pretty princess, and I'll be the hedge wizard."

His expression of mock outrage sent her over the edge. She laughed so hard that she nearly fell all the way back down the stairs and had to beg him to stop.

Leigh was gasping for breath by the time she and Brandish made it to the top of all those stairs. Perhaps she'd been wrong to think of this castle as vulnerable. Any attacking army would have to hike up all that—in armor no less. She paused at the top, trying not to puff too loud, but Brandish didn't notice anyway. He stood at the foot of the castle, staring straight up with his mouth open as the moonlight glinted off the white stone.

"Gorgeous," he breathed. "I've always wanted to know what it looks like inside."

She considered knocking but decided against it. After all, if she was the princess, this was her castle, wasn't it? Besides, she didn't want the official tour full of factoids about this architect and that designer, none of whom she'd know anyway. She wanted a chance to see the place on her own terms and compare it with her childhood dreams.

If anything, it was more opulent than she'd imagined. The enormous front doors opened into a foyer dominated by a giant chandelier and two enormous staircases with swans carved into the bannisters. To one side was a pretty sitting room full of delicate furniture, the frames of the chairs so elaborate that they looked painful to sit in. To the right, a pastel library with shelves crammed with books and a comfy reading nook full of pillows. Brandish stared inside with hearts in his eyes for a long moment before tearing himself away.

They continued on through room after room full of pastel furnishings against spotless white walls. A conservatory full of instruments both familiar and not, a huge and imposing formal dining hall, an enormous kitchen of such pristine cleanliness that it might not have ever been used. They didn't see anyone in their rambles. Brandish pointed out a bell in the kitchen, but she decided not to ring it. It was late, after all, and she was having fun exploring.

They climbed yet another staircase. This time, even Brandish was faltering by the top, putting the back of his hand to his forehead and declaring in strident tones that he was never climbing another stair so long as he lived. Leigh plopped down on the top step and tried not to gasp. After they caught their breath, they continued down a long hallway that seemed promising. The doors on either side were closed, but at the very end, a pair of double doors had been thrown wide to reveal an elaborate bedroom suite.

It looked like the designer had gone to Pottery Barn Kids for inspiration, took a look at one of the princess-themed rooms, and immediately ordered two of everything. Leigh had loved those catalogs when she was a kid and spent hours planning dream rooms that they couldn't have afforded in a million years. Little Leigh would have taken one look at the bed, with its lace trimmed pillows, floral sheets, and gauzy curtains, and fallen in deep, deep love. Teenage Leigh thought it was all a bit too much, although one thing caught her eye—a mannequin head covered in snowy white fabric atop which rested a delicate silver crown full of glittering pastel diamonds in pink, purple, and blue.

This must be her room. For a moment, she wondered what it would be like to fall asleep in that frilly, fluffy bed, cradled in a nest of pillows. She'd get a good night's rest without being woken up by screaming drunks at the bar across the street. If she was hungry in the morning, someone would bring her food from that enormous kitchen. She'd never have to worry about coming home only to find that her dinner choices consisted of macky cheese or nothing. It sure was tempting. She trailed her fingers over the crown, too nervous to actually touch it.

"Is this yours?" asked Brandish, a little awed.

"Uh...yeah. I think so." Her cheeks began to redden again. Although she wasn't a prude, she also wasn't in the habit of inviting guys she barely knew into her bedroom alone at night. Even if this room wasn't really hers in the ways that counted, it still felt incredibly intimate. She cleared her throat, trying to look anywhere but at him. "We should go. Find those maidens. They're probably somewhere close by."

"Right. Sure."

His voice was all too bright as he rushed toward the door. Maybe because the tension between them pushed him bodily out of the room? Regardless, she was puffing for breath again as she exited into the hallway and closed the doors behind her, and so was he. Although maybe that was because he'd just sprinted out like his life depended on it; she honestly couldn't tell.

With determined casualness, she strode down the hallway.

"The maidens are probably in one of these rooms. After all, they're supposed to be my ladies-in-waiting. I imagine they sleep close by in case I need them to do some waiting in the middle of the night."

"What do ladies-in-waiting do exactly?" asked Brandish.

"Honestly? No clue."

She rapped on the first door to the left and was relieved to hear the sound of light footsteps on the other side. The knob turned; the door opened. But instead of a maiden in a frilly dress with some magical bunnies living in her hair, she saw a plump middle-aged woman with rosy cheeks and an apron, her graying hair swept up into a frilled bonnet.

"Princess!" she gasped, dropping into a curtsy. "I didn't know you were here!"

After a moment's shock, Leigh recovered.

"I'm sorry; I didn't mean to startle you. Honestly, it's a relief to find anyone living in here. I was starting to think the place was deserted," she said.

"Oh, well, there isn't much for us to do when no one is at home. I come in every day to dust and straighten up. I would have been here earlier, but it was market day, and I lost track of time," said the maid.

Leigh and Brandish exchanged a worried look.

"No one's here? We were looking for the maidens. Curlycrown and..."

"Fairhair?" asked the maid. They nodded. "I'm afraid you're out of luck. They've been kidnapped again, the poor things. They barely ever sleep at home these days. It's always one dungeon or another for them, although in their spare time, they do some lovely needlework. I think it's a comfort for them."

Leigh hissed in frustration, shutting her eyes to avoid swearing in frustration at this poor, innocent woman.

"Princess, are you well?" asked the maid, concerned. "Do you need to sit down?"

"It's been a long day," soothed Brandish. "Lots of stairs. Do you know where they are? Who has them?"

"Please tell me it's not Ravenwaves," added Leigh without opening her eyes.

"I'm not entirely sure," said the maid in uncertain tones. "They went out to pick moonflowers yesterday and never came back."

"Show us where," ordered Leigh, determined.

CHAPTER 16

THE HOUSEKEEPER LED THEM TO A SMALL CLEARing in the forest that looked like every other small clearing Leigh had been in over the past few weeks—pretty, pastoral, and ponytailed. The ground was undisturbed, with no signs of a struggle that Leigh could make out. Then again, she wasn't exactly a hunter. She wasn't sure she could identify signs of a struggle without a handy diagram.

Brandish shrugged when she looked at him, so she turned to the maid, who stood at the edge of the clearing, wringing her hands.

"You said they were picking moonflowers," said Leigh. "I don't see any flowers here."

"Oh, well, moonflowers grow in the caves," said the maid. "That way." She pointed, her hand visibly shaking. "But please don't make me go in there. I don't want to die!"

"Die? Who said anything about dying?" asked Brandish.

But Leigh waved him off. She had bigger questions.

"Let me get this straight," she said. "The maidens went into some sort of death cave on purpose? We are talking about the same people, right? Their hobbies are needlework, hairstyles, and getting kidnapped?"

"And musical instruments," added the maid.

"And they went in?" Leigh asked incredulously.

The maid nodded, the tremors spreading to her entire body. Leigh could hear her knees clicking together. Leigh and Brandish exchanged glances, and he shrugged again.

"I take it you've never heard of this so-called death cave," muttered Leigh.

"No clue," he murmured back. "But I say we check it out. Whatever we find in there, we can take it."

Her eyes met his, and the complete confidence in his gaze warmed her. She found herself overcome by the urge to rise up on her tiptoes and kiss him, just to get it over with. If she did that, maybe she could get it out of her system. But then he winked at her, and the moment passed. She snorted instead.

"Can you point us to the cave entrance?" Leigh gently asked, turning to the woman. "Then you can go back to the castle where it's safe."

Overcome with relief, the maid gave them some hurried directions before running off as fast as her legs could carry her, which wasn't very fast at all.

"Shall we, milady?" asked Brandish, offering his elbow with a flourish.

Leigh bonked him with her staff, snickering, and the two of them set off to find the cave. Luckily, for all her nerves, the maid had given them excellent directions, and they had no problems finding it. Then again, it was an enormous yawning mouth of a black cavern, with rocks jutting over the entrance like jagged teeth. It would have been hard to miss even without the directions.

"Gorgeous," she said. "I bet this place is a real tourist trap."

He snorted, cracking his knuckles.

"Let's do this," he said.

Leigh crept toward the entrance to the cave with Brandish at her heels, trying not to trip over the sticks that littered the ground. They rolled under her feet as she slipped beneath the rock teeth and into the dim recesses of the cavern. The inside was bigger than she'd expected, with a single path leading down into the depths of the earth. Crystalline formations on the roof of the cave let out a soft, insufficient glow.

"Well, this looks lovely," she said.

The cavern rumbled ominously, and she tensed, waiting for it to stop so she could wipe her forehead with the back of her hand and say something pithy like, "Well, that was close." But it didn't. If anything, it shook harder. Debris began to rain down on their heads, pinging off the ground.

"Get back!" shouted Brandish, grabbing her around the waist and flinging them both off to the side.

They got out of the way just in the nick of time. The mouth to the cavern collapsed, rocks clattering and groaning as the earth closed over them, cutting off the sky. They lay breathless on the ground, his arms around her waist. Leigh's eyes began to adjust as the dust continued to settle. At least she could see. The dim, reddish glow of the walls wouldn't be enough to read by, but she could make out basic shapes. Brandish's face swam out of the haze, his eyes wide with shock. They exchanged a stricken look, and Leigh's blood ran cold as she contemplated what could have been.

"Thanks," she croaked.

"Yeah," he whispered back.

She wanted to stay there just for a moment, safe in the circle of his arms. But another wave of dust and debris rained down on them, and the groaning noises coming from the newly constructed ceiling didn't exactly inspire confidence. They scrambled up, darting for the entrance to the tunnel, where the structure was a bit sturdier. There they paused, coughing, to shake as much of the dust from their clothing as they could. Leigh sighed as she fingered a rip in her skirts, but there was nothing she could do about that now.

The shaking stilled, and silence settled over the cavern once again.

"You think—" she began.

As soon as she spoke, the cavern began to quake anew, cutting off her words, but as soon as she clamped her mouth shut, it grew still again. She'd gotten the picture. No noise. They'd accidentally triggered the cave's burglar alarm, but now they'd be quiet.

Brandish put his finger to his lips, coming to the same conclusion she had. She nodded, and when he offered his hand, she took it. After all, it would be safer that way. Less likelihood of getting split up since they couldn't talk.

They made their tentative way down the path. About halfway down, Leigh slipped on a stick and picked it up to hurl it away in disgust. But as she lifted it into the dim pink light, she realized that it wasn't a stick at all. It was bone. Probably a tibia, if her memories of Bony Tony served her right. Squealing, she flung it away with a clatter.

Something massive shifted in the darkness down below.

Brandish's wide-eyed look mirrored her own. They tiptoed into the depths, Leigh's heart hammering in her ears. Would they be trapped in here forever with some enormous, ravenous whatsit? She didn't intend to join the skeleton party; there had to be another exit. She was going to find it and the maidens, and then she was going to get the heck out of here. Those death cave jokes no longer amused her.

Down and down and down. The path went on for what felt like forever but was probably only a few minutes. The glowing crystals grew sparser here, but at least she didn't hear any more movement. Maybe whatever they'd accidentally awoken had gone back to sleep.

The path curved, leading into deep darkness. Brandish stopped to look at her, but there was no question of what to do. The only way out was through. They edged into the unknown together, squeezing each other's hands tight. She couldn't see a thing, not even her own fingers when she wiggled them in front of her face. Water trickled somewhere in the distance. The wall next to Leigh dropped away, leaving her to paw at nothing. Something in the air changed, and Leigh had the sensation that they'd entered an enormous cavern, although she couldn't risk speaking aloud to ask Brandish if he felt the same. She squeezed his hand instead, and he squeezed back. It would have to be enough.

They inched forward, bones clattering beneath their feet.

From somewhere in the darkness, a young woman said, "I-is someone there?"

Moron. Leigh's relief at finding at least one of the maidens—or so she presumed—was tempered by her desire to throttle the girl. Did she want to bring the cavern down, or was she just that dumb?

The ceiling rumbled high above in warning. Luckily, the maiden didn't speak again. Leigh didn't dare make a sound, but she tugged on Brandish's hand, pulling him in the direction of the maiden's voice. They had to get out of here.

The tumult above subsided, but she still heard a low rumble from somewhere off to the right. But the voice had come from farther down; she was sure of it. She couldn't risk a single delay. If this ceiling came down too, they'd be trapped in here forever. They'd passed no other exits. Her mouth went dry as she contemplated the very real possibility that they could die here.

She took another cautious step and accidentally kicked another bone. She really got it good too; it made an impressive amount of noise before it finally rolled to a stop.

The gentle rumble off to the right cut off like someone had flicked a switch, and a burst of hot steam wafted over her, swirling her skirts. A sharp smell entered her nose that reminded her of the burnt tang of the air in her apartment every time the furnace clicked on. Something huge chuffed in the darkness, and with dawning horror, she realized that some enormous creature was breathing on her.

Before she could come to terms with this knowledge, a giant glowing eye opened in the darkness, its iris about the size of a compact car. The creature blinked once, muzzily, its gaze sweeping the room. Brandish's hand went clammy in hers, sweat slicking their palms.

The eye swung out of sight, and bones clattered as the unseen beast shifted its bulk on the floor. Its body stretched far into the darkness, and Leigh's stomach sank even further. But as tempting as it was to call on her Pixietails and blow this joint, she wouldn't leave Brandish to face this gigantic whatsit alone. He was here only because of her. She couldn't abandon him.

Another huff of hot steam. A third. Then *whoosh*! The air high above them filled with bright flames that threw the cavern into stark relief and made red motes dance before Leigh's eyes. But she could see enough—the cavern, the cage at the far end, the two young women standing at the bars—oh, and the dragon.

Its red-black bulk filled the entire right-hand side of the cavern, scales gleaming in the firelight. Leigh gulped, her blood running cold. She'd thought the *T. Rex* skeleton at the Academy of Natural Sciences was huge, but this thing could have eaten that and still had room in its belly for a second course. Its head was about the size of her entire apartment. Her stomach fluttered as it huffed again, its annoyance clear. Apparently, it didn't like having its beauty rest disturbed.

Brandish released her hand. As the last embers of the dragon's breath faded, they outlined him as he held his hands up in a familiar pose, his lips moving silently as he cast one of his illusions. A flicker of light appeared on the far end of the cavern as Fake Brandish ignited a torch. Next to him, Fake Leigh swung her staff, baring her teeth with a ferocity that Real Leigh found rather flattering. Was that how he saw her? She could get behind that.

The dragon let out an angry chuff that was quickly silenced by a threatening rumble from the ceiling. It swung its heavy body around, crashing against the wall so hard that the whole thing might come down anyway. With every step, it let out a little gout of flame, illuminating the space in a series of strobe-like flashes.

There was no time to waste. Leigh grabbed Real Brandish's hand and tugged him toward the cage where the two maidens cowered. They scrambled over bones and falling debris as the dragon roared out a gout of furious fire, engulfing the two fakes in flames. But when the fire ebbed, the illusions remained. In perfect tandem, they stuck their tongues out at the already-furious beast.

Leigh and Brandish reached the cage just as another gout of flame illuminated the cavern. *Flash.* She leaned close, his hair tickling her face.

"Pick it?" she breathed.

She felt him nod, and he released her again, metal clanking quietly as he maneuvered the lock. Leigh's heart skipped a beat, but the dragon didn't notice. It was too busy trying to barbecue the nonexistent adventurers.

Either Brandish was a master thief in disguise or the lock was utter crap. It slid open within seconds. *Flash.* With deft fingers, he lifted the lock silently from the cage. *Flash.* The maidens—one brunette, one redheaded—rushed the door, jostling each other in their obvious desperation to escape.

Clang!

The cage door flew open and banged against the bars as both maidens tried to cram through the opening at once. The ceiling rumbled, rocks plummeting down as the very walls reacted to the sound. The dragon spun, opened its mouth, and shrieked in fury.

The response from the cavern was immediate. The ceiling began to crumble to pieces in slow stages, the entire room quaking as if the ground might split and swallow them whole. The redhead went down to one knee, crying out in pain, and Brandish lifted her by the elbow.

"How do we get out?" demanded Leigh, since the place was falling to pieces anyway.

The brunette pointed wordlessly toward the back of the room, behind the dragon. As the creature lumbered toward them, she could see the faint light of an open doorway set into the wall. Too bad they couldn't get to it without going through an angry beast the size of a football stadium.

What should she do? She wasn't sure the Pixietails were strong enough to restrain this thing, and she couldn't risk it. She'd have to take the beast out herself, and she knew exactly how. The dragon had only one eye; the other socket was puckered and scarred. That was its weakness. That was where she would strike. She just had to get there before it fried her like a chicken wing.

"Go, go, go!" she shouted, sprinting toward the monster.

She didn't stop to see if Brandish listened. Instead, she dashed through the disintegrating cavern, dodging falling stone and debris, and slammed her staff against the ground. The saber-spear hummed to life, illuminating the space around her. Her heart choked her throat as she closed in on the furious dragon. Was she really doing this? What was she, nuts?!

But there was no other choice, and to her surprise, a wave of elation drowned out the fear. As she leaped into the air like an avenging anime warrior, she couldn't keep from whooping aloud. Maybe she would die here, but at least she'd go out feeling like a total badass.

The hit struck true. She landed on the dragon's nose, sinking her blade into its eye. It shrieked in pain, tossing its head and flinging her toward the wall.

"Pixietails, save me!" she shouted.

Bright pastel sparkles immediately enveloped her in a way that suggested that her magical friends had been waiting for the call without a whole lot of patience. She twisted in midair, narrowly missing a plummeting boulder the size of a sofa.

“Whew!” she said. “Pixietails, get us out of here.”

She heard the startled exclamations of the maidens as the Pixietails complied, and Brandish let out a whoop, too, his delight evident. As they soared out of the trembling cavern and into the fresh night air, Leigh realized she couldn’t stop grinning.

They’d done it. For the first time, she felt like maybe she actually deserved to be here after all.

CHAPTER 17

THE PIXIETAILS DEPOSITED LEIGH, BRANDISH, AND the maidens on a neighboring hilltop just in time to watch the cavern collapse. The ground shuddered and churned, crumbling to pieces, as the dragon launched itself into the air, roaring in fury. It circled once, twice, and then flew away without seeing them. As it disappeared into the dark sky, Leigh's death grip on her staff began to ease. They really had done it. They'd freed the maidens and fought an actual dragon. When Ari heard about this, he was going to flip.

She grinned at Brandish, who seemed to share her elation. His eyes danced as he gazed down at her. The fond expression he wore made her stomach do slow flips, forcing her to tear herself away.

The maidens clung to each other, their eyes wide with shell shock after their ordeal. They looked to be about her age, tall and willowy. The one on the left had long brown hair and wore a powder-blue medieval kirtle over an obnoxiously poofy blouse. The other girl had curly red hair down to her knees, with an identical outfit in shades of yellow. The redhead clutched at her friend with the panicky strength of a drowning person with a life preserver. With deliberate care, the brunette peeled her friend's fingers from her arm one by one.

Once she was free, the brunette maiden—Fairhair, if memory served correctly—dropped into a deep curtsy.

"Thank you for saving us, Princess. Thank you, brave adventurer," she said, her voice surprisingly throaty.

"Happy to help," said Leigh. "You two okay? Are either of you hurt?"

"I am unscathed," said Fairhair. "Maiden Curlycrown?"

They all turned their attention to the redhead, whose hands fluttered nervously from her hair to her dress to her face as she looked at Leigh.

"You look so different," she murmured. "And you..."

Her eyes snagged on Brandish, widening. Then, with a graceful sigh, Curlycrown fainted at his feet.

"Oh no," said Fairhair. "Not again."

Brandish dropped to his knees, worry pinching his handsome features. Leigh's breath caught, too, as she considered the relativc lack of medical care here. At home, she could call 911, and her dad's coworkers would come. But here, there was only her. Then she took in Curlycrown's flickering eyelids and the exasperated expression on Fairhair's face, and the clenched worry in the pit of her stomach slowly eased.

Curlycrown must be faking it to get the attention of the cute hedge mage.

The cute hedge mage in question was fanning Curlycrown with one hand while the other hovered over her bodice, too nervous to actually touch anything. He looked up at Leigh with obvious panic in his eyes, and although she found the whole thing incredibly funny, she decided to take pity on him.

"Check to see if she's breathing," she suggested, the corner of her mouth twitching.

He leaned down to do so, and Curlycrown's eyes flew open. She seemed way too shocked to find a cute guy right there, but that didn't stop her from fluttering her lashes at him fast enough to cause a noticeable breeze. Not that Leigh was jealous. After all, she and Brandish were just partners. Or friends. Definitely not anything more.

"Thank you for rescuing me, brave knight," said Curlycrown, laying it on thick.

"I... uh..."

Brandish's eyes flicked up to Leigh and back down again, his expression vacillating between outright concern and intense skepticism. He seemed to have noticed that Curlycrown had woken up at an awfully convenient moment. Then her hand fluttered up to cup his cheek oh so delicately. He froze like a deer in headlights.

That was enough. Leigh cleared her throat, and Curlycrown jerked upright. Leigh was trying to keep a poker face, but something in her expression still made the maiden leap to her feet, miraculously recovered.

"Thank you, sir, for aiding me in my distress," she said, curtsying. "I'm sorry. I didn't catch your name."

"Uh... Brandish the Distractor. I'm a hedge wizard."

"Thank you, Sir Brandish. I am in your debt," Curlycrown cooed.

"Right."

Brandish stood up and very deliberately put Leigh between himself and Curlycrown. Was this the same guy who had been flirting nonstop with her ever since they'd met? She would have expected him to eat up Curlycrown's obvious interest. But that would mean that his behavior to Leigh hadn't just been empty flirting.

That would mean he was truly interested. In her.

She couldn't believe it, and even if she did, she wasn't sure what to do about it. They didn't even live in the same world all the time. Even if she could deal with the stressors of a long-distance relationship, he wouldn't get any of her jokes. Meet her friends. Watch her favorite anime. Nothing.

"Princess?" asked Fairhair. "Are you okay?"

"You look ill," exclaimed Curlycrown. "Perhaps the brave hedge wizard could whisk us away to safety lest you faint away at his feet."

"I'm not going to faint. I just fought a dragon, remember? I'm tougher than that," said Leigh.

"Damn straight you are," added Brandish.

"That was so brave!" Fairhair said, her eyes sparkling. "However did you learn? I wish I could do such things."

"Funny you should say that," Leigh replied. "I've got a request for you both."

Curlycrown brightened.

"Of course! What do you need? Will you let me braid your hair? It's been so long since I got to do that," she said, pouting prettily.

"I'm afraid the braids will have to wait," said Leigh, elbowing Brandish as he snickered. "I've got other things on my mind. But let's go back to the castle first, in case that dragon comes back."

Instead of answering, Curlycrown shrieked, lifting her skirts off the ground and daintily running in the wrong direction, as if the dragon might swoop by at any minute and deposit her back into the cage.

"Uh... this way?" said Leigh.

Back at the castle, the maidens excused themselves for just a moment to freshen up, and Leigh and Brandish settled down in one of the ornate sitting rooms to wait. The maid brought a pot of tea and some delicate, doughnutlike pastries decorated with the Lady Lovely Locks cameo from the cover of Leigh's storybook.

Without a clock, she had no idea how long it had been since she'd eaten, but her stomach snarled audibly at the sight of food. She helped herself and took a single bite. Sugary sweetness filled her mouth, cut by the sharp tang of some fruit she'd never tasted before. It was like a berry but citrus-tart, and it smelled like flowers. The coating on the top crackled as she took another bite, shoving half the thing into her mouth before she remembered that she had company and said company thought she was a princess. She stared at him, eyes wide, and tried to decide if she could force out an apology without spraying him with bits of chewed-up food.

He threw back his head and laughed.

"Keep that up, and I'll throw one of these delicious pastries at you," she said, swallowing.

"Promise?" he shot back. "Nice work in the cave. That could have gotten nasty."

"No kidding. You too."

They beamed at each other.

"Leigh, I—"

The sitting room door flung open, interrupting whatever Brandish had been about to say. His delicate mouth twisted in annoyance, but he quickly brightened when the maidens returned. They wore fluffy robes over nightgowns of such overwhelming frilliness that they threatened to swallow them whole. Those things must have been heavy. Leigh wasn't even sure the maidens would be able to sit down without being enveloped entirely in tulle.

Fairhair flounced over, fabric rustling, eyed the delicate wrought-iron chair, and stood next to it.

"Are you sure you don't want your hair braided?" she asked. "I find it very soothing after a traumatic experience."

"I'm good, thanks," replied Leigh. "Would you like some tea or refreshments?"

"Ladybuns! My favorite!" exclaimed Curlycrown.

The two maidens helped themselves, and for a moment, they snacked quietly. As she ate, Curlycrown kept edging closer and closer to Brandish, who was determinedly pretending not to notice. If she kept this up, she'd end up in his lap. Leigh decided to take pity on him and say something before things got truly awkward.

"I'm glad you're both okay," she said to the maidens. "We need your help."

"But not with hairstyles," said Curlycrown, pouting prettily.

"No, we're stealing a painting."

The moment the words escaped Leigh's mouth, she regretted them. Why hadn't she phrased it more gently? She could have said "liberating a painting" or even "temporarily borrowing" it. She braced herself for their inevitable dismay.

"A heist?" asked Fairhair, brightening. "I've never been invited to participate in a heist before. How fun."

"What do you think is the proper attire for a heist? The yellow dress with the ribbons or the one with the lace?" asked Curlycrown.

"Ribbons. Definitely the ribbons."

Leigh looked from one to the other as they chattered away in excitement. She couldn't believe what she was hearing. Brandish's mouth hung open, and he kept blinking in shock. Maybe this would go better than she'd thought.

"Great!" she said. "You don't know how much this means to me. The duchess hid the painting somewhere, and I figure since you've been imprisoned in her tower so many times, you know the place better than anyone in the village—"

The maidens froze, their excitement giving way to obvious alarm.

"What did I say?" asked Leigh. "What's wrong?"

"I'm so sorry, Lady Leigh, but I think you've got us all wrong." Fairhair wrung her hands, refusing to meet Leigh's gaze. "We're gentle maidens. Tangleland is treacherous. I don't see how we could help."

"I don't want to die!" wailed Curlycrown, working herself up into a tizzy. "I'm too young!"

"We'll train you. There's no need to panic," said Leigh desperately.

"The snagfires will eat me!" continued Curlycrown.

She burst into tears. Fairhair hugged her, turning pleading eyes to Leigh. So much for an easy solution. If she didn't calm them down pronto, she'd be back to square one again. She'd have to approach random villagers at the market. Maybe she could set up a stall and recruit them there, like the military but with better hair.

No, she needed the maidens. She leaned forward, reached past the mountain of fabric, and patted Curlycrown on her shoulder. But the girl kept on sobbing.

"I know it's scary," she said. "But..." She racked her brain for something that might soothe their worries. Across the table, Brandish helped himself to another pastry. Curlycrown's red-rimmed eyes followed his every movement. *Bingo.* "Brandish is a talented wizard. He'll keep you safe. Right, Brandish?"

Brandish nodded, projecting an air of confidence that he promptly ruined by winking at her. She rolled her eyes, but luckily, the maidens didn't seem to notice anyway.

"I have faith in you. You're our princess, and the magic doesn't choose the unworthy. But I still think we would not be useful on this quest of yours, and I'd hate to be the reason it fails," said Fairhair. "Methinks you'd be better off without us."

Leigh launched to her feet and began to pace. She felt like such a jerk. In her determination to get her hands on that painting and figure out what had happened to her mom, she had forgotten to consider how the maidens might feel about this. Maybe they were a little naive, but that didn't mean that they lacked feelings. She was treating them like chess pieces on a board instead of actual people, and she had good reason to feel ashamed.

"Listen," said Brandish hesitantly, "I know Lady Leigh. You can trust her—"

"They're right," Leigh interrupted.

They all stared at her. Brandish looked startled, Curlycrown shaken, Fairhair somber. Although it was the last thing she wanted to do, she stopped her pacing and faced them head-on.

"It's dangerous," she continued. "I'm asking you to do something dangerous and pretending that it's not. That's not fair, and I'm sorry. But I don't know what else to do. I just thought that because you have

Pixietails, you could help. Don't you hate getting kidnapped all the time? Can't you use your magic and save yourselves?"

As she took in their puzzled expressions, her heart sank. They'd never even considered saving themselves. They didn't even need to say it aloud. When there was no princess to rescue them, they just sat around waiting for her to return. She could picture it all too well: the endless days of passive helplessness, waiting for a rescuer who rarely showed up. In a way, they were just as much prisoners as Shining Glory in his crystal ball. Heck, it was a miracle that they were still sane.

"How do you manage?" she asked, awed. "What do you *do*?"

"When we're not locked up somewhere, we practice appropriate accomplishments for young maidens," said Fairhair, trying to force a smile that still appeared strained. "Like needlework."

"And we play music. I know only twenty-six instruments, but I'm working hard at a new one. Fairhair has twenty-eight," said Curlycrown. "If you'd like to hear a duet on the harmonichord, we've been working on a lovely one."

"But you have Pixietails!" Leigh exclaimed, clenching her fists. The more she heard, the more upset she got. She couldn't—wouldn't—stand for it. "There are two of you. You could protect the village when I'm not here. Go places. Live your lives. If you can't do it for yourselves, do it for the people."

"Protect the village?" Curlycrown covered her mouth with both hands, shocked. "I wouldn't know how to begin."

"I don't know..." said Fairhair. She stood suddenly, walking to the window and looking out into the darkness. Her mouth was tight, her expression pensive. "I've always wanted to travel. Meet new people. See new places."

"There's no reason you can't." Leigh joined her at the window. "Just think about it—you could go anywhere you wanted. Take a weekend trip to the Color Valley Kingdom or whatever the heck it's called. You wouldn't have to be afraid anymore. You'd be free."

Fairhair's brown eyes were hopeful as they stared into Leigh's.

"You really think we can?" she asked.

"I do," said Leigh.

Fairhair took a deep breath, looking over Leigh's shoulder at Curlycrown. Whatever she saw there seemed to reassure her. She straightened, standing tall and proud despite the ridiculous floof of her nightclothes, and nodded.

"What do we have to do?" she asked.

CHAPTER 18

THE NEXT DAY WAS SATURDAY, AND LEIGH SLEPT IN late, waking only when Ari tapped on her door. They'd barely had time to catch up since her big confession. Their lunchtime conversation on Friday had been taken over by homework, since Leigh was struggling to keep up. Ari had been forced to set aside his laundry list of Lady Lovely Locks questions to drill her on anatomy facts. At work, they'd been swamped, so they couldn't talk without being overheard. By the time the rush ended, she'd needed to go to Lovely Locks or miss the opportunity, and she'd been too tired to talk when she returned. He couldn't restrain his curiosity any longer, and she didn't have the heart to turn him away even if she would have preferred to sleep a little more.

Although she really wanted to stay in bed for the next decade or so, she got up and ran a brush through her rat's nest hair and brushed her teeth. Ari had brought gifts—a giant mocha and a gas station chocolate croissant, which made her feel a lot better about being awake. Since the weather wasn't too bad, they took a walk so they could talk without being overheard, and he pelted her with questions. Some of them she'd answered before, but he didn't seem to care. He was enamored with everything she'd told him—the snagfires, the castle with its bad knock-off Pottery Barn decor... everything. He'd even let up with the judgy comments about Brandish.

"He hasn't slobbered all over you yet, so that's a plus," he said.

"I'm not even sure if I'm interested," she replied through a mouthful of croissant. "I mean, he's gorgeous and all, and there's definitely a spark, but beyond that? I barely know the guy."

"And he's giving you the space to get to know him. I can respect that. It's not like you don't have your hands full anyway. You really think you can make those girls tough?"

"I've got to try. If I don't do something, they'll spend their entire lives waiting for someone to save them."

"Oof." Ari shuddered, kicking an empty aluminum can off the sidewalk.

They walked in companionable silence for a half block or so before Ari cleared his throat.

"So I've been thinking about your mom," he said.

"Yeah?"

"If there's a picture of her in there, how did it get there? And what about the wig? Did that vendor specifically go to the con to sell it to you? Is this one of those fate things?"

"Oh, don't even get me started. I've been asking these questions ever since I saw that painting. Think about this—let's say that my mom did own the wig, and she went into Lovely Locks Kingdom, and she stayed there, disappearing from our world forever. But if she did that, she'd still have the wig, right? Unless there are two magic wigs, and potentially two Lady Lovely Lockses. Ugh. That plural might not be right, but you know what I mean."

"I gotchu." Ari sighed. "I've had no luck with tracking down that vendor so far. I talked to my connection on con staff, and there's no record of a wig vendor in that area. They didn't recognize her when I described her either. I think she must have sneaked in."

"Damn it," muttered Leigh.

"I haven't given up yet," he promised. "I'm working my way through all the con photos I can find. If I can spot her in the background, maybe I can read the sign on her table. I'm also working my way through the other regional cons to see if there are any signs of her there. It's a fairly small community. She's got to pop up again at some point. When she does, I'll be there. I don't know if it'll change anything, but I'm really curious to find out where that wig came from."

"Thanks for going to all this trouble, Ari. I really appreciate it."

She stopped at the crosswalk to look up at him, warmed more by the kind gesture than by the coffee in her hands.

"You deserve to know what happened to your mom," he continued doggedly. "Want me to keep watch while you travel today? Is your dad still suspicious?"

"I have no idea what goes on in that man's head. But I'd love to bring the cosplay over to your place if you wouldn't mind. That way you won't have to sit around bored while I'm there, and as long as I get back early enough, we could work on your wings."

"My wings?" He blinked, struggling to follow the topic change, but then the pieces clicked together. "Oh, *those* wings! Yeah, you still owe me, don't you? That would be great. I'll see if I can talk my mom into ordering pizza."

"Then I'll owe you again. It's just a never-ending cycle of owing, but I'm here for it."

The plan worked out great. Leigh suited up in Ari's closet since he shared a bathroom with two sisters. If anyone saw her coming out of the closet, they'd claim she was looking for cosplay materials or it was a jump scare gone wrong. Ari had insisted on coming up with multiple cover stories depending on the situation. If she hadn't stopped him, she was pretty sure he would have written actual scripts.

When she arrived in Lovely Locks, the sun hung bright in a cloudless sky, and birds chirped as they flew overhead. Even the air smelled better here. Cleaner somehow.

The market was bustling, and everyone wanted to say hello and touch her hair again, but once they'd gotten it out of their systems, they largely left her alone. She was able to wander the booths undisturbed and complete her business in record time. By the time the sun began to dip beneath the clouds, she was already waiting on the castle steps with all her equipment at the ready and a small sack of goodies at her side. She'd found more of those flat doughnut pastries and bought every last one in the stall.

She had just stuffed one into her mouth when Brandish sauntered up, pausing to inspect the enormous contraption standing a short distance from the steps. She'd cloaked it with some pink bedsheets begged off the maid to avoid spoiling the big reveal.

"What's this?" Brandish asked, trying to peek beneath the cover.

"Hands off, bucko. It's not for you," Leigh shot back.

He jerked upright, holding his hands up innocently. She rolled her eyes, and he joined her on the steps. She held out the bag to him, and he helped himself to a pastry with a grin.

"Good, aren't they?"

"I might never eat anything else again."

They munched in companionable silence for a moment.

"So what do you want me to do here? If you're teaching those girls to fight, I won't be much help. These hands were made for magic, not maces," he said.

"You're the carrot; I'm the stick."

"I've never been called *that* before." He grinned.

"Don't be an idiot. It's easier to persuade a horse to move with a carrot than with a stick. I'm going to push them out of their comfort zones. At some point, they'll balk, and that's your cue. Compliment them. You're a cute guy. Curlycrown's desperate to impress you."

"Oh." He absorbed this for a moment. "How cute am I, exactly? On a scale of one to ten."

He leaned back onto one elbow, grinning. A lock of sandy hair fell into his eyes. She couldn't decide what color they were. On a license, they'd probably be listed as hazel, with flecks of green and brown and tan, but the word didn't do them justice. The grin slid from his face as she stared into them. Her cheeks heated. They inched toward each other in slow motion. Her heart jackhammered in her chest, and suddenly the air had gotten a lot thinner...

"Lady Leigh!"

Curlycrown's excited shout drove them apart like a pair of flipped magnets. She hurried toward them, holding her long skirts up off the ground, ribbons and hair streaming behind her. Fairhair followed a few steps behind, smiling to herself. Leigh hoped she was amused by Curlycrown's antics and not by whatever had just almost happened between her and Brandish. It was probably a good thing they'd been interrupted before she could do something she might regret later. Right?

Her cheeks were blazing, but she tried to act casual, standing up and brushing off the back of her skirts. Brandish coughed, suddenly engrossed in straightening the pouches that lined his belt. Curlycrown didn't even seem to have noticed as she slid to a stop, huffing, a hand held melodramatically to her chest.

"I hope we're not late," she said. "I changed my dress three times. Is this one okay?"

She spun around, skirts swirling. It was not what you'd call a good outfit for fighting. Or running. Or breathing. But Curlycrown wore this sort of thing every day. It wasn't worth the argument.

"It's fine," said Leigh. "Are you ready to get started?"

"As ready as we'll get," said Fairhair, joining them. "I've got to admit I'm a little nervous. And excited. It's been so long since I tried something new. Unless you count musical instruments or handcrafts. Oh, and then there's hairstyles..."

"What are we doing?" Curlycrown bounced on her toes. "There isn't a snagfire beneath that tarp, is there? I can't decide if I'm frightened or thrilled! It's ever so confusing!"

Leigh pulled the sheet off to reveal a makeshift punching bag hanging from a wooden stand. The contraption would have looked out of place in a kickboxing gym, with its lumpy homespun bag and plain wooden stand, but she was proud of it anyway. Although it was a simple thing to build, she'd had to accomplish it with the rudimentary materials available in the village market. If it held up, she'd promised the smith he could have it later.

The bag spun lazily at the end of its chain as the maidens circled it, oohing and aahing. They liked the gentle tinkle of the chain and the neat stitching around the circumference of the overstuffed sack.

Finally, Fairhair asked, "What is it, Princess? A decoration? I've never seen anything like it."

"We call it a punching bag. It's much easier to learn to hit a bag than it is to hit a person. Let's give it a try."

Leigh had never been able to afford the martial arts lessons she'd always wanted, but she'd taken a little stage fighting and a few karate seminars at an after-school program. She just had to make it look good to get the maidens used to the idea of hitting something, and she could do that.

Fairhair took to the fighting lesson like a duck to water, but Curly-crown needed a bit of extra encouragement. A smooth comment or two from Brandish pushed her to throw a few shaky punches, but she had the ridiculous habit of apologizing after every one. It was a real pity, too, because she had more natural aptitude. Her final punch hit with so much power that the swinging bag came back and hit her in the face, and no amount of cute-boy compliments could entice her to try again. Resigned, Leigh called for a pastry-and-tea break.

Fairhair seemed to have sucked up all the excitement that Curly-crown lacked. She bounced over, chowed down on two Ladybuns in quick succession, and then sprawled on the stairs with a satisfied sigh.

"Fun, right?" asked Leigh.

"I don't want to stop! Although I'm not very strong," Fairhair responded, her happy smile beginning to wobble. "I don't think I'll ever be able to hit as hard as you."

"Pff." Leigh waved a hand. "Look at me. I got arms like twigs, but I can still throw down. A good punch is all about form. It doesn't matter if you're smaller than the other guy if your form is better. That's what they say, anyway."

“Really?” Fairhair’s eyes shone. “They only recruit big, strong men to be knights, you know. I always wanted to try, but I can’t.”

“It takes hours and hours and hours of practice, but you could totally do this if you put the work in.”

“I know how to play twenty-eight instruments, Lady Leigh. I have time coming out my ears. May I borrow the punching bag?” Fairhair punctuated the request with a set of rather impressive puppy-dog eyes. “I’d like to continue learning on my own.”

“It’s yours,” replied Leigh.

“Thank you! Thank you!”

Fairhair flung her arms wide, throwing them around Leigh and nearly upsetting her drink in the process. Leigh hadn’t expected a hug, and for a moment she froze before tentatively returning the gesture. A warm feeling spread in her belly.

She pulled back, unsure of where to look or how to act. Her cheeks were red again, but this time she didn’t care.

“Right,” she said. “Thanks. Now let’s go on to phase two: Pixietails.”

The girls exchanged hesitant glances.

“I don’t know how much good that will do,” said Curlycrown. “My Pixietails aren’t as useful as yours. I use them to play games sometimes.”

“What powers do they have?” Leigh asked. “We can brainstorm.”

Curlycrown looked down at her feet, scuffing at the dirt with one toe like a reluctant child. It took her a moment to screw up the courage to answer, and when she did, her voice wilted with embarrassment.

"Pixie Copper can summon balls of fire. Pixie Brunet can summon balls of rock. Pixie White can summon balls of ice," said Curlycrown mournfully. "Isn't that awful?"

Leigh and Brandish exchanged looks of complete dumbfounded confusion.

"That's not the word I'd use..." he said.

"What's the problem?" Leigh asked. "Are they tiny fireballs? Do they just plop down at your feet?"

"No, they shoot out all over the place and make a huge mess. I still have a hole in my canopy bed from a fireball gone wrong." Curlycrown sighed, holding her hands out in front of her, sketching a shape about the size of a golf ball. "They're about this big. I used to play target games with them, but I'm afraid that's all they're good for. I think I still have the targets if you want to play."

After a moment, Leigh realized her mouth was hanging open. These girls had been hiding inside all this time when one of them could shoot fireballs? And ice and stone! Leigh was honestly a bit jealous. Curlycrown got elemental magic, and what did she have? Pixie Shine had a magic lasso, Pixie Beauty could levitate things, and she still hadn't bothered figuring out what Pixie Sparkle did. Maybe it summoned an invisible jet, and Lady Lovely Locks was secretly a hairier, pastel version of Wonder Woman.

"I'm almost afraid to ask this question, but what do your Pixietails do?" she said, setting that aside and turning to Fairhair.

"Pixie Growth makes things bigger. Pixie Cut shrinks them. And Pixie Luscious makes them stronger." Fairhair preened a bit. "You should see my rose garden."

"Can you use their powers on yourself? Make yourself big and strong and punch through walls?" asked Leigh.

"I've never tried," Fairhair said, startled. "Do you think that would work?"

Why had she wasted all this time teaching the maidens how to punch a bag when they had all that power at their fingertips? It almost wasn't fair. She growled, and they all looked at her with matching expressions of concern.

"I just need a minute," she muttered. "Get your targets, Curlycrown. And maybe some flowers, Fairhair. I want to see what you can do."

With one last worried glance, the girls scampered off, leaving her and Brandish alone in the courtyard. She began fussing with the punching bag, trying to distract herself from her roiling emotions, but he could read her too well. He sidled right up to her, bobbing and weaving to remain in her field of vision despite her attempts to look elsewhere.

"Hey. Hey!" he said. "You okay?"

"I don't even know what I'm so upset about." Leigh threw up her hands. "It's so stupid! Augh!"

"I mean, take your pick. All that time wasted. All that wasted potential. And the pastries? Also wasted," he joked.

"Tell me about it."

"I noticed you don't use your Pixietails very much," he persisted, craning his neck to force her to meet his eyes again. "Why is that? Are they as awful as Curlycrown's?" He sketched quotation marks in the air at the word "awful."

"They're idiots. And they're loud. But mostly I like doing things myself. If I get used to relying on the Pixietails, and then they're gone, I'll be miserable. It's better not to get too used to it." She sighed. "I know; I'm an idiot."

"No. I know exactly what you mean. You don't know what you've got until it's gone."

She glanced up at him, expecting another of his grins, but his expression was somber. The empathy didn't really change anything, but she felt better anyway. Less alone.

"Maybe you should teach this bit, since you're the wizard and I barely use my Pixietails," she said.

"No thanks. I don't do Pixietails, and besides... I like watching you teach. You're good at it, Leigh."

The compliment warmed her just as her success had earlier. She needed to quit being so hard on herself. Brandish was right. She was a good teacher, and she'd accomplished something important here.

"Yeah, okay," she said, nodding. "Although you aren't supposed to work your charms on me, you rascal. We're business partners, remember?"

"Is that what we are?" he asked, his voice soft. "I wasn't quite sure."

She cleared her throat, looking away.

"I don't think we can—" she began.

"Brandish," shouted Curlycrown from somewhere high up above them. "Could you help me carry these targets? They're so heavy!"

"You don't think what?" he demanded.

But that was the problem; Leigh couldn't think. Couldn't force the words out, even though she knew what she needed to say. Instead, she just gaped at him. Didn't he see that any relationship between them was impossible?

His shoulders drooped, and for a moment his eyes held Leigh's, his mouth slightly open as if preparing to speak. But then he turned away. Leigh's heart lurched, sadness chilling her veins. It just wasn't meant to be. It never had been.

"Right," he said, sighing. "Coming!"

With one last unreadable glance at her over his shoulder, he began to climb the steps toward the castle doors.

Chapter 19

THE NEXT DAY WAS SUNDAY, AND LEIGH WAS scheduled for another full shift with Ari. She wouldn't have enough time in Lovely Locks to make the trip to Tangleland, so she decided to hold one more training session before the heist on Monday. The maidens needed it. If left to their own devices, they got distracted easily. Curlycrown had the attention span of a hyperactive squirrel and would wander off midsentence, while Fairhair liked to tell long and convoluted stories. Hopefully a little more practice would help settle them down.

As Fairhair worked with the punching bag and Curlycrown tried desperately to hit the targets with her elemental projectiles, Shining Glory rounded the corner. The moment she saw him, a wave of guilt ran over her. She felt bad for the maidens, but Shining Glory had things worse. The maidens had the potential for change if they could only work up the courage, but Shining Glory was still cursed.

Guilt tightened her throat as she approached and patted Prince on the head.

"Princess," Shining Glory said warmly. "I hope you don't mind a little visit. I heard you were training with our young ladies, and I wanted to offer my support."

"I'm so sorry." Leigh swallowed, her throat tight with tension and shame. "I haven't put any effort at all into removing your curse."

He arched a brow.

"You have no obligation to me. It is I that am here to support you," he said.

"But why is that? Why am I so special that the entire kingdom revolves around me? The snagfires attack the village, and nobody does anything. You're cursed; the maidens get kidnapped all the time, and nobody blinks. But the minute I need help, everyone hops to it. It's not fair!"

Her voice rose, propelled by frustration. There was so much to be done, so much to change. This place had seemed like a fairy-tale utopia at first—so perfect that it made her want to vomit—but now she knew better. You'd have to be blind not to see the problems and heartless not to try to help.

"I don't know," he replied, his voice calm and steady. "I could speculate if you wanted, but I'm not sure how much use it would be. I suppose what's important is that you're doing something now."

"But I'm not. I'm mostly trying to help myself."

"Oh?" Shining Glory arched a brow. "I don't think that's how the maidens see it. During my hair mask, all they could talk about was their excitement over your training session. I've never heard them so confident. I think you're selling yourself short, Lady Leigh. You cannot solve all the problems of the world at once. Pick one."

She took a deep breath. "I have. We've got a plan for that hypothetical heist we were talking about. We go tomorrow."

"Good. Reach that goal and then reevaluate. The rest will come." Shining Glory smiled. "Now tell me about your hypothetical plans."

They talked for a long time. Occasionally, he'd make a low, frustrated noise in the back of his throat, which she knew meant he had observations that he couldn't force out. Sometimes she managed to dance around the point enough to get the gist of it, but in a handful of cases, they had to give up after an aggravating attempt at talking in circles on both their parts.

The conversation stretched on so long that the maidens finished up, and Brandish offered to walk them inside, as Fairhair wanted help setting the punching bag up in her room again. Shortly after he left, Leigh realized she'd missed an opportunity to finally introduce the two wizards, but she'd been so engrossed in the conversation that she didn't realize it until too late. Next time. Brandish kept saying that hedge wizards and royal wizards didn't mix, but she thought they'd get along just fine.

She had to admit that her feelings might have been coloring that opinion. Shining Glory reminded her of the good old days with her dad. He'd worked days when she was in elementary school, and when he picked her up from after-school care, they'd go on adventures. Nothing special—just trips to the grocery store or to the park. Sometimes, they'd do silly things like cook only orange foods for dinner. Mostly, they talked. He'd listened to her back then, and even if he wasn't into her favorite cartoons or books, he'd made her feel like he cared anyway. But then, he got rear-ended by a car, and the insurance screwed him over, and everything fell to pieces. The medical bills got so bad that they had to downsize. Then move. Then move again, until they were stuck in a tiny apartment in a bad Philadelphia neighborhood. Their stove had only one working burner, but it didn't matter. They didn't cook orange meals anymore anyway. He'd switched to night shift since it paid a little better. She'd picked up a job. Neither seemed to make any difference in digging them out of the hole they'd gotten into. They'd never reconnected, and she'd convinced herself that she didn't want to.

But talking with Shining Glory made her miss it. Made her miss *him*.

She hid her growing sadness, keeping it stuffed down inside as they chatted, and eventually Shining Glory slapped his hands on his knees to signify the end of the conversation. Sometimes, he seemed like he would stick out like a sore thumb in the real world, but at times like this, she thought he would have fit right in.

"It's been lovely to chat," he said. "I'm impressed by all that you're doing. It feels like you're taking on multiple quests rather than just one, but if anyone can make a success of that, I believe it's you. I hope you'll keep me posted."

"Thanks," she said, trying to keep hold of herself and failing. "Of course I will. I'll come keep you company whenever I can."

She waited until Shining Glory and Prince were gone to let herself cry. She did so silently, letting the tears snake down her cheeks, and allowed herself to feel the depths of her own loneliness for the first time. Her mom had left her. Her dad used to be her best friend, and now they barely spoke. Sometimes it felt like that had to be her fault. After all, parents were supposed to love their kids no matter what. One of them had to be defective, and sometimes she thought it had to be her.

But for the first time, she had the opportunity to get what she had wanted so badly for so long. She could finally find out what had happened to her mother all those years ago, and maybe, if she was lucky, she could heal her own broken heart. She couldn't give up now, not when the answers were so close. The maidens had a few ideas of where Ravenwaves might have hidden the painting. This plan really could work.

She found herself suddenly exhausted. Once again, she'd lost track of time, but Ari had promised to wait at the store for her to return, so they could walk home together and debrief. That would be a good thing. She needed a friend right now, and although Brandish would listen, he also stirred up feelings that she really didn't need to deal with right now.

"Pixie Shine! Pixie Beauty! Pixie Sparkle!" she said, waiting for the little pastel pests to come zipping out and send her back to the real world.

But they didn't show.

How odd. They'd been complaining because she hadn't been paying much attention to them, but they still came when it was time for her to go home. Were they sulking? She plunged her hands into the masses of her hair, marveling at how light it was. It ought to make her neck hurt, but it seemed to have a gravity of its own. What it didn't have was a set of Pixietails, at least not anywhere that she could reach.

She considered consulting the maidens, since they had Pixietails of their own. Curlycrown's had been upset at her, too, since she'd been neglecting them all her life, but they'd always obeyed her. After all, they couldn't resist a direct order.

"Pixie Shine, Pixie Beauty, and Pixie Sparkle, come out right now and send me home," she said.

Nothing happened.

If they were hiding, they wouldn't have gone far. She'd seen them briefly at the beginning of the lesson when they'd come out to tentatively ask to participate. She'd turned them down, and maybe she shouldn't have done that, but punishing her like this was a bit too much. She was going to give them a piece of her mind when she found them.

They weren't in her castle bedroom. She climbed all those darned stairs for nothing. She crouched to look under the bed and opened every drawer and closet. Listened at every door—including the maidens'—for the telltale jingle of Pixietails at work. But she heard nothing except for the rapid whump of Fairhair's fists against the punching bag.

She made a quick circle of the castle grounds, calling out their names every few minutes. At some point, they'd hear her and be forced to obey. But still no dice, so out the gates she went.

Worry quickened her steps, driving her out into the courtyard. They weren't there either. Maybe in the village somewhere? Full night had fallen long ago, and there was no moon in the sky, leaving her adrift in a sea of darkness. One quick slam of her staff against the ground surrounded her in a pool of glowing light from the blade out the top. Perfect. Now she was protected from snagfires and from trip hazards.

The fear took hold again, driving her desperate search. If she didn't find them, was she stuck here forever? Or would some cosmic timer eventually run out and plop her back into the real world again? If not, she was doomed. She'd never see her dad or Ari again. She'd never cosplay. Never graduate high school.

She stumbled again, barking her knee against a thick branch, and swore aloud. This was stupid. Once she got her knee to stop screaming, she'd wake up her friends. The maidens could deploy their Pixietails; the wizards could use their magic. That's what friends did. She turned back toward the castle, but before she could take a step, a faint, familiar jingle caught her attention. She froze in place, straining to hear. There it was again. Either she'd found her Pixietails, or some late-night bell vendor was traveling home on foot.

"Pixie Shine! Pixie Beauty! Pixie Sparkle!" she shouted. "I want to go home!"

Still no response.

She began to limp in the direction of the noise, favoring the injured knee. It creaked with every step, sending twinges of pain up into her thigh, but she could make it work so long as she didn't go too fast. She placed her feet carefully, squinting at the ground to avoid hurting herself even worse. The ground here was uneven, full of loose shale and the gnarled branches of flowering bushes that snagged at her boots.

It took all her concentration to avoid falling flat on her face, which probably explained why she walked right up to Ravenwaves without noticing her. The duchess's dark hair and equally dark dress probably didn't help either. In the dim light of Leigh's staff, the only thing visible in the black was the white oval of her face and the triumphant glint of her eyes.

Leigh stopped short, clutching the staff with both hands. They were deep in the woods surrounding the village; she couldn't even see the lights through the trees. But she could smell the stink of snagfires and hear the wheeze of their breath all around her. Another faint jingle suggested the Pixietails were nearby, but where? She tried unsuccessfully to look everywhere at once, cold with the knowledge that this had to be a trap.

“Well, hello, Princess,” said Ravenwaves. “We’ve been waiting for you.”

“Oh?” replied Leigh, playing it more casual than she felt. “I didn’t realize you were throwing a party. If you’d sent me an invitation, I would have avoided it.”

“Don’t be rude. We’re friends, aren’t we?”

“Friends don’t lock friends in their creepy tower and threaten to cut off all their hair.”

“Oh, come on. It wasn’t all your hair. Just a piece. But since you’re offering, I’ll take it all this time.”

Leigh rolled her eyes.

“Save it, Ravenwaves. I’m too tired for your melodrama. Where are my Pixietails?” she said.

“Oh, them? Say hello to your princess, Pixietails.”

Ravenwaves bared her teeth in a fierce grin that made Leigh’s stomach sink. There was another jingle. Then the faintest of pastel glows illuminated the huddled forms of her Pixietails, trapped in a small cage behind Ravenwaves. The contraption couldn’t have been more rudimentary, with a wooden floor, barred walls, and a drop-down door. It looked like the sort of trap you’d see in a kids’ cartoon—or a storybook. If someone had brought it to a cosplay contest as a prop, she would have laughed her butt off. But it had worked, so maybe it wasn’t that funny after all.

Inside, Pixie Sparkle had its arms wrapped protectively around the other two Pixietails as all three of them huddled in the center of the cage. As they shivered in fright, little sparkles of Pixietail magic floated out of their bodies only to be immediately sucked into the bars of the cage. Some sort of magical trap, Leigh assumed. If that was the case, they wouldn't be able to get out on their own. A snagfire leaned down over them, huffing a burst of hot air through the bars and making them all jingle in alarm.

"So," Ravenwaves said, "what do you think about that haircut?"

"Back up your goons, and then we'll talk. If you barbecue my Pixietails, then you won't have any magic to steal, you know."

"Oh, fine." Ravenwaves gestured like she was shooing away some pesky flies. "Back off, snagfires. You stink anyway." She waited while the snagfires retreated back into the darkness, although Leigh could still hear them. They were the loudest breathers she'd ever heard. Probably chewed with their mouths open too; she hated that.

"Happy now? Let's trim those lovely locks of yours," said Ravenwaves.

Leigh sighed. "Honestly, this is all so stupid. Do you really expect to inherit my Pixietails by cutting my hair? Has anything like that ever worked? How stupid are you gonna feel when you've got a handful of hair and no Pixietails?"

"I... what do you mean? Of course it'll work! Magic hair, magic Pixietails... they have to go together. I can't believe I have to explain this to you. It isn't fair that you get Pixietails and I don't!" exclaimed Ravenwaves.

"You're right. It isn't."

Ravenwaves paused midrant, tilting her head in confusion.

"But there are other ways to learn magic, aren't there?" continued Leigh, pressing her advantage. "Why not become a wizard? You don't need to kidnap people and shave them bald for that."

The duchess hesitated, thoughtful. Then she lit up again as she scraped together another argument.

"Wizards are all male. Everyone knows that," she declared triumphantly.

"So boys can learn magic all on their own, but the only way girls get any power is by growing some magic hair—or by stealing it? That's the stupidest thing I've ever heard. I'm more than just a pretty face, and so are you. Aren't you?"

"Well... y-yeah. But..."

"But nothing! Lady Knot was a sorceress, right? So it's possible."

"I'm not talking about Lady—her! We don't say her name, and I'd be happy if I never had to say it again. I'd rather forget she existed, the backstabber!"

"Then why do you have her painting in your study? Who is she?" Leigh tried to keep her voice from shaking with excitement. She chose her words carefully. "We can work together, you know. Here's a thought. What if you give me the painting and tell me what you know, and I help you become a sorceress?"

Ravenwaves snorted, but she didn't outright refuse either. Leigh continued.

"You don't have to be a villain to get what you want. Honestly, why do you waste all your time on these ridiculous plots anyway? If you want magic, learn some. It's much better than a life as a frustrated hair thief."

"You're... that's..." Ravenwaves spluttered for a moment before stiffening up again. "You're making this all up to trick me. Just like everyone else. But I won't fall for it, not again."

Clearly, she'd struck a nerve. Something must have happened to Ravenwaves to make her so distrustful. Maybe something with

Lady Knot? Leigh couldn't afford to betray the fact that the sorceress might be her mom, not until she had her answers.

"How do you think I'm trying to fool you?" Leigh held one hand out to the side. "There's just me and one staff against you and a whole gaggle of snagfires. The numbers aren't exactly to my advantage."

"I'll have your hair, or my snagfires will roast your Pixietails, and I'll eat them for dinner." Ravenwaves sneered. "I'll tell you one thing—you won't call me a frustrated hair thief again. I'll have my own power if I have to take it off you."

The venom in the duchess's voice shook Leigh to her core. There would be no talking her way out of this one. If they fought, Leigh was fairly certain she would lose. She needed to even up the odds. As Leigh looked around in the darkness, she tilted the staff ever so slightly in an effort to make out something—anything—nearby that would help. The pastel light glinted off the slanted, hungry eyes of a creature in the underbrush. They shone briefly in the glow as the unseen beast blinked, a slow lowering and lifting of the lids.

Great. Now either she'd get fried by snagfires or eaten by some freaky Cheshire cat wannabe.

The eyes disappeared, but that only made her more nervous.

When the eyes opened again, they floated in the darkness behind the cage, stalking with slow deliberation toward the Pixietails inside. The snagfires hadn't noticed its silent approach. Leigh hesitated, unsure whether this was a hungry whatchamajigger that planned to eat the Pixietails or the whatchamajigger cavalry come to the rescue.

It stepped cautiously into the faint glow of the staff, its outline barely visible against the darkness. She could make out a long, lithe body and a beautiful bushy tail...

Prince!

The locksfox padded silently toward the cage where the terrified Pixietails huddled. Then he stopped as one of the snagfires snuffled in the dark, huddling against the ground like he was trying to disappear. But there was nowhere to hide. It was only a matter of time before he was spotted.

Unless Leigh caught their attention.

While she was distracted, Ravenwaves had pulled out a pair of golden scissors. Her mouth twisted into a cruel grin, and her eyes glittered.

Leigh swung her staff in a wide loop over her head before pulling it down and crouching to signal that it was game on.

"You want to take me on, Ravenwaves?" she shouted. "You think you've got what it takes to defeat the real Lady Lovely Locks? Because you don't. You're just a two-bit has-been."

"What's that?" Ravenwaves sounded puzzled more than anything. "Should I be insulted?"

"Very. And what are you going to do about it? Send your pet snagfires to fight me? Of course you will, because you're too weak to face me yourself, even without my Pixietails."

It was the most transparent of manipulation attempts, but Ravenwaves bought it anyway. She let out a snarl of fury, and the snagfires responded with more of their hooting barks, reacting to her obvious rage. Leigh could hear them behind her now; they'd surrounded her while she'd been talking. This plan had better work, because she wouldn't be retreating that way. But she didn't dare look at Prince. If she reacted at all, it would tip Ravenwaves off. So she kept her eyes on the duchess, taunting her with a cheery smile and a quirk of a finger.

"Come on," she prompted. "Or are you chicken?"

"I'll cut off all your hair and leave you bald. I'll chain you up and make you scrub my floors and brush my hair," spat Ravenwaves.

Clang!

Metal rang against metal as the door to the cage fell open. Ravenwaves stiffened, her eyes widening. Leigh didn't dare wait; she just called out to her Pixietails and hoped that the noise had been Prince setting them free. Otherwise, they were all in the soup now, and it wasn't going to be good.

"Pixie Beauty, lift us up! Pixie Shine, restrain the snagfires!" she commanded.

For one heart-stopping moment, nothing happened. Then magic gathered around her, coating her in a pastel glow and shooting her up into the air like a rocket. The tense bands constricting her chest slowly eased as she flew out of range. She saw Prince, ears flat against his head, as he flew alongside her. Golden lassos of power filled the air.

They were free. Her only regret was that the Pixietails had whisked her away so fast that she hadn't gotten to gloat.

CHAPTER 20

IT DIDN'T TAKE LONG FOR LEIGH TO GET PRINCE AND the Pixietails settled in the castle, but she was much later returning home, to reality, than intended when she took the wig off. Without a clock, she didn't know exactly how tardy she was, but Wing It must have closed hours ago. She owed Ari big-time.

As soon as the magic teleportation sparkles faded from her vision, she knew something had gone sideways. She reappeared in the darkness, but she'd definitely left the bathroom lights on. She remembered staring into the mirror to get the wig on straight. The door had been locked from the inside, so why was it open now? She hesitated in the darkness, broken only by the faint red glow of the emergency exit sign near the back door. The store was silent and still.

"Ari?" she asked, her fatigue washed away by a rush of concern.

No response. That didn't bode well; he was supposed to wait. Had he gotten abducted by hardware thieves? Forgotten all about her? She couldn't decide which would be worse. Her fingers grazed the light switch, but she decided against flipping it. A private security company patrolled the shopping center, and although the guard was often napping in his car when they closed the store, the guy had to wake up sometime. So she fumbled around in the dark, trying to find her bag. It wasn't on the edge of the sink. Had it fallen? She flailed around near the ground, her fingers brushing against the damp porcelain exterior of the toilet. Ew.

From somewhere in the main room, she heard the unmistakable buzzing of a phone on vibrate. She whirled around to see a screen light up, the bright white light floating in the dark. Within its nimbus, she could make out the vague outlines of her backpack, perched on the edge of Sal's rickety old desk with her cell sitting face up on top. She lurched toward it, something damp clinging to the expanse of bare leg between her skirt and boot. A piece of her expensive wig had stuck to her. She didn't want to think about how it had gotten wet and decided to leave it there for the moment.

She grabbed her phone and skimmed through her notifications. Ari had DMed her. The sight of his name made her almost dizzy with relief; at least he was okay. He'd been sending her messages every fifteen minutes or so. Most were just her name, over and over again, punctuated by "answer me, damn it!" and "where are u????"

"wut happened?" she typed, her thumbs flying.

She noted the time—well past eleven. She had intended to return right around nine to help close the registers. He must have been frantic with worry when she didn't show. His messages started pinging in, one right after another.

sal showed up right b4 closing to do that tax crap
couldn't stay
u ok???

yah
got attacked. couldn't get out
but i fixed it.

u scared the crap outta me

sorry
am i fired?

There was a long pause, and then she got a notification—he'd video called. Her heart sank. He wouldn't want to deliver bad news via text. She pressed her lips together, trying not to freak out at the thought of being unemployed. She'd be stuck in that crappy apartment for the rest of her life, eking out a meager existence in a series of increasingly bleak customer-service jobs, because no way was she going to afford design school without Wing It. At that point, she might as well say screw it and go to Lovely Locks for good. At least there she had free rent.

The phone kept buzzing, and she answered with her stomach screwed up in knots. Ari's face popped up on the screen, dimly lit by the glow from his phone. Worry pinched his features and furrowed his brows.

"So I'm fired," she said, resigned.

"I don't think so," he replied. "I told Sal he just missed you puking and I sent you home. He got a little pissed when he realized the door to the john was locked. The dude picked it, if you believe that. I guess he really needed to take a leak? Anyway, I hung around as long as I could, hoping to distract him so you could sneak out when you finally came back, but he sent me home. I've been frantic ever since."

"I'm so sorry," she said. "My Pixietails got kidnapped, and I couldn't get out. I had to find them, and . . . it was a mess. I owe you big-time."

"You need me to come get you? I couldn't sleep. I'm so worked up I might never close my eyes again."

"I'll just take the bus."

"You got cash? You can't take your phone with you, so no bus pass. Sal knows you left the cell with your bag. If it's gone in the morning, he'll know something wasn't copacetic."

Leigh hissed in aggravation, but he was right. If she pressed her luck, she really would get fired. Or Sal would refuse to let her close with Ari anymore. It had taken a while to convince him that they could be trusted to do it without a manager, and he wasn't the sort of guy who believed in second chances. Especially if he was in the middle of a hissy fit about the taxes.

"Okay, I'll pick it up tomorrow and give him the 'It must have been something I ate' line," she said. "I might squeak out of this thing after all, thanks to you."

"Don't mention it. I'm just glad he was gone when you popped back up. I had this awful vision of you reappearing in the bathroom while he was using it."

"Stop!" she exclaimed, shuddering. "I don't even want to think about it."

"Exactly."

"I better get walking, I guess."

"Message me when—crap, you can't without your phone, can you? Are you sure you don't want me to come get you? I can hop on a bus and be there in a half hour."

"If I have to sit around waiting that long, I'll fall asleep. I'll get on my laptop and send you a DM on Insta when I get home. Should take me forty-five minutes tops."

"Deal." He hesitated. "Glad you're okay."

"Me too. I nearly had a heart attack when I came back to a dark room and an open door. It felt like the setup to a bad postapocalyptic thriller."

He groaned, and they signed off.

She grabbed her keys from the inside pocket of her bag and inched an oversize black hoodie out from the bottom, trying to keep the top layers just the way she'd found them. The hoodie nearly covered her entire cosplay, with only the longer section of the skirt poking out underneath. It would have to do. She took a minute to examine the soggy wig. Luckily, only a bit had dropped into the toilet, and she dried it with a paper towel before tucking it into her hood. No way was she going to risk losing that along with her link to Lovely Locks.

She eyed the security keypad next to the back door. This part would be a bit sticky, but she had no choice. If she went out the front and was spotted by security, they'd ask questions she didn't want to answer. They'd call Sal, and he'd definitely fire her then. Maybe Ari too.

The keypad beeped as she punched in the exit code, disabling the alarm for thirty seconds. As long as she avoided setting it off, Sal would have no reason to check the logs. Then she took a deep breath, steeling herself, and exited out the back.

Normally, she and Ari left through the front door, since the back opened up into a sketchy alleyway. Piles of discarded boxes and disintegrating pallets choked the space, and sometimes when she went to take out the trash, she'd find empty bottles in brown paper bags or see a huddled figure sleeping beneath an insufficient cardboard tent. The thought of running into someone back there in the middle of the night with no way to call for help made her heart pound. But she had no other choice.

She clutched her keys in her hand, squeezing them between her knuckles like the self-defense videos suggested. After the dragon, she was more confident than ever in her ability to throw down, but somehow, fighting in the real world still scared her more than it did in Lovely Locks Kingdom. Maybe because she didn't have magical bunnies living in her hair, or the benefit of a magic staff. Regardless, she wasn't keen on getting into a scuffle with anyone crazy enough to be out in this neighborhood late at night.

The back alley was just as dark as she remembered. She turned left, hurrying toward the road as the heavy security door boomed shut behind her. She winced at the noise, but it was too late to do anything about it now.

"Hey!" The voice was startled, male, and accompanied by the bright beam of a flashlight. "Who's there?"

Just her luck. She'd managed to encounter a rare security guard who actually patrolled the grounds instead of dozing in the car all night. He was down near the back corner of the strip mall and closing in fast. The flashlight bobbed and weaved as he searched for her in the darkness. She couldn't afford to get caught. Run or hide?

Her heart leaped into her throat, choking her with nerves. The piles of garbage beckoned, but he might stop and search them. She couldn't risk it.

She ran.

Gym had never been her favorite subject. When it came time to run the mile, she'd always jogged the first bit just to get the teacher off her back and then walked the rest, squeaking by just under the fifteen-minute time limit. She'd never be a track star. Then again, she'd never really tried either.

Now she sprinted full out, catching her foot on the edge of a pallet and nearly face-planting. But she recovered, arms pinwheeling, and kept on going. The beam of the flashlight swept over her before returning to lock on her back.

"You there! Stop!" shouted the guard.

She ran as if her life depended on it, not daring to look behind her. But despite her best efforts, the thump of the guard's footsteps drew closer and closer. Her side burned; she gasped for air. She should have run those stupid laps in gym. Maybe then she could have avoided getting arrested tonight.

The guard let out a muffled curse, and something clattered loudly as he fell. She risked a glance behind her, slowing. He'd stumbled over the same pallet that had tripped her and had fallen hard, the flashlight rolling all the way over next to the building. As she watched, he flipped over, groaning and flailing around. She didn't wait to see what happened next. She hightailed it out of there, keeping up a staggering, pained run until she reached the main drag.

The next day, Leigh plodded through school. After she got home and took a nice long shower, she knocked a bunch of things off her to-do list. She aced a take-home quiz, read a few pages of *Romeo and Juliet* for English, and ran a load of laundry, carting the basket down into the basement of their building to snag the last open washer. She even scrubbed down the kitchen counters before making another pot of macky cheese. She was just settling into a spot at the kitchen counter with a steaming bowl when her dad came trudging out of his bedroom in rumpled pajamas.

"Good morning," she said. "Or evening, I guess. Macky cheese?"

She didn't really expect a coherent answer. Neither of them woke up well and never had. But working nights had turned her dad into a bit of a zombie. He usually couldn't squeeze out a coherent sentence without a cup or two of instant coffee to lubricate his brain. In fact, she was feeling a bit charitable since she hadn't gotten arrested the night before, so she decided to make him a cup.

But as she slid out of her seat, he reached over and put a hand on her shoulder, holding her in place. She stared up at him in confusion.

"You want coffee?" she asked. "I was going to make you a cup."

"Why did you lie?" he demanded, folding his arms.

Her heart stuttered. She'd never seen him look so disappointed and angry—not at her.

"L-lie?" she asked.

"I called your work last night. Sal said you went home early."

"I was sick..." she began. "Must have been something I ate."

"Yeah, so I got some wonton soup and brought it home. Surprise, surprise, you weren't here! And don't say that you went to Ari's, because I checked there, too, after my next call. And then when I returned home again, you were miraculously asleep in your bed."

"So what are you, a stalker now?" she snapped.

Maybe it didn't make sense for her to be so offended, since she'd lied in the first place. But the way he was talking to her only proved her point. She wouldn't have been able to trust him with the truth. He'd stopped truly listening to her long ago. Between that and his continued refusal to tell her anything related to her mom, she couldn't trust him at all.

"A stalker?" he asked. The pitch of his voice climbed to match the brows. "A stalker?! No, Leigh, I'm a parent. It's my job. Just like it's my job to know where you go at night. All I ask is that you respect your curfew. That seems pretty reasonable to me, but maybe I'm wrong."

"You want me to confide in you? Then act like the kind of guy who will care enough to listen for once!"

"Jesus, Leigh. Of course I care." He sighed, running a hand over his thinning hair. When he spoke again, his voice was smaller than she'd ever heard it. "Are you on drugs? Just tell me. We'll get you help."

"No! Jeez, Dad. You know me better than that."

"I thought I did. But you're sneaking out at all hours. Your grades have gotten shaky. The school emails me one of those weekly reports, you know. You've got missing assignments."

"I also have a job! And a tough course load. And maybe I slacked on a couple of things, but I still have a B or higher in all my classes."

"You have a B- in gym. Gym, Leigh. All you have to do is run around and throw a ball."

"Yeah, well, I'm not sporty like you. I hate sports. Sometimes I just don't want to be reminded how uncoordinated I am—"

"You aren't uncoordinated. Gimme a break," he interrupted.

"Let me finish! Sometimes I don't participate in gym, but it's a pretty big leap to get from gym slacker to drug addict. Don't you think you maybe missed a few steps there?"

"Then explain it to me. Do it in small words so I understand," he said, his eyes wild. "Because you're not telling me the truth, and we both know it."

She stared at him for a long moment, anger and hurt churning her stomach. How could he of all people accuse her of keeping secrets when he had the biggest one of all? But she couldn't say that out loud, could she? Because he was the adult, and she was his daughter, he had to be right. She had to be wrong. It didn't matter that his lies were much bigger than hers. He'd robbed her of her mom. Of knowing where she came from.

Just like that, she was done.

"I learned it from you," she said. "After all, you're the expert in keeping secrets, aren't you? You kept my mom from me for all these years. Oh, sure, you gave me a couple of pictures, and you told me she left, but that's it, and I'm supposed to be content with that? And you have the nerve, the absolute gall, to sit here and lecture me about being forthcoming? Don't make me laugh, Dad."

He stared at her for a shocked moment, his eyes wide.

"That's not fair," he finally forced out.

She couldn't stop. Deep down inside, she knew she needed to, but the dam had broken, and all her feelings spilled out. All the frustration. All the fear. She couldn't hold it back anymore.

"You know what the worst part is?" she said, staring him down. "At my worst moments, I'm convinced that you're not telling me what happened because it's all my fault that she left. That she hated me. Because otherwise, why wouldn't you tell me what happened? For all I know, you resent me for it, and that's why you're so... so..."

"Say it," he said, his voice bleak. "Go ahead and say it."

But she couldn't. One look at his bloodless face made her shut her mouth. For one long, tense moment, they stared at each other. She wondered what he was thinking. Did he hate her for lashing out at him? If so, did he have a right to?

Her pulse thundered in her ears.

“I think we’re done here,” he said, taking in a shaky breath.

“Done?” she demanded. “That can’t be it! At some point, I deserve to know!”

He held out both hands, his fingers trembling. He looked like a man standing on the edge of a steep precipice. A man at the end of his rope.

“Not now,” he said. “Just... stay home tonight. No more sneaking out. No more...” He winced. “Just no more. I can’t take it anymore.”

“Dad,” she said, all the heat leaking out of her. “Look, we can...”

But she didn’t get to finish her suggestion. He turned his back on her and marched into his room, slamming the door behind him. She sat there for a long time, but he didn’t come back out again.

CHAPTER 21

AFTER HER DAD LEFT FOR WORK WITHOUT HIS USUAL goodbyes, Leigh invited Ari over. They sat down on the sagging couch, and she explained everything that had happened. The longer she talked, the more somber Ari became.

"I know you and your dad aren't exactly tight, but that sucks," he said. "And he didn't say anything to you on the way out?"

"Not a word. Maybe I was right. Maybe he really does hate me."

"No way. He sounds scared, what with all the drug questions."

"What did he say when he came over to your place?"

"Nothing much, I don't think. I didn't even see him. Martin answered the door, told him you weren't there, and slammed it in his face. In his defense, it was midnight, and Martin's working mornings, but still. Typical Martin."

Ari's oldest half brother had never been the communicative type. Leigh could count the number of times she'd heard him speak on one hand and still have fingers left over.

"And typical Dad," she said. "He's allowed to keep me in the dark for years, but I've got to tell him everything. It's so hypocritical."

"I never understood why he wouldn't tell you anything in the first place. Like, I get that the man has trauma, but he couldn't communicate his way out of a paper bag."

"My grandpa was like that too, though. When he got pissed, he'd just clam up. You haven't lived until you've seen a grown man giving everyone the silent treatment."

"Boomers, man," said Ari, rolling his eyes. "You think therapy would—what's that?"

She followed his pointing finger to an envelope propped up against a box of macky cheese next to the stove. In her dad's chicken-scratch handwriting, it said *Leigh*.

He'd left her a letter. A wave of dread ran over her, the hair on her arms prickling. He scribbled the occasional Post-it reminder and left it on the fridge, but he had never written her a letter before. It felt significant. Terrifying. Final.

She was afraid to feel. Afraid to think. She kept her mind carefully blank as she picked up the envelope and ripped it open. Inside, she found a single sheet of notebook paper half full with his handwriting. She flipped it open and devoured it, her hands shaking.

> LEIGH,
>
> I'M SORRY. I KNOW YOU'RE RIGHT. KEEPING YOU IN THE DARK ISN'T FAIR. I TOLD MYSELF I WAS DOING IT TO PROTECT YOU, BUT THAT'S ONLY HALF TRUE. I'VE BEEN PROTECTING MYSELF TOO. I'M . . .

Here, there were a series of thick ink blotches where he'd scribbled out a few words. Try as she might, she couldn't make them out.

> I DON'T KNOW WHAT TO SAY, SO I DON'T SAY ANYTHING, AND I'M SORRY FOR THAT.

SOMETIMES YOU REMIND ME OF HER. NOT IN A BAD WAY, NOT AT FIRST. IT'S IN THE WAY THAT YOU CURL A LOCK OF HAIR AROUND YOUR FINGER WHEN YOU'RE THINKING, OR SNORT WHEN YOU LAUGH REALLY HARD. SHE WAS SO CREATIVE, SO DRIVEN, AND I SEE THAT IN YOUR COSPLAYS. BUT LATELY, YOU REMIND ME OF HOW SHE WAS RIGHT BEFORE SHE LEFT. DISAPPEARING WITHOUT EXPLANATION. DISTRACTED. DIFFERENT. THE TIGHTER I HOLD ON, THE MORE YOU SLIP AWAY. IT SCARES ME. THAT'S WHY I LOST MY COOL. I'M SORRY.

I DON'T WANT TO LOSE YOU TOO. I HATE THIS.
I LOVE YOU.

DAD

Leigh sat back, her throat tight with guilt. She should have been thrilled at the mention of her mom, but somehow, that didn't matter so much to her right now. Her mom was a stranger, a myth, a dream. A woman in a painting. Maybe even a villain. Her dad had been the exact opposite. A constant, until he wasn't. She'd never realized he missed their closeness as much as she did.

Reverentially, she folded the letter and slipped it back into the envelope. Her eyes prickled with a jumble of emotions she couldn't even begin to untangle. Maybe she didn't always agree with her dad. Maybe he didn't get her. Maybe he should have told her about her mom. But for all his faults, he loved her. She couldn't deny that. Wasn't that enough?

"Well?" prompted Ari.

He was practically vibrating with impatient curiosity.

"He's sorry. It's..." She broke off, her throat tight. "Maybe I've been too hard on him."

“Oh.” He took in her expression. She wondered what he read there. Maybe it would tell her how to feel about this. “Do you need a hug?”

“I’ll kick you in the shin if you come anywhere near me right now. No offense. I’m just trying to hold it together.”

“I gotchu. What now? Nachos?”

She snorted and considered the question. Her dad’s letter had solidified one thing for her—he deserved answers as much as she did. They’d waited long enough. It was time to go to Tangleland, and she had an idea that might just tilt the scales in their direction. Her dad’s bragging about her cosplays had provided the final piece. They said she was an artificer. It was time to see what she could do.

“Help me build a new cosplay,” she said.

“Now?!” he asked, his confusion clear.

“My props do things over there. The staff. The mirror. My dad and I deserve some answers. Let’s make something that will help us get through all those snagfires.”

“You have my axe, my bow, and my heat gun,” he replied.

That night, Leigh arrived to her scheduled meeting with Brandish and the maidens in the castle drawing room and nearly got punched in the face. She wrenched her mask off just in time to avoid getting socked by Fairhair, who was howling in fear and fury at the prospect of another snagfire attack. The maiden pulled up short, her fist still cocked back, disappointment and confusion mingling for dominance on her face. But as she took in Leigh’s getup, both vanished and her jaw dropped open. Behind her, Curlycrown kept on screaming.

"You look so real!" she exclaimed. "It's okay, Curlycrown. It's just Lady Leigh."

Curlycrown broke off midshriek, gasping for air. Fairhair patted her on the shoulder before turning apologetically back to Leigh.

"I nearly hit you! I'm so sorry!" she said.

"I can tell you've been practicing with the bag," replied Leigh. "Sorry I frightened you. I should have taken the mask off. Be honest. Does it look real?"

She put the head to her snagfire cosplay back on and crouched, clicking her beak hungrily. A black gauze covering hid her face from view in the depths of the mouth. Her claws scratched the ground. The costume moved differently in Lady Locks Kingdom. Back in the real world, the mask had sat lightly on her head, wiggling slightly as she moved. The body insulated her from the outside world, cocooning her in foam. But now, they felt like her claws. Her beak. Her hunched body and loping stride. Once again, the magic had taken her creation and made it real.

"It sure does," said Curlycrown, tremulous. "You're terrifying."

Brandish entered the drawing room, fiddling with one of the overstuffed pouches that hung from his belts and straps. He stopped short before giving her an appreciative grin that made her stomach flip-flop a little.

"Leigh," he said. "You look different. New hairstyle?"

"Ha ha. I'm glad you're here. New plan. We're going to pull a *Star Wars,*" she said, taking the mask off again so she could breathe.

"What's that?" asked Fairhair, leaning forward eagerly.

"You're my prisoners. I'll be territorial over you. Protect you from the other snagfires. I've been watching them with my Looking Room when I have a free minute; they respond to aggressive displays.

I should be able to keep most of them off us on the way there since we haven't been able to find a way to sneak around them."

"And what happens on the way back?" asked Curlycrown.

Leigh couldn't help but notice the red blotches in the middle of Curlycrown's pale cheeks and the way she kept wringing the fabric of her dress in her hands, her sweaty palms leaving damp streaks in their wake. She seemed an inch away from bolting upstairs and hiding under her bed, but she'd shown up anyway. Leigh had to respect that. She wished she had a more reassuring response, but she had to be honest. They deserved to make their own decisions rather than being tricked into something dangerous.

"That all depends on whether or not we avoid Ravenwaves, I think," she said.

"I'll handle the retreat," said Brandish. He didn't swagger up to them exactly, but his obvious confidence made Curlycrown straighten up a little, patting her hair into place. Leigh wasn't affected by him, though. No, that lurch in her stomach had to be nerves. "You get us in, Leigh. I'll make sure no one sees us on the way out. You have my word."

"Thank you, Brandish!" Curlycrown clung to his arm, giving serious damsel-in-distress vibes. "I don't know what we'd do without you."

Brandish patted her hand before gently pushing her away. Then he winked at Leigh. She looked away, flustered.

"Curlycrown and I have been talking," said Fairhair. "We think the dungeon is the best place to check, since you searched the main tower already. It's concealed behind a secret door, which makes it the perfect hiding spot. If you get us inside, we can get you there."

"Perfect," said Leigh. "You get us in. Brandish and I will do the rest, just like we planned. Everyone remembers their jobs, right?"

"Yes! Let's do this!" exclaimed Fairhair, clenching a fist and pumping it in the air.

"I feel sick," moaned Curlycrown.

Her eyelids fluttered in what looked like actual distress this time. She needed some sort of distraction before she gave herself a panic attack.

"Curlycrown, could you help me with my hair?" asked Leigh, as casually as she could. "I've got it tied up, but I don't want it to fall out the back of my costume and give me away."

The maiden jerked to attention, perking up at the prospect.

"Of course," she said, pulling a hairbrush from who knew where. "I can plait it up for you and tuck the excess down your back."

"I'd appreciate it."

The two of them stepped off to one side while Fairhair and Brandish chatted quietly. Curlycrown got to work, her fingers deftly sectioning Leigh's long tresses and twisting them into some elaborate arrangement that Leigh could only hope would fit inside the helmet. But the request had been a smart one. The longer she worked, the more Curlycrown's obvious agitation ebbed away. She even began to hum as she worked.

"Curlycrown?" asked Leigh. "Are you sure you want to do this?"

Curlycrown sighed.

"I know it's the right choice," she said. "But I'm not brave like you are. You're not scared of anything."

"Are you kidding? I'm afraid of *everything*. For years, I wanted to know about my mom. I told myself I asked my dad; I told myself I did everything I could to find out... but I didn't. He cares about me. I think he would have told me if I'd really pushed. But I was too scared. I'd rather face snagfires than hurt him," said Leigh.

“You love him,” said Curlycrown. “There’s nothing wrong with that. But...”

She trailed off, although her fingers kept on moving, binding Leigh’s hair to her head with some sort of hair wizardry.

“But what?” prompted Leigh.

“I guess I understand. Fairhair wants to travel, but the idea of waking up and not seeing her is worse than the idea of getting eaten by a snagfire. She’s always been here. I don’t know how to be without her.”

“You could go with her?”

“I belong here. And I can’t hold her back.” Curlycrown tied off the long braid and tucked it into the back of the snagfire suit. “I’m not as brave as you two are, but I’ll help. She deserves to have her dream.”

Leigh didn’t know what to say to that. She certainly hadn’t expected such thoughtfulness from a girl she would have brushed off as superficial and airheaded just a short time ago. For the first time, she could see Curlycrown as a friend. That first day she’d come here, she wouldn’t have believed that she could care so much about such a ridiculous place, or its ridiculous people. But in a weird way, this felt like home too. She only hoped she wasn’t about to screw it all up.

“You’re a good person, Curlycrown,” she said.

Curlycrown’s cheeks pinked, and she launched herself at Leigh, surprising her with a hug.

“Out of all the princesses we’ve had, I think I like you the best,” she whispered. “Now let’s do this.”

They released each other, beaming. Leigh put her helmet back on and summoned her best coughing roar. Curlycrown let out a little breathless squeal.

“Let’s do this,” echoed Leigh.

Chapter 22

The small group of adventurers set off for Tangleland. Leigh had expected the trek to suck, since foam bodysuits aren't exactly made for hiking. But either her artificer skills had resulted in an exceptionally comfortable cosplay or all her fairy-tale exploits had given her some stamina, because she bounded over the increasingly rough terrain. She'd scamper ahead and perch on a rock or a log, opening up her beak to scent the air and breathe a little while the others caught up, and then repeat the whole thing over again.

Gentle, sloping hills carpeted in soft grass gave way to loose dirt and sparse vegetation. The ground became jagged, the path weaving through narrow gaps etched between rock formations. As they moved farther into Tangleland, the twisted branches of empty trees reached toward the sky, and on the rare occasions when they encountered live vegetation, the huddled forest looked less like inviting wilderness and more like the kind of place that fairy-tale characters went to get eaten by witches living in sticky candy houses.

The maidens had kept up a steady stream of excited—or maybe nervous—chatter as they'd left the castle, but as the landscape had grown increasingly bleaker, their babble had faded into a silence that made no secret of its nervous origins. Brandish kept making soft jokes, his tone light and carefree, but his eyes never stopped their roaming, and his hands didn't stray too far from his pouches. Leigh wondered what he carried in there. Spell components? Potions? Love letters from his many admirers? Whatever it was, he seemed to draw some comfort from it.

A sharp stink came wafting into her mask, and she sniffed hard, trying to figure out what was making such an awful stench. Possibly snagfires, or maybe that foul greenish pond off to the right with all the sickly bubbles floating on top. Hard to tell. She dashed around another pile of rocks to get upwind of the pond and try again, but the smell had faded. Still, she remained on high alert, her nerves jangling.

The rapid crunch of footfalls announced the approach of one of her companions, running full out. Had one of the snagfires circled around to flank them? Was it chasing them even now? Leigh tensed, snapping her jaw shut and readying herself to pounce. Brandish rounded the corner, his shoulders tense with strain, which quickly evaporated as soon as he saw her.

"Don't disappear like that!" he exclaimed. "You nearly gave me a heart attack."

"Sorry. I thought..." She shook her head. "Never mind. I think I'm getting a bit too into character."

"If you start breathing fire, that's where I draw the line," he said, offering her a hand down.

She couldn't feel his hand through the thick gloves of her cosplay, but the touch still sent a shiver through her. Damn it. Maybe she'd written off the possibility of a relationship too soon, because ignoring her feelings wasn't helping. Brandish was smart and charming and funny, and it seemed like he genuinely liked her; why shouldn't she at least give him a chance?

She let him help her down. This time, she didn't blush as she had every time they'd made even the most accidental of contact. She was done fighting her feelings. Brandish leaned down toward her, examining the mask more closely. If the beak hadn't been in the way—if she'd worked up the courage—they could have kissed.

"You really made this?" he asked, tilting his head to look at the seam between the chitinous plastiformed beak and the rest of her cowl. "It's a work of art."

"Thanks," she said. "I hope the eyes glow enough to be convincing."

"Definitely..."

He leaned closer. Too close for friends. All of a sudden, the mask was stifling. She couldn't get enough air, so she wrenched open the jaws and clawed aside the fabric that covered her face.

He was right there. His gaze was locked on the hooked tip of her beak, and he reached up to touch it with the tip of one of his long, delicate fingers. His eyes flicked down to hers, and the corner of his mouth quirked up into that damn smile that made her knees go wobbly. Her instincts screamed at her to back away, a wave of nervousness running over her, but now she understood it. In some ways, she was just like her dad. She pushed things away out of fear.

She was done pushing him away.

Brandish's hand dropped from the tip of the beak to the edge of her jawline. He ran a thumb soft over her skin, tilting her head up. She could feel his breath as he inched closer, his lips hovering over hers. Duty and longing warred for dominance inside her. At any moment, the maidens were going to turn the corner, and Curlycrown had been flirting with him pretty hard. Leigh didn't want to make things awkward. The aftermath wouldn't be good; she needed to pull away.

But she didn't. She couldn't.

A scream split the silence, and she instinctively squeezed her eyes shut, not wanting to see the expression of betrayal on Curlycrown's face. Brandish released her, the tension between them evaporating like smoke in the wind.

"Come on!" he snapped, shaking her shoulders. "What are you doing?"

Her eyes flew open again. The maidens were nowhere in sight. Curlycrown hadn't shouted about the almost-kiss. Her initial sense of relief was quickly dampened by the realization that something else must be dreadfully wrong. She yanked her face covering up and snapped the beak shut. This was her fault. The maidens had been passive victims all their lives; they shouldn't have been left alone out here while she played kissy-face with Brandish. She could only hope that she wasn't too late to avoid tragedy.

Without a word, she bounded back around the rocks. The maidens had flattened themselves against the sheer wall. An entire pack of snagfires encircled them, hulking forms spitting out breaths of eager fire. One lay prone on the ground, and based on Fairhair's fierce expression, her lifted fists, and the birdlike Pixietails hovering over her shoulders, she'd used her magical strength to knock one of them out. In stark contrast to her fierce friend, Curlycrown appeared to be having a panic attack. Her chest heaved as she hyperventilated, panicked eyes darting around as she searched desperately for escape. Leigh needed to intervene before the whole plan went up in smoke.

Showtime.

She leaped into the gap between the maidens and their kangorilla attackers, turning to face the enormous beasts. One of them coughed out a challenge, its aggressive stance familiar from her time spent watching them in the Looking Room. Time to assert her dominance. She rose up on her hind legs, tossing her tangled mane, snorting and coughing in response. Her hind claws scraped the dirt. A few of the beasts edged back, their shoulders dropping as they acknowledged her superiority. But the aggressive one coughed again, digging its feet in. Okay then. Game on. She pulled out all the stops, beating her chest and shuffling her feet, huffing with all her might and hoping that none of them noticed that no steam erupted from the tiny holes set into the sides of her beak.

Snagfire dominance postures were ridiculous, but this would work only if she committed, so she gave it her all. Early on in her cosplay career, she'd noticed that good performances often elevated her final ranking. The first time she'd done Princess Bubblegum, her scores had been only so-so. But she'd returned in the same cosplay for another contest and placed third only a month later, and she honestly thought her performance had made all the difference. That second time, she'd worked on choreography, but more importantly, she'd really committed to *being* Princess Bubblegum. Her belief had allowed everyone else to believe it too. There was no room for doubt, no way to keep from looking a little stupid. Either she was a snagfire... or she wasn't.

It worked. The snagfires retreated before her furious display, and one after another put their beaks to the ground in a show of subjugation. Finally, there was only one left, the one who had challenged her in the first place. She charged at it, and finally it, too, bowed down before her.

She whipped her head around to stare at her friends. Brandish had joined the maidens, and they clung to his arms, squealing in fright. They'd remembered their cue. Even Fairhair appeared like nothing more than a frightened young woman once again, her earlier bravado evaporating like so much smoke. Leigh hopped closer, snuffling at his hair and claiming him as hers. Brandish flinched. His acting skills were impressive, understated. The aggressive snagfire let out a sad, disappointed little cough, and just like that, she knew she'd won. None of the snagfires were willing to fight her to get to her prisoners.

She nudged them down the path. Curlycrown cried outright as they stumbled along, big fat tears streaming down her face. Leigh wasn't sure if the maiden was acting. If so, she had a real future as the star of Lovely Locks Kingdom's first teen drama. As she cowered, Brandish hugged her close. Leigh's attention kept snagging on the sight of his arm around her shoulders. It was ridiculous to be jealous—he was acting—but she couldn't help it. In a desperate effort to ignore her jumbled feelings, she nudged her attention toward the tower in the distance, silhouetted against the red embers of the Tangleland sky. That was her goal. Everything else could wait until she got the painting and returned their entire group to safety.

As they crept toward the tower, more and more snagfires joined them. Leigh had to confront a few, frightening off new challengers eager to claim her captives. But she was feeling pretty good about it all until the most enormous snagfire she'd ever seen blocked the entrance to the bridge, coughing out a warning. She gulped as it towered above her, so huge that it would have had to hunch down to get through the tall castle doors. Its tangled ruff had grown so long that the ends dragged on the ground, and a deep gouge had been ripped into the side of its beak as if a single long claw had torn a furrow into the chitin. Leigh didn't want to contemplate what kind of beast could do such damage to this monster. No way was she going to scare this thing off, but fighting it was even less palatable. It would dangle her upside down by her feet.

She launched into her dance of dominance, trying to ignore the sinking feeling in the pit of her stomach. It watched her quietly, without any attempts to counter with moves of its own. She finally stopped, clicking her beak one final time, and tried not to gasp for air. She couldn't afford to show an ounce of vulnerability. They'd all die.

It let out a strange, soft hoot. Almost a coo. Then it did it again, leaning down to lock her gaze with its burning red eyes. All the other snagfires popped off, hooting and screeching in a way that made Curlycrown hysterical again. The huge, scarred snagfire—Scar, she'd call him—preened a little, but he didn't make a move toward them. Leigh took a cautious hop toward her prisoners, and Scar simply watched her.

Okay then. She nudged her friends down the path with her beak, the back of her neck prickling as Scar fell into step behind her. She could feel the heat of his breath on the back of her head. As they reached the doorway, the other snagfires peeled off, hunching low to the ground as if afraid to go inside. Perfect.

There was just one problem—Scar didn't join them. His eyes darted around as he hesitated at the archway, but he followed them into the courtyard. Leigh watched him cautiously, trying to figure out what his deal was. He hopped closer to her, pressing his bulk against the foam of her costume. Then his enormous head dipped down toward her, rubbing against her tangled mane. He cooed again.

"I think it likes her," said Curlycrown, hiccupping, the waterworks over for the moment.

Leigh's stomach dropped to her toes. She had to agree, unfortunately. Maybe she'd designed a particularly hot snagfire. Or perhaps the garbage she'd rolled the foam in to disguise the scent smelled a bit too much like snagfire pheromones. It didn't matter; Scar's lovesick interest couldn't have been clearer. Somehow, this nonverbal creature's flirting was easier to read than Brandish had ever been. He was still cuddling Curlycrown. She'd thought the *Twilight* love triangle was bad, but this put it to shame.

She thought back through everything she'd seen and learned about the snagfires, but she didn't recall any obvious mating rituals. She'd have to wing this. No big deal. She just had to find a way to let an enormous fire-breathing kangorilla down gently.

Scar proceeded to perform what she could describe only as a chicken dance of love. He strutted back and forth, darting his beak here and there. As the ridiculous performance progressed, he began to huff little gouts of flame into the air to punctuate each step. He moved with the swagger of a snagfire who knows he's a total pimp.

Leigh hated this sort of thing. Sometimes guys like Scar showed up at contests in skimpy cosplays, expecting everyone to fawn all over them while they posed. At Steel City Con, a Sexy Mario in blue-overall short shorts, a bare chest, and an overgrown mustache had spilled a coffee all over her hand-sewn *Steven Universe* Rose Quartz outfit and then tried to flirt his way out of paying for the damage. The memory alone made her want to scream.

Scar was just another Sexy Mario who thought she was a push-over. He was about to learn the error of his ways.

She bodychecked him, putting all her weight into it. Her shoulder crunched against Scar's bulk; it was like trying to mosh with a mountain. Scar looked down at her and trilled like she'd just done something thrilling.

"Aw—"

She choked off the rest of the annoyed exclamation before it could give her away. Last thing she needed was for Scar to realize she wasn't a cute little snagfire after all. He'd probably barbecue her. But she didn't know what else to do. Try as she might, she couldn't get rid of him. She backed away slowly. Maybe it was time to accept failure and move on.

He watched her with avid devotion, clicking his beak all slow and inviting-like. But as long as she didn't move too fast, he let her go. With slow caution, she crossed the dim antechamber to the maidens. Scar followed close on her heels.

The maidens cowered as they approached. Brandish glowered at them, his hand tightening on Curlycrown's shoulder. She couldn't speak without giving away her disguise, so she cough-barked at them, hoping they'd get the hint. In a daze, Brandish shook Curlycrown on the shoulder.

"Open the door," he muttered.

Fairhair was one step ahead of them. She moved to one of the blank walls, unremarkable from the surrounding dull stone. Her fingers trailed over the stones, pressing them seemingly at random. What if she couldn't find the right combination? Leigh's stomach dropped as she considered the possibility that after all this work, she still might return home empty-handed. She wasn't sure she'd be able to accept failure. Not this time. Her dad needed this, and so did she.

But she'd worried in vain. Fairhair pressed one final brick, eliciting a loud click from some unseen mechanism buried somewhere inside the walls. A section of brick swung soundlessly out, releasing a waft of dank, stale air. Inside, Leigh could see a narrow wooden passage with a set of rough-hewn stairs leading downward into dim, flickering light.

Brandish released Curlycrown and edged forward, his eyes glued to Scar. The enormous snagfire remained docile, his attention glued to Leigh. She let out a snagfire cough, just to keep up the ruse, jerking her beak toward the stairs.

"Right," murmured Brandish. "Follow the plan. Guard the door. We'll be back."

"Don't worry about us," said Fairhair quietly.

That was easier said than done. Curlycrown could barely stand for all her trembling, but Leigh couldn't give her another pep talk with Scar glued to her side. She would just have to trust that Fairhair had everything under control. With her Pixietails and that narrow doorway, she should be able to hold off any attackers, and so far, Ravenwaves hadn't shown her face. Maybe they would luck out and find the painting without so much as seeing the duchess.

Right, and pigs fly.

But they were committed now. Leigh nudged Brandish onto the stairs with her beak, Scar following close behind. His attention was so locked on her that he seemed to have forgotten about the maidens altogether. Good.

The staircase was almost claustrophobically tight, and for a moment, Leigh wondered if Scar would be able to fit. But the snagfire crammed his bulk into the small space like a cork in a bottle, his shoulders brushing the walls and the top of his head skimming the ceiling. She had to give him props for determination, but she wasn't about to show it. He didn't need any encouragement.

They descended the stairs unscathed, and with every step, she grew more confident. The stairway opened into a wide chamber of wood and stone, segmented by a row of iron bars. On one side sat a heavy desk, its surface covered in a thick layer of dust. Beyond the locked door sat a sizable windowless cell, empty save a pair of thin straw mattresses on the floor, a broken bucket sitting on its side, and a rat scurrying through the thick shadows at the back of the room. Leigh examined the space with dawning horror. Was this where Ravenwaves kept the maidens when she took them? She couldn't contemplate spending a night here, let alone multiple in a row.

Based on all the dust, it didn't look like anyone had been here for a while. She didn't know where Ravenwaves had gone off to and honestly didn't care as long as it wasn't here. She crept farther into the room, Scar at her heels like an overgrown fire-breathing puppy. With every passing moment, she became more used to his presence.

"I'll search the desk," said Brandish.

He leaned over to look beneath the desk and pull open the drawers. Leigh tried the cell door and found it locked. The bars were fastidiously clean and free of dust. Someone had been in here recently, and why would the cell be locked if it was empty? Was Ravenwaves trying to hold rats prisoner now?

The painting was in there. Leigh was sure of it. She almost said so aloud before remembering she was in character. She hooted to get Brandish's attention and tapped her beak on the lock.

He jerked upright, hitting his head on the bottom of the desk. Clapping a hand to it, he edged around Scar to join her at the cell door. She tapped her beak on it again, rolling her eyes in exasperation. This whole no-talking thing was really getting to her.

“I’ll pick it,” said Brandish, the corner of his mouth twitching as he rolled his eyes in response.

Scar huffed his stinky fish breath all over the side of her face while Brandish worked on the lock. The smell infiltrated her mask, marinating her nose. She couldn’t wait to get her hands on that painting and get out of this thing.

This lock must have been more complicated than the last one, because it took Brandish a few minutes of muttering and twisting his lockpicks before the door clicked and sprang open. He bowed with a flourish that bothered Scar for some reason. The snagfire barked and snapped, and Brandish straightened, his face gone pale. Leigh thwacked Scar on the arm, drawing his attention away again before things got out of hand.

She needed to find that painting.

Brandish picked up the first mattress, sending another rat scurrying for cover. Scar pounced on it before it could make its escape, shoving the rodent into his mouth and chowing down with a loud crunch. Gross. Leigh tried to block out the chewing noises as best she could and kicked over the other mattress.

The painting sat on the floor beneath it.

Finally.

She paced closer, hunkering down on her haunches to get a better look at it. After all this effort, she was going to be really pissed if it wasn’t her mom. But it really looked like her. The eyes, the shape of the head, the birthmark... they all lined up.

Then her pulse literally stuttered. Grasped in one hand, the woman held a sheet of paper that said *Leigh*. She hadn’t noticed it last time; the paper wasn’t very big, the writing tough to make out.

That was definitely her name. But how? This was the clue she'd been waiting for her entire life. Excitement thrummed through her, and she barely restrained herself from crowing aloud.

She jerked her beak at the painting, and Brandish knelt by its side. Moving with the rapid assurance of experience, he reached into one of his pouches and produced a small screwdriver, loosening the hardware from the back of the frame. Within moments, he cut the canvas from its moorings, rolling it up neatly and securing it to his belt.

Triumph swelling in her veins, she turned to leave. Ravenwaves blocked the exit, those stupid scissors clutched in one hand. The duchess grinned as she took them in.

"Funny thing about hidden doors," she said. "Sometimes there's more than one of them."

Leigh barked, trying desperately to sell her character. If Ravenwaves didn't see through her disguise, she might just lock Brandish up. He could pick the lock as soon as she left, easy peasy.

He must have come to the same conclusion, because he stepped forward, hiding Leigh partially from view. He struck a casual pose, looking Ravenwaves up and down.

"I don't think we've met," he said. "I'm Brandish the Distractor. If I'd known an angel lived here, I would have introduced myself properly."

"Oh, don't even try charming me," said Ravenwaves. "I'm not that gullible. I'm not stupid either. I know you're in there, Princess, and it's about time that I got that lock of hair I've been asking for."

Leigh's veins ran cold. This was not in the plan. She, Brandish, and Scar could take care of Ravenwaves, but she worried about the maidens. And if Ravenwaves sounded the alarm and summoned all the snagfires, all bets were off. She wasn't sure where Scar's loyalty would fall if he was forced to choose.

"Hello?" Ravenwaves clicked her scissors, taking a step forward. "Quit playing stupid."

Leigh shot a reluctant glance at Scar. She had to reply, but how would the enormous snagfire take it when she suddenly began to speak?

"Just let us leave," she said, keeping her beak closed so Scar couldn't see her face. "And we won't hurt you."

Ravenwaves snorted. Scar didn't move. He hunched there, letting out little gouts of smoke with every breath. So far, so good.

"All we want is the painting," said Leigh.

"Oh, give me a break. Why are you so obsessed with that dumb painting? If you're thinking that Lady Knot will help you defeat me once and for all, don't bother. She'll turn on you just like she did me."

"Quit insulting my mother," spat Leigh.

Ravenwaves took a step back, her eyes wide with horror and fear.

"That's not funny," she said. "Not funny at all."

Her obvious terror made Leigh hesitate for a moment. But Ravenwaves was a lying liar who lied. The one person in this entire place who was exactly what she seemed.

"I'm not joking," said Leigh.

"In that case, I can't possibly let you leave," said Ravenwaves. "Hairball! Attack!"

Scar lifted his head, glaring at Ravenwaves with baleful red eyes.

"What are you doing, you imbecile! I'm your master, remember? Attack!" screeched Ravenwaves, gesticulating with her scissors.

The snagfire still didn't move, and Ravenwaves marched over, prodding at him with the scissors. As she drew closer, he let out one of his warning coughs. Leigh got the message loud and clear—he wasn't going to put up with this—but Ravenwaves wasn't paying attention. She was too busy complaining about how no one listened to her and it was difficult to get good help these days.

She stabbed the scissors at Scar—Hairball—again and snipped off a lock of his shaggy mane. The chunk of matted hair plopped to the ground. Hairball stared down at it, snarling and clicking his beak. Then he threw his head back and roared.

Leigh had seen the snagfires huff out little bursts of fire before, but they were more like lighters than flamethrowers. But not Hairball. He breathed out a great gout of flame that engulfed the ceiling and billowed through the air. The sheer heat of it drove Leigh back a step. When he clamped his mouth shut, the heavy wooden beams that held up the ceiling still crackled with flame.

The wood must have been dry, because the fire spread quickly, running across the ceiling and dropping burning motes onto the floor as they all tried to cover their heads. A few motes fell onto the dusty desk and went up with a *whoomph.* Ravenwaves let out a cry of alarm, backing away from the flames, and ran into the cell door. She went down like a ton of bricks, striking her head on the bars, and didn't get back up again.

"We've got to get out of here!" exclaimed Brandish, dashing for the stairs. "Come on!"

Hairball seemed to agree. His bulk pushed against Leigh, herding her toward the door. One of the mattresses caught aflame, the dry straw going up in sparks. The ceiling rained glowing embers onto their heads, and she could smell the foam of her costume burning. If it disintegrated into ash, Hairball would realize she'd tricked him.

She allowed him to herd her toward the door as the fire spread, howling. Every breath burned her lungs, and for the first time since she'd gotten here, she felt the mask pressing in on her, the plastic beak growing hot against her skin. If she didn't get out of here, she might die.

Brandish yelled in inarticulate fear, gesturing toward the stairs. She moved toward them like a sleepwalker. Above her, the fire crackled and popped. Something fell off the ceiling, emitting a shower of sparks. She yelped as they sprayed her back; Hairball hissed, shielding her with his bulk as best as he could. She cowered against him, thankful for his protection despite the awful stench of his fur. They reached the door; the hallway burned now too, the fire spreading across the ceiling and beginning to creep down the walls. Would Hairball even fit? He'd annoyed the crap out of her, but she refused to abandon him down here.

Wait. She couldn't leave Ravenwaves either. Yes, the duchess would shave Leigh's head bald and not care one bit that she'd never be able to go home. But if Leigh let her burn, she'd be just as bad.

Swearing beneath her breath, she tore free, flinging herself back into the burning room. The air scorched her throat as she huddled toward the floor, where it was marginally cooler. The ceiling above had turned into a blinding inferno. She could see Ravenwaves, still motionless on the ground. She sprinted to the rescue, dodging burning debris. The ceiling groaned. From the sounds of it, it would give way at any moment. She grabbed an arm and began to drag the duchess toward the door, grunting and heaving with all her might.

The inferno pounded at her face; tears streamed from her eyes. A dark shape rushed at her just as something above her cracked.

Hairball leaped out of the smoke. Her cosplay must have burned clear away, and here he was to finish her off. He hit her like a freight train, knocking her backward. A moment later, a mountain of burning debris fell right where she'd been standing, burying him. Stunned, she waited for the giant beast to heave himself free, but burning wood and stone kept raining down, creating an enormous pile.

But still, she stared. She hoped. And nothing moved.

Dazed with shock and a lack of oxygen, she sprawled on the floor, the arm of her costume igniting as the fire continued to spread. Then Brandish was there, patting out the flames with frantic movements. He hauled her to her feet, and she stared for one blank moment at the dark outline of Hairball's claw-tipped hand sticking out from beneath the pile of rubble. She couldn't leave him there. He'd sacrificed himself to save her. Then one of the ceiling timbers ripped free, falling onto the pile. The entire roof began to tear itself to pieces on top of their heads; there was no time.

Crying in grief and terror, she scrambled for the door. Brandish had managed to lift Ravenwaves in an awkward fireman's carry, following her.

As they escaped into the stairway, the ceiling collapsed in.

CHAPTER 23

LEIGH FOLLOWED BRANDISH AS HE CARRIED RAVEN-waves out of her burning tower, coughing and staggering. The tall stairway had begun to fill with choking smoke, and the walls burned steadier now. It was only a matter of time before the whole building came down, leaving only an empty husk. They couldn't afford to be inside when that happened.

Brandish staggered beneath the duchess's weight, nearly toppling down the stairs as he gasped for air. Eyes watering, Leigh tore off the hot mask and threw it to the ground, preparing to help share the load. Then her Pixietails hovered up next to her. She hadn't even called them, but it was past time to accept their help.

"Pixie Beauty, get Ravenwaves outside," she croaked. "You two others stay with me."

For once, they didn't stop to fuss or argue. Pixie Beauty streaked away, the purple sparkles of its magic barely visible against the red glow of the flames. Ravenwaves lifted off Brandish's shoulders, floating gently up toward the door. Brandish choked out a thank-you, offering his hand. Leigh took it, pieces of her costume flaking off as she moved, the foam disintegrating beneath the intense heat to reveal her Lady Lovely Locks getup underneath. They helped each other up the stairs, each supporting the other's faltering steps.

When they reached the top, they found the door wide open and the maidens nowhere in sight. Hopefully, they'd found somewhere safe to wait outside. Once she caught her breath, Leigh would find them. In the courtyard, they paused, gulping up the cool, sweet air. Ravenwaves still hovered in the air, motionless. Between coughing jags, Leigh checked to make sure the girl still breathed. She was surprised at how relieved she was to confirm that Ravenwaves was only unconscious and not dead.

"Leave her alone!" shouted Curlycrown from outside the tower. "Stop!"

Leigh jerked to attention, her eyes still watering. Brandish caught her by the wrist as she made her way toward the noise, pulling her close and whispering in her ear.

"I'll hide in the shadows just in case we need my illusions," he said. "If it goes sideways, I'll make you all disappear. Meet up at the rendezvous point."

She nodded, her heart racing once more.

Out on the bridge, Fairhair and Curlycrown had been captured by a mass of hungry snagfires. Fairhair had fought hard. A few limp beasts littered the ground around her, but there had been too many of them. Now she'd been knocked over, and a snagfire crouched on her chest, its beak snapping shut just short of her skin. One of her eyes had swollen shut, but she still fought back. A short distance away, Curlycrown struggled against the restraining grips of two snagfires. Tears streaked her face, but she lacked the strength to break free.

Leigh marched toward them, trembling with anger. One of the snagfires charged her, letting out a bark of challenge. She coughed and couldn't stop as the beast grew closer and closer. But at the last moment, she moved. Maybe she'd absorbed more stage combat than she'd realized, or maybe she was just that pissed, but she moved with impeccable instincts, tossing the snagfire up and over in a perfect hip throw. It teetered on the edge of the bridge before toppling into the foamy water far below. Although Leigh couldn't see, she could hear the thrashing as the fish began to feed.

She staggered then, racked by another round of coughing. Her stomach began to heave, desperate to work all that soot out of her system. Two more snagfires closed in on her. She dodged a swinging arm, stepping in for a counter, and then coughed so hard she threw up.

The snagfires didn't seem to care. They grabbed her none too gently, pushing her to the ground. She clung to consciousness with desperate stubbornness. Brandish would save her.

Fairhair shrieked as snagfire claws dug into her soft flesh, but she couldn't dislodge the heavy weight of the beast on her chest. Something about the sight of her struggling friend grabbed Curlycrown's attention, stopping her tears. She screamed at the top of her lungs, chest heaving.

"Leave her alone!" She threw her arms wide, dislodging the surprised snagfires and flinging them to the ground. "Pixie Copper! Pixie Brunet! Pixie White! Take the snagfires down!"

Her voice shaking, the gentle maiden called out to her Pixietails, and they answered. Balls of pure elemental power came whizzing out of her body in all directions—fire, ice, and rock flew through the air like vengeful comets. Although the barrage appeared random at first, each projectile found a target. A ball of fire whumped against one of the snagfires holding Leigh, pushing it over the side of the bridge.

A ball of ice slammed against the beast on Fairhair's chest. Leigh's remaining attacker tried to run for it, but a chunk of rock whacked it in the back of the head, knocking it out cold. Within moments, the entire field had cleared.

At that precise moment, Ravenwaves stirred.

Leigh staggered toward the maidens as Curlycrown helped Fairhair up, and the two hugged each other in desperate relief. They'd survived.

But maybe not for long. They could hear the coughing barks of snagfires in the distance, and Ravenwaves rolled over to one side before sitting up with one hand clapped to her head. She took in the burning tower, her mouth open. Then she whirled on them, teeth bared in fury.

"You took my home from me!" she screeched, fury giving her the strength to launch to her feet. "I'll make you pay for that."

"It was an accident," croaked Leigh, her throat raw from all that coughing.

"An accident! I'll show you an accident! Snagfires, to me! To me!"

The duchess's eyes turned an eerie green, and a chorus of snagfires responded to her. Leigh thought she'd faced a lot of them before, but now it sounded like Ravenwaves had summoned them *all*. Could they stand against an entire army?

"Go ahead and fly away," said Ravenwaves, snarling. "We'll shoot you out of the sky and take your Pixietails by force."

Leigh exchanged nervous glances with the maidens. Fairhair straightened her clothes, visibly gathering herself for another fight. Curlycrown gulped, her nerves asserting themselves again. But she didn't cry. She didn't run.

"I'm so proud of you both," said Leigh, dragging her tired body over to join them. "Whatever happens, I want you to know that."

"Thank you," whispered Curlycrown.

"We're going to be fine," added Fairhair. "I believe in us."

"Fine?" cackled Ravenwaves. "You'll be snagfire chow before the night is through. I won't stop them from eating you this time. Except to cut your hair first, of course."

"Of course." Leigh sighed.

"That's not nice," added Curlycrown, frowning. "Should I . . . ?"

Leigh knew how the question ended. Curlycrown wanted to know if they should fight. But far in the red gloom, she saw undulating masses of snagfires, too many to count. Her cosplay was in shreds. She had no weapon save her Pixietails; her staff hadn't fit beneath the costume. If the fight went poorly, she could teleport out and go back to the real world, pretend that none of this had ever happened. But what fate would she be leaving them to? She couldn't. She wouldn't.

Perhaps it was time to make a deal. Salvage as much as she could from this awful situation. Her reckless insistence on getting her hands on that painting had gotten her friends into this mess; it was her responsibility to get them out of it.

"If I give you my hair, will you let them go?" she said, stepping forward.

"No . . ." moaned Curlycrown.

"Lady Leigh," added Fairhair. "You'll be stuck here. Forever."

Leigh ignored them. This was the right thing to do, the only thing she *could* do. Her hands shook as she thought about what this decision would mean; her throat went dry with panic. She'd never see her dad again. Never hang with Ari. Never graduate from high school or work another full-moon shift at Wing It. Those losses hurt. But it was the right thing to do.

Ravenwaves grinned even wider, her mouth stretching into a self-satisfied curve. She didn't answer for a moment, reveling in her triumph or maybe in Leigh's defeat. It didn't matter.

"I knew you'd see sense," she said. "Haircut first, and then I'll let your friends go."

"No deal. You make one move toward me before they're safely away, and I'll teleport back to the real world. I'll never come back. You'll never get my hair. You want to make a deal? This is my only offer," declared Leigh, her voice trembling only a little.

The silence stretched out, broken only by the tumult of the snagfires as more and more of them arrived, hooting and coughing in the darkness. There were so many that the air filled with their stink. If Ravenwaves ever decided to go to war, it would not go well.

"Oh, fine." Ravenwaves wiggled her hand at the maidens, dismissing them. "Go on, you two. Get out of here. Hurry up before I change my mind."

Curlycrown flung herself into Leigh's arms. Although her mass of hair hid her face from view, the snuffling noises made it clear that she was crying again. Fairhair pulled her away, her expression drawn.

"We can't leave you!" cried Curlycrown, clinging with all her strength.

"Stop it," hissed Leigh, a bit harsh in her desperation not to break down herself. "Pull yourself together. The villagers need you. You know what you need to do. Don't forget what I taught you; you're stronger than you realize."

Her face drawn with sadness, Fairhair pulled Curlycrown free. She hugged Leigh then too, whispering in her ear.

"We'll send help," she said, but Leigh shook her head. She appreciated the offer, but the help wouldn't come in time. Besides, who in their village could stand up against a snagfire army? Shining Glory should be able to protect the castle; that would have to be enough. The maidens couldn't help, and Brandish hadn't come to the rescue.

He wouldn't leave her, which meant that he had to be dead. Unconscious. Something.

She pushed the maidens away, trying to face this moment with pride and composure if nothing else. She could fall apart later. She'd have plenty of time at the bottom of whatever dungeon Ravenwaves threw her into, since the last one had burned down.

"Take Fairhair and Curlycrown back to the castle, Pixietails," she said.

"Noooo," said Pixie Sparkle, hugging her with surprising strength.

But they complied. They had no other choice. Crying softly, the maidens clung to each other as the Pixietails lifted them into the air over the gaggle of snagfires.

"If you bolt, I'll go after them," said Ravenwaves with a disturbingly conversational air. "With all my snagfires. It won't be pretty. I'll level the village while I'm at it."

"Do I look like I'm running?" asked Leigh, pretending to yawn.

"I can't wait until I snip that satisfied expression off your face."

Ravenwaves subsided, pacing and grumbling. The maidens shrank as they flew off toward the castle, leaving nothing but a shower of sparkles behind. That would probably be the last time Leigh saw her Pixietails or heard their mismatched trio of voices.

The last time they'd argue with her or drive her nuts with their lack of common sense. She'd even miss their obnoxious jingling.

But she'd made her choice, and as the maidens vanished from sight, she couldn't regret it. The maidens would carry on, regardless of what happened to her today. She'd given them the opportunity to live rather than hiding in fear. Maybe she hadn't succeeded in figuring out what had happened to her mom, but she'd still accomplished something important.

It would have to be enough.

"I'm ready," she said.

As the duchess advanced, the gleaming scissors held out in front of her, she felt the faint stir of breath on her ear, wisps of hair tickling her face.

Brandish whispered, "Get ready to run."

He was alive. And invisible.

Her knees went weak with relief, and she sagged off to one side. Ravenwaves laughed again, taking this as a gesture of weakness. Leigh barely noticed. Brandish had come through after all. She could have kissed him for it.

She heard the lowest of murmurs, too quiet to make out the words. Not that she'd understand all his hocus-pocus incantations anyway. Whatever Brandish said made electric energy dance along her limbs. The tingle grew and grew until she couldn't help but twitch. Ravenwaves stared at her, eyes narrowed.

"What . . . ?" asked the duchess, squinting. "You're sparkling."

With an audible pop, Leigh vanished. This was a different illusion than the ones he'd cast before. Instead of creating a Fake Leigh, he'd made the real one disappear. She couldn't even see her own hand as she waved it in front of her face. The sight—or lack thereof—dizzied her, so she tore her eyes away, trusting in Brandish's magic. He would not let her down.

"Where'd she go?" exclaimed Ravenwaves, charging toward the spot where she still stood. "Find her!"

"Run!" whispered Brandish, the word almost inaudible beneath the snarls of the enraged snagfires.

They fled for the rendezvous point together, hand in hand.

CHAPTER 24

LEIGH AND BRANDISH HAD A SHOCKED, JOYFUL reunion with the maidens at the castle. They'd gathered all the villagers behind the walls, and the smith had almost taken Leigh's head off with the sledgehammer when she poked her head through the gate, but luckily his aim wasn't all that great. The maidens came rushing out as soon as they heard his shout and promptly swamped her in relieved hugs. As soon as she extricated herself, she sent her Pixietails back to scout. If Ravenwaves was mounting a counteroffensive, they'd need more than a big hammer to hold all those snagfires at bay. But the Pixietails reported that Ravenwaves had her hands full saving what was left of her tower. They were safe for now.

They sent everyone home, and finally the four companions said their goodbyes.

"Are you sure you can't stay?" asked Fairhair.

"I've got to go home, but I promise I'll be back tomorrow," responded Leigh. "Pinkie swear."

"Thank you ever so much," said Curlycrown, hugging her again. "You saved us."

"You moron," said Leigh fondly. "You never needed saving, just help. You're perfectly capable on your own."

Curlycrown's cheeks flushed, and she looked down at the ground for a moment. When she looked up again, her eyes shone with unshed tears.

"You know, I think you're right," she said.

"Of course I am," said Leigh.

"I think maybe..." Curlycrown hesitated. "I'll ask Shining Glory to train me. I want to learn more about magic, find new ways to use my Pixietails."

"Go for it."

Leigh and Brandish finally managed to extricate themselves, setting off down the quiet pathway to the village beneath a glittering twilight sky. They stopped at Brandish's tree house, and without so much as a word, he pulled down the ladder and gestured for her to climb. He didn't even need to be asked; he just knew what she wanted.

Once inside, Leigh hovered near the doorway while Brandish crossed the room to light an oil lamp. A match hissed in the dark. He hung the glowing lamp on a hook before clearing off a space on the desk, gesturing for her to come closer. Only then did he pull the canvas from his belt, holding it out to her.

"I think you should do the honors," he said, giving her one of his crooked grins.

She couldn't take it any longer. She batted the painting out of the way and hugged him hard. After a shocked moment, his arms wrapped around her, squeezing the breath from her body. She didn't care. Who needs oxygen anyway?

"Thank you for saving me," she gasped, unable to draw a full breath. "That was so stupid. I almost got you all killed."

"Hey, I volunteered," he argued, his mouth against her hair.

"Well, you're an idiot."

He let out a muffled laugh. "Maybe. But I'm still not letting you hog all the credit."

"Blame. The word you're looking for is 'blame.' "

"No, it isn't."

He released her reluctantly, and she looked up into his shifting hazel eyes. She wanted very badly to kiss him, but it didn't seem like the appropriate time. When she finally took the leap, she wanted to be able to concentrate on him and him alone. Right now, she felt pulled in seven hundred different directions, her emotions jumbled up into a tangled ball. So she looked away.

"Right," he said. "About that painting."

She unrolled it, holding it flat against the desk. Her mom smiled that enigmatic smile. Brandish tilted his head, looking from the painted face to Leigh and back again.

"I can see the resemblance," he said. Leigh pointed out the paper with her name on it, and he whistled softly, amazement flooding his eyes. "I guess that settles it, then," he continued. "It really is her, isn't it?"

"Yeah."

"Anything on the back? Any other clues? I didn't really have the time to look when we grabbed it."

She flipped the canvas over, her heart hammering eagerly.

But there was nothing.

"Well, it's a start," said Brandish. "I'll see if I can find a magnifying glass. Maybe we'll be able to make out some detail that would help us learn more. I don't see a signature anywhere, but maybe it's just tiny."

"Good thinking."

"Should I hold on to it, or would you like to take it up to the castle? I assume you have to go back home, and I've got to confess that I'm about two steps from total collapse."

Leigh considered the question briefly, but there was no need. She trusted him.

"I'll leave it here," she replied. "Maybe you'll notice something helpful. Some hint to where it came from."

"I mean, I'm pretty new here, but I'll try my best. You can trust me."

"Always," she said, beaming at him.

The next day, Leigh returned to the tree house to find Brandish pacing back and forth on the ground near the ladder, his hair standing up in all directions. He kept running his hands through it, muttering to himself. Back and forth. Back and forth. Something sure had riled him up.

"Do I need to shank someone?" she asked as she drew closer.

He halted, straightening, and lowered his hands. Worry seized her, but it quickly faded as a grin spread across his face, lighting his eyes.

"Wait till you see," he said.

"See what?"

"Nah. I can't tell you. You wouldn't believe me if I tried. Come on; I'll show you."

He led the way up the ladder and into the tree house. As soon as she reached the door, she scanned the room, trying to figure out what had gotten him so excited. But nothing appeared out of place. Well, some of the clutter had been moved off the desk, where the painting had been pinned down by a few random pieces of crockery, but otherwise the space looked exactly like it had before.

"Well? The suspense is killing me," she said. "If I die, it'll be your fault."

"Over here."

He took her by the elbow, his long fingers wrapping around her arm.

"Look," he said, tapping on the desk.

She didn't want to look away from the bright excitement on his face but tore herself away before she did something embarrassing. Then she hissed out a few swear words as she realized what he'd been trying to show her.

The painting had completely changed.

The last time she'd seen it, her mom had been sitting with her legs off to the left. Her head had been turned to give the viewer that enigmatic *Mona Lisa* smile. In her back hand, she'd clutched the sheet of parchment with Leigh's name on it. But now, inexplicably, she'd *moved*. Her legs had turned forward, and she held out the sheet of paper with both hands, the writing on it as clear as day.

It said, *Leigh, rip the painting.*

A shiver ran over her, excitement thrumming like electricity through her veins. She could barely force the words out through her trembling lips.

"Oh my god," she said, sinking into his desk chair. Her lips—no, her whole body—had gone numb with shock. "Is that...?"

"Magic," said Brandish. "I never would have thought of it."

“Is my mom in there?! I don’t want to get my hopes up if...” She trailed off again, unwilling to say it aloud.

“I’ve never seen anything like it,” he admitted, running his hands through his hair again. “But I think so. She moves incredibly slowly. The paper was only halfway up this morning. And now... well, you can see it for yourself.”

“This could explain everything,” said Leigh, clutching the edge of the desk like it was a life preserver. She was so lightheaded with relief that she thought she might fall out of the chair. “She’s been in the painting this whole time. Brandish, she didn’t leave me. Ravenwaves imprisoned her and hung her on a wall. My quest was to find my mom, and *I’ve done it.*”

The realization hit her like a freight train. No matter what came next, no matter what the answers were, she’d done it. She’d found the truth, and no one could ever take it from her. For the first time, her life felt full of possibilities instead of obstacles. She was more capable than she’d ever allowed herself to believe. When she’d come here, she would never have imagined that this ridiculous place would teach her that, but here she was.

He reached out to squeeze her shoulder.

“I’m so proud of you,” he said. “Should I leave? I thought you might want to do this alone.”

“Stay, please. If something goes wrong, your magic might be helpful.” Leigh watched his expression fall, eyes dropping to the ground. “And I’d like you to be here!” she hastily added. “Without you, I never would have gotten this far! I’m sorry; I’m just excited.”

His face cleared, and he nodded.

"Yeah, of course. Now rip the thing already, or the suspense might kill *me*!" he joked. "I don't want to die before the payoff."

She laughed, turning her attention back to the painting. Her hands felt clammy with sweat as she reached for the heavy canvas. Never in her wildest dreams would she have imagined that she might meet her mom today. The most she'd dared to hope for was a clue. But this was happening. She could barely believe it.

She grabbed the corner of the painting, working at the heavy fabric. One tug, and she knew that ripping this thing with her hands would be impossible. She'd have better luck drilling through stone with her fingernails. But Brandish held up a pair of scissors.

"Here," he said. "I thought you might need these, so I picked up a pair."

Leigh hesitated, her fingers hovering over the handle.

"I'm nervous," she said, joking in a vain attempt to relieve some of the tension that made her hands shake. "I think Ravenwaves gave me a phobia of scissors."

"Quit stalling," he urged. "You've got this."

Taking a deep breath, she cut a little snip at the edge of the canvas and set the scissors down on the desk. She grabbed the corner and yanked with all her might. The fabric gave way with an almost deafening tear, the pieces fluttering to the desk. Ever since she'd first put on the wig, Leigh had gotten used to the feeling of magic coursing through her body. She'd described it to Ari as being tickled with electrified feathers. But what she felt in this moment was completely different; the wave hit her like a typhoon. Her hair stood on end and her heart skipped a beat. All the breath was squeezed from her lungs in a scream she hadn't intended on uttering. Brandish bellowed beside her. The entire room turned white.

Then it was over. The light faded; the air returned. Bright spots danced across Leigh's vision. She blinked desperately, trying to see, wanting to know. Had it worked?

"Mom?" she asked, her voice tremulous.

A portal of some sort hung in the air over the shreds of the painting. Arcing around the torn pieces where the frame would have been, a pulsing purple energy swirled and spit, emitting sparks that hissed on the desk. The image inside flickered like the display on her grandparents' giant old console TV, a constant roll that made her stomach churn. When she looked down into it, she saw the dark, foreboding room from the painting. And her mother.

Moving.

Her long black hair had been woven into a complicated plait atop her head. The wide neck of her gown exposed a triangular birthmark that Leigh had stared at in grainy pictures for so long that she could have drawn it in her sleep. As Leigh watched, her mom reached up and tugged nervously at the neckline.

"Leigh?" called her mother. "Can you—"

The image rolled, and a hiss of static drowned out the remainder of the sentence. Leigh's hands hovered over the edges of the portal, but she was too scared to touch it. The last thing she needed to do was meet her mother for the first time and then promptly electrocute herself.

"Mom?" she asked, her voice shaking.

Hiss. Crackle. Her mother's lips were moving, but no sound came out. The image was too broken up for lipreading, but Leigh still squinted desperately at it anyway.

"—punkin. I knew you'd—"

"Mom?!" Leigh's voice was choked with tears. "Can you hear me?"

She leaned closer, and the portal belched out another gout of sparks. One landed on her hand, burning, just as Brandish's hand closed on the back of her collar, yanking her out of the way before she singed her own eyebrows off. She shook him off, intent on her mother's face.

"Careful," he murmured.

"You know how to work this thing?" she asked.

"Not a clue, I'm afraid." He winced. "Is it just me, or is it shrinking?"

She fixated on it, hoping against hope that any shrinkage was only in his imagination. But the portal was definitely smaller than it had been just a few seconds earlier. At this rate, it would be gone in minutes.

"Mom!" she shouted. "Where are you? I'll come get you!"

"No, you can't—" Another wave of static drowned out whatever Leigh's mother said next. "—fight my way out."

"Where are you?" demanded Leigh. "We're at Lovely Locks Castle."

"—broke the curse—" *Crackle. Piff. Hiss.* "—but now I have a chance."

The portal was definitely shrinking. Just a few seconds ago, it had been the size of a serving platter. Now it was a dinner plate.

Leigh's heart leaped into her throat. She had to do something, but she didn't even know if her mother could hear a single thing she'd said, and that portal had almost fried her face off already. Then her eyes settled on her staff, leaning against the desk. If her mother had to fight her way free of whatever prison Ravenwaves had presumably stuffed her into, she could use a weapon. Especially a magic one.

She turned to Brandish, who had a white-knuckled grip on the edge of the desk. He stared at the portal with his brow furrowed and startled when she tugged on his sleeve.

"Can I put this through the portal?" she demanded, shaking the staff.

"I—I'm not sure," he stammered.

"Worth a try."

She lifted it over the portal, holding her hands well away from the sparks. It was now the size of a dessert plate. She dropped the staff into it. The portal squealed as the staff vanished into its depths, spitting out another burst of sparks that threatened to ignite the desktop. Brandish upended a cup over the smoldering wood.

Leigh barely noticed. She was too busy craning her neck, trying to see if her mom had the staff. But she couldn't make anything out in the darkness beyond the purple glow of the portal.

"Did you get it?" she shrieked.

"Yes," said her mother. Another wave of static. "—there in three days."

The portal hummed as it grew smaller and smaller. It was now the size of a quarter.

"Mom! I love you!" Leigh shouted desperately.

"I—"

The portal snapped shut with a burst of energy that made Leigh's ears pop. Little purple sparks rained down on the desk, scorching the ripped remains of the painting. Desperately, Leigh smothered them, peering into the ripped pieces in the hopes that she might see what was happening. But all she saw was the empty chair, upended now. Leaning against one of the legs was the paper with her name on it.

“Reopen it,” she begged, holding the strips out to Brandish. “Please. Whatever you have to do. Don’t you have anything about portals in your books? We could look it up.”

“Leigh.”

His calm voice cut through her growing agitation, stopping her short.

“You’ve done what you could,” he said. “It’ll be okay.”

“How do you know that?” she demanded, the words tumbling out of her. “After all this time I finally found her. She’s . . . I’m . . . man, my dad is going to flip the heck out. But what if she doesn’t survive?”

“She survived all this time, right? If the two of you have anything in common, she’ll find a way. Have a little faith, Leigh,” he said gently.

She tried to take a deep breath, her throat suddenly tight.

“I know you’re right. It’s just that I finally have what I’ve always wanted right at my fingertips. What if it’s taken away when I’m so close? I don’t think I could stand that.”

“I think you could stand anything. You’re astounding.”

“I bet you say that to all the girls,” she said.

“No, I don’t.” He stepped a little closer, his multicolored eyes uncertain. “You know that, somewhere deep down. Don’t you?”

“Yes,” she whispered.

“Leigh, maybe this is awful timing, but I can’t resist any longer. Can I kiss you . . . ?”

All of a sudden, she couldn’t breathe. She wouldn’t have noticed if a bomb hit the tree house; all her attention was locked on his lips as they slowly inched toward hers. His hand slid up to cup her face. Hers lifted to his collar. For a breathless moment, they hovered there, lips barely brushing, frozen in a moment of anticipation. Her heart beat so loud he could probably hear it. Then his mouth closed over hers, featherlight and gentle.

Her knees turned to jelly, but somehow she managed to remain standing. It wasn't just her. When he finally pulled back, he rested a hand on the desk as if he'd gone lightheaded.

"You know," he said, "if you'd like to march into certain death again sometime soon, I'm in. You talked me into it."

She pushed him a little, playfully.

"Stahp," she said. "Be serious."

"I am being entirely serious. Kiss me like that again, and I'll give you anything."

"I think if I did that, I wouldn't be able to stop."

The corner of his mouth quirked up.

"You say that like it's a bad thing," he said.

CHAPTER 25

WHEN LEIGH FINALLY MANAGED TO PRY HERself away from Brandish and call for her Pixietails, she couldn't stop smiling. Everything had turned out better than she'd dared to dream. She couldn't wait to see her dad's face when she brought her mom back. Three days, she'd said. That wasn't that long to wait, but it felt like eternity. Having her back would be weird at first, and Leigh didn't know exactly what their life would look like, but maybe they could be some sort of family once her dad realized that her mom hadn't wanted to leave them after all. It could really happen.

Back in her real-world bedroom, she changed clothes and pulled the pillows out of her sheets. She'd made her own Fake Leigh just in case her dad checked on her. They hadn't been disturbed, so the ruse must have worked. Once she had the space, she toppled onto the mattress and dashed off a couple of DMs to Ari, bringing him up to speed. Ari replied in long strings of exclamation points, random keyboard smashes, and even more random emoji. For him, a text string of pregnant-guy emoji, coral, and six green apples followed by two lines full of exclamation points was the height of excitement. She snickered to herself as the random combos and memes kept rolling in.

The next day flew by. She took two quizzes and couldn't remember a thing, and after school, she fell asleep on her homework. She awoke to a gentle tap on the door. When she responded, her dad cracked the door open and stuck his head in.

"Hey," he said hesitantly. "You feeling okay?"

"Yeah. I just needed to catch up on sleep."

They stared at each other for a long moment. After everything that had happened, Leigh had forgotten about their fight, but now it hovered over them. She wasn't pissed anymore, but that didn't make the things they'd both said magically go away either.

"Listen," said Dad, "I won this week's fantasy football pot. Maybe I could take you out to that ramen place you like before I have to get to work?"

"You don't have to do that," she said. "Put it toward bills. Or do something for yourself."

"This is me doing something for myself." He took a deep breath before meeting her eyes. "Making things right. Did you read my letter?"

"I did."

"Good. I'm sorry, punkin. I was out of line."

"It's okay. I get it."

"No, you don't." He entered the room, swallowing nervously, and sat down next to her. He couldn't even meet her gaze and kept his eyes on the floor. A sliver of worry pierced her happy little bubble, but she ignored it. Nothing could take away her excitement. She was closer than ever to having her mom back. "I owe you a real apology."

"I told you; it's no big deal. We both said some things we didn't really mean. I'm sorry too."

"That's not it." He clasped his hands, staring down at them. "Leigh, I did you dirty. I didn't mean to. I meant to protect you.

But it was wrong of me to refuse to tell you anything about your mom."

She almost laughed out loud. He was going to freak out when he realized what she'd done. She wanted to tell him so badly, but of course he wouldn't believe her, and she wanted them to all experience that reunion together. In fact, she couldn't wait.

"It's okay," she said. "Maybe I wasn't always cool with it, but I know you. You wouldn't hurt me on purpose."

"That's kind of you to say." He looked up at her then, and to her surprise, she realized that his eyes were filled with tears. "I've always wanted the best for you, and I feel like I've always fallen short. I couldn't protect you. I really tried."

"Protect me? Protect me from what?"

But he didn't even seem to hear the question. He just kept on talking, his eyes glued to his hands.

"I didn't realize anything was wrong," he said. "I thought we were both just tired, that her odd behavior was just sleep deprivation. We were supposed to go to my parents' house for the weekend, but your mom said she wasn't feeling well and didn't want to throw up all over the inside of the car, so she stayed home. When I got back with you, she was gone."

Leigh couldn't imagine how difficult that had been for him. Thinking her mom had just up and left him. How could he have known that some dark-haired psychopath had kidnapped her and stuffed her into a magic painting?

"I'm sorry," she began, but he held up a hand.

"I'm not finished. She took everything with her. She wiped us out, Leigh. All this time, I've been telling you that the car accident got us into financial trouble, and it sure didn't help, but it all started with your mom. After she left, I started getting bills in the mail. Credit cards with my name on them. She racked up a lot of debt, and she left us with it. I didn't want to tell you. I didn't want you to feel betrayed like I did."

Leigh's mouth hung open. That didn't make any sense. Her mom had gone into Lovely Locks and couldn't come back out; she didn't need money for that. Had she left before she'd been imprisoned? The timeline didn't quite add up.

Surely, there had to be a reasonable explanation.

"What?" she stammered. "Why didn't you tell me this? I would have understood. Maybe not when I was little, but now I get it. People are complicated. Besides, how can that be when—"

"Let me finish," Dad interrupted. "After she left, people started showing up at the house, looking for her. I'm not sure what they were into. Drugs maybe? But they just acted shady, in ways I just can't explain. Always asking too many questions and snooping around. They set me on edge. But I never expected that one of them would try to take you."

"Take me?!" Leigh exclaimed.

"Out of your room. I caught him in your bedroom. I don't even know how he got in. The guy said he was taking you to your mom. I'm not a violent guy, Leigh, but... well, I defended you. I beat him within an inch of his life and dumped him outside. You never even woke up. We moved later that week, and we haven't stopped running since. Every time I thought she might have found us, we moved again. I was just terrified I might lose you. One day, I'd turn around, and you'd be gone."

He paused for a moment, his voice breaking when he finally continued.

"I'm sorry," he said. "I hope you don't think I'm crazy. The cops sure did."

Leigh didn't know what to think. None of this jibed with the woman she'd just met, who just wanted to talk to her. But she also knew her dad. He wasn't lying. And then there was the question of Lady Knot. Everyone was terrified of her. Which woman was real? There had to be some way to figure that out, but she didn't know how.

"I don't think you're crazy," she said.

"You're being awfully calm about this. Let me buy you some ramen. If you have any other questions, I'll answer them. No more secrets, I promise."

"Yeah, okay. Let me put my shoes on."

"Come on out when you're ready."

He planted a kiss on the top of her head and left. She sat there for a moment, shocked, but she couldn't dredge up a handy explanation that would make sense of all this weirdness no matter how hard she tried. She'd have to ask her mom about it; there had to be a reasonable explanation.

She and her dad had to rush to make the train to head crosstown to her favorite ramen place. She would have been fine with something closer, but her dad seemed determined to assuage his guilt by treating her and wouldn't take no for an answer. They sprinted up the stairs and onto the SEPTA platform just in time to dash through the closing doors of the six forty-seven. She stood just inside the doors, panting, as the train began to pull out of the station.

"You okay?" asked Dad, patting her on the shoulder.

"Yeah."

She straightened, looking out the window as she tried to catch her breath.

Wait a minute. Was that *Brandish*?!

He stood on the platform in a pair of jeans and a black button-down, his hair smoothed back and plastered to his head. Overall, the effect was much more clean-cut than she was used to from him. But it was him. Their eyes met, and a shock of recognition ran through her body. It was him.

The train pulled away.

The last vestiges of her earlier happiness faded away to be replaced by an anxious ball in the pit of her stomach. Clearly, there were things she didn't know. Secrets to unravel.

She had no idea whom to trust.

But she was going to find out.

ACKNOWLEDGMENTS

I've had such a blast working on this book. I remember playing Lady Lovely Locks as a high school babysitter, and I have to thank Ryan Wiesbrock and the entire team at Cloudco for letting me play with those toys again and being such supportive creative partners. The team at Running Press is the absolute best. Allison Cohen is a terrific editor and amazing person, and I'd like to take this opportunity to formally declare that I'd like her to be my friend. A whole team of people offered their editorial expertise to help me sound like less of an idiot, and I owe them all a nice fruit basket: Leah Gordon, Jess Riordan, Julianna Holshue, and Sarah Chassé. Tricia Tamburr and Nikki Ioakimedes lent their keen proofreading eye to make the words pretty, and Mary Boyer and Rossi Gifford provided the gorgeous art and design. I can't art my way out of a paper bag, so I couldn't be more appreciative of their talents. Becca Matheson and Kara Thornton in marketing and publicity helped spread the word, and I know firsthand how big of a task that is. A billion thank yous to all of you.

Thank you to my family, especially Andy, Connor, Lily, Ryan, Keith, Aunt Marian, Lee, and MaryEllen, and to my friends, especially Sarah, Marcy, Emily, Jen, Lee, Patty, Jay, and James. You are appreciated for your general awesomeness and also for providing inspiration for hairstyles I may or may not have used in this story.

A SNEAK PEEK AT

TENDRILS

A Lady Lovely Locks Novel

BOOK 2

CHAPTER 1

IT WAS A BRIGHT, GORGEOUS EARLY EVENING IN THE Kingdom of Lovely Locks, and Leigh Carroll was on the warpath. As she made her the way into the village, she stalked past a pair of happy villagers leading livestock—also obnoxiously happy, for the record—in from pasture. Instead of enjoying the scenery, however, she resented all of it, including the cheery sunlight, the musically burbling brook alongside the path, and the gently undulating cornrows of the hedges.

She wasn't a violent person, but when she got to Brandish's tree house, he'd be lucky if she didn't punch him right in the mouth. He deserved it. The more she thought about seeing him on that Philadelphia train platform a few hours ago, the more upset she became. He'd lied to her. That story about being a hedge wizard from another kingdom? Not an ounce of truth in it. He'd looked right into her eyes and told her he learned real-world slang from books. He must have thought it hilarious when she bought that load of crap. What else had he lied about? For all she knew, he had a girlfriend already. She wouldn't put it past him to be a cheater atop everything else.

As she stomped through the market square, a sobering thought occurred to her. What if everyone in Lovely Locks—all the villagers, the wizards, the maidens—was from the real world, and she was the only one not in on the joke? Had they all been laughing at her this whole time? A small but rational voice buried deep inside her whispered that this was impossible, but she was too far gone in the depths of anger to listen to it.

To her left, a farmer with a bushy beard set out baskets of enormous vegetables for the Night Market that evening. To her right, a young girl fussed with a display of bejeweled hairbrushes. Leigh veered toward the brush vendor, her jaw clenched.

"Princess!" exclaimed the girl. "Can I interest you in a brush? Or perhaps some jeweled hair combs? I have some shaped like your Pixietails; wouldn't that be funny?"

"Hilarious," said Leigh flatly. "Have you ever heard of Philadelphia?"

The question was met with confused silence.

"Philawhatsia? Is that a hair product?" asked the girl hesitantly.

"What about Hot Pockets? Wi-Fi? *Family Guy*? *Lord of the Rings*?"

"There's a jewelry vendor down at the other end of the market if you'd like a ring, but I don't think he's royalty," said the girl, her eyes wide and nervous. "Is everything okay, Princess? You're scaring me."

Leigh sighed. The shopgirl didn't seem to recognize the random pop culture references, and berating her wasn't going to make Leigh feel any better. She was beginning to suspect that nothing would.

"Never mind," she said, forcing a smile. "I have something important to take care of, but I'll come back later and do my shopping."

"Of course!" The girl's brow smoothed, the worry draining from her face. "I hope you're able to resolve whatever troubles you."

"Oh, I'll resolve it all right," muttered Leigh. "I'll punch him in the face."

"Boy problems?" asked the girl, the corner of her mouth quirking. "The smith is running a special on mallets if your mystery man needs a whack on the head."

Leigh snickered as she walked away. Of course she was still furious—and rightfully so—but she couldn't let the emotion get the best of her.

Although she might just check out those mallets later.

When she reached the tree house, she had her Pixietails levitate her up to the door. She didn't want to give Brandish the Coward an opportunity to sneak out the back while she was noisily climbing up the rope ladder. Instead, she glided up, landing on the smooth wooden planks of his porch without a sound. The last time she'd been here, he'd kissed her goodbye with such gentleness that her knees had gone gooey. Except . . . none of it had been real, had it?

Tears sprang to her eyes. But she wasn't going to give him the satisfaction of knowing she cared, so she brushed the offending moisture away and focused on the comforting fury still simmering beneath the surface. Brandish would be lucky if she didn't have her Pixietails string him up by his toes.

She burst through the door like an avenging angel. It was a good entrance. Too bad no one was there to see it. The tree house sat empty, the windows shuttered. She squinted in the gloom, but there was nowhere to hide in this tiny room unless he'd shrunk himself. Then again, he was a master of illusion, and he'd turned them both invisible before. She circled the space, flailing her arms around, but didn't hit any lying, invisible situationships.

"Brandish?" she called.

No answer. He really wasn't home. He was probably still on that train platform in Philly. All the strength went out of her legs, her fury spent. She sat down heavily on the stuffed mattress and sniffled. She would not cry, not for him, but it sure was dusty in here.

Her Pixietails flitted out of her magic hair, jingling with an offensive level of joyfulness. The last thing she wanted was to be cheered up, and especially not by a bunch of hyperactive hair bunnies.

Pixie Sparkle floated up next to her with a perky little jingle-jangle. Sparkle had always been Leigh's favorite. The Pixietail had fluffy pink fur, a surprisingly deep bass voice, and a snarky streak a mile wide. But this time, the sarcastic little creature didn't make a pointed comment. It just patted her hand. Her other two Pixietails, Pixie Shine and Pixie Beauty, clustered behind Sparkle with funereal expressions that were somewhat ruined by the cheery jingle that accompanied every movement.

Great, now even her stupid magic hair bunnies knew she'd had her heart broken. If they started giving her relationship advice, she was going to throw herself out one of those windows. *Ugh.* That lovesick garbage made her want to hit her head against a convenient wall.

She straightened. The only thing she could do was what she always had—keep on moving. Yes, she felt betrayed, and yes, everything that could go wrong had, in fact, done so. But she'd never been the sort of person who folded under pressure, so why should she start now? She couldn't sit around moping about some boy; she had crap to do.

"Okay," she said. "I'm okay."

“Are you sure?” asked Pixie Shine in its squeaky bunny voice.

“We can sing you sad songs if you need them,” added Pixie Beauty. “The last Lady Lovely Locks liked it when we did that. She’d cry and cry and cry.”

Pixie Sparkle nodded soberly and then rolled its eyes. Leigh snorted.

“I think I’ll pass, but thanks,” she said. “I need information. Did you know that Brandish is from my world?”

Beauty shook its head in rapid horror. Shine’s eyes went wide.

“He is?” asked Shine. “The nerve!”

“He was lying all along!” exclaimed Beauty.

“What a jerk. To answer your question, there’s no real way to tell, Princess,” said Sparkle. “I’m sorry.”

They had no reason to hide the truth from her. She nodded.

“I need to know why he lied to me. If you know anything potentially helpful, now’s a good time to spill it. Otherwise, I’m going to search the place,” she said.

The Pixietails exchanged sober glances.

“We could help you look?” suggested Sparkle.

With their small size, they could fly into all kinds of nooks and crannies that she couldn’t reach. Leigh nodded.

“That would be great. Anything you find with writing on it, you bring to me,” she said.

“Yes, Princess,” they twittered.

“Let’s get to work,” said Leigh.

She opened up the windows to let in a little of the fading sunlight and sat down at the desk, rummaging through the stacks of books and papers piled atop it. His handwriting was atrocious, but she could puzzle it out. She sifted through notes on magical theory and prices in the marketplace. There were stacks of storybooks, containing a mix of familiar and unfamiliar fairy tales. He'd scribbled notes in the margins, but none of them jumped out at her as particularly important.

She moved on to the next stack as the Pixietails tossed the bed, working together to lift the blankets and pillows and search beneath them. The little buggers were stronger than she'd realized. She left them to it.

At the bottom of a tall stack of books, she found a copy of *Lady Lovely Locks*. It was the same edition her mother had left her, covered in pink with a gold-foil cameo of the princess stamped on the front. Her heart thumping, she flipped through the pages. He'd scribbled all over it; she didn't see a single page without his chicken scratch crowding the margins. She skimmed, trying to figure out why he was taking notes on a kids' storybook like he'd be tested on it later, but the notes were unintelligible. Half of them weren't even words, just strings of random letters.

Frowning, she flipped to the beginning of the book, hoping that would help her make some sense out of all this weirdness. As she rifled through the pages, a few loose papers slid out and fell to the floor. Hopefully they contained something coherent, because she was starting to wonder if maybe good old Brandish had lost all contact with reality. Maybe the guy wasn't a liar as much as certifiably insane.

She unfolded the pages, revealing her own face. Brandish had sketched her out in pencil, her eyes bright and mouth open in mid-laugh. Pastel locks of hair streamed around her face, flowing to the edge of the paper. Tucked in the corner, he'd signed his name.

Heart racing, she flipped the page to reveal another drawing. This time, she was crouched in her patented anime-meets-Black-Widow attack stance, staff clutched in one hand and planted on the ground, free hand held out to the side. Her lip curled in a snarl of defiance. Ribbons streamed from her cosplay. She looked like a total badass, gorgeous and fierce.

She stared at the drawings for a long moment, her heart thumping. He wouldn't have spent so much time sketching her if he didn't care, right? But if he genuinely liked her, why hadn't he told her the truth?

"Look out!" squeaked one of the Pixietails.

A loud, rapid thumping filled the air. Leigh immediately dropped the drawings and ducked her head, shielding it with her arms. Something bopped her shin, and she turned to see a mass of brightly colored balls bouncing and rolling across the floor.

The Pixietails hovered over the mess with guilty expressions, a large box held aloft between them with each one at a corner. As she watched, one final green ball teetered over the edge of the box, bounced off the floor, and winged past her head. A yellow one bumped off her foot.

"Jeez, guys," she said. "You nearly gave me a heart attack."

"Sorry!" said Shine.

"We didn't mean it!" added Beauty.

"Meh. No harm done, I guess," replied Leigh.

As she surveyed the mess, her gaze snagged on something very odd. A small door had opened in the middle of the wall. But there hadn't been anything there before; she could have sworn it.

"What's *that*?" she demanded.

"A secret hiding place! I think one of the balls opened it!" exclaimed Pixie Shine.

"Ooooh, how exciting!" squealed Beauty. "I love secret hiding places!"

Leigh peered inside but saw only black nothingness. The opening wasn't very big—just wide enough for one of the Pixietails to fit through—and the insufficient light from the window wasn't enough to illuminate the inside. She had no desire to stick her hand in and get it bitten off by some miniature unknown whatsit.

Brandish had an oil lamp on the desk, and she'd watched him light it using the flint and tinder, but she'd never tried it herself. She struck the hard stone a few times, trying to figure out the trick to making a spark. It was harder than it looked, and it didn't look easy in the first place. She tried five times, huffed at it in exasperation, and went for a sixth. Still no luck.

"I'm going in," declared Pixie Sparkle.

"Wait..." said Leigh, but the Pixietail didn't even pause before darting into the deep black hole.

"Oh dear," said Pixie Beauty, wringing its little hands. "I'm so scared!"

Pixie Shine clung to Leigh's shoulder as she crossed the room to look into the hole, kicking those stupid balls out of her way. But she still couldn't see a dang thing.

"Pixie Sparkle, you okay in there?" she called.

"Yeah, I'm—"

The Pixietail's voice cut off abruptly, interrupted by a whumping noise. The tiny door rattled on its equally tiny hinges.

"Pixie Sparkle?!" squeaked Shine and Beauty in high-pitched unison.

"Oof!" shouted Sparkle. "Ow!"

There was another series of thumps. Something was beating the tar out of her hair bunny. Leigh looked around for a weapon, wishing with all her heart that she hadn't given her mother her staff. She needed a replacement, but Brandish didn't even own a broom.

Whump! Wham! Bam!

"Lady Leigh, do something!" begged Beauty.

"Please help!" urged Shine.

The door swung to and fro with the force of the repeated blows. Leigh put her ear to the wall, trying to pinpoint the noise. If she had to, she'd bust a hole in it to save Sparkle. The obnoxious hair rabbits drove her nuts, but that didn't mean she'd sit around and let someone—or some*thing*—hurt them.

WHAM!

The wall trembled right beneath her ear. There! She just needed something sharp to break through the wall. Didn't Brandish own a fireplace poker? A sturdy knife? Did he just rip his food apart with his teeth like a caveman?

As her eyes raked the room for a suitable tool, a black shape came flying out of the tiny doorway. It definitely wasn't Pixie Sparkle. It was about the same size and general shape, but there wasn't a hint of pink anywhere on it, and instead of all the obnoxious jingling, it moved in complete silence. It came streaking out of the wall like it was on fire and made a beeline for the window.

Leigh launched toward it and would have caught it, too, except for the fact that she stepped right onto one of those bleeping balls. It rolled out from beneath her foot, and she slid into an awkward almost-split that strained a muscle in her inner thigh. She bleated out a startled oath as the black Pixietail-like mystery thing escaped through the open window. As Leigh scrambled gracelessly to her feet, Pixie Sparkle flew unsteadily out of the wall, its normally immaculate fur coated in dust bunnies. One of its eyes was blackened and swollen.

"Catch that Pixietail!" shouted Sparkle.

"Wait. What?!" gasped Leigh, but this wasn't the time for conversation. She staggered for the door without waiting for an answer.

ABOUT THE AUTHOR

CARRIE HARRIS writes novels, comics, and games for exciting licenses including Marvel, *Warhammer 40k*, *Miraculous Ladybug*, *Arkham Horror*, and the World of Darkness. She's a five-time Scribe award finalist for best licensed fiction, and her young adult horror comedy *Bad Taste in Boys* was a Quick Pick for Reluctant Readers. Carrie lives in New York with her family and an anxious dog named Slartibartfast.

Over the past few years, Carrie has had amethyst, mermaid, and sunset hair, but none of them have teleported her to a magic kingdom . . . yet.